County Justice

Thomas E. O'Brien

PublishAmerica
Baltimore

ISBN: 1-4241-1387-3
PUBLISHED BY PUBLISHAMERICA, LLLP
www.publishamerica.com
Baltimore

Printed in the United States of America

To my family

Acknowledgments

One obvious thing that I have discovered while writing my book, and it's a fact I'm sure. I am convinced that no one, I repeat, no one has ever written a book alone.

I couldn't have gotten started without the support and understanding of my wife Mary Ann. She kept picking me up, dusting me off and telling me I could do it.

This was followed immediately by continuous encouragement by my good friend Barry Horne who did the first proofread. My old mentor Al Daula also encouraged me to continue.

The research and guidance supplied by John Folk and Einar Bohlin was invaluable. How they found time to respond to my nagging needs while living normal lives and maintaining respectable golf handicaps is beyond me.

Thanks to my doctor, Grant Jenkins MD. He immediately observed the negative affects the publishers' form letter rejections were having on my blood pressure, so he took the time out of his busy schedule to put me in touch with author Cheryl Brown-Avery. Cheryl led me to PublishAmerica.

I would like to mention the constant support from my daughters, granddaughter's son-in law, and sister and brother in-law, some of whose names might be familiar to the readers, Kathleen, Colleen, Jamie, Bridget, Meghan, Sally and Richard.

I would like to acknowledge the fact that although this is a fictional book, the Vietnam Wall in Washington D.C., and the names listed on it are not. Two of the American warriors listed on that wall are:

EDWARD WALTER JR CONNELLY CAPT MARINES AGAWAM MA 1/10/1944-5/5/1968. He is honored on panel 55E, Row 7 of the Vietnam Veterans Memorial.

LELAND RICHARD COTTIN SP4 ARMY DALLAS TX 2/1/1945-6/20/1966 He is honored on panel 8E Row 65 of the Vietnam Veterans Memorial. He was Army Airborne.

It was never my intention to confuse the names of the above heroes with the fictional characters' names in my book.

Chapter 1

The Weaver 10X variable scope mounted on the Remington Model 700 was focused perfectly. The cross hairs were set firmly on the heart and the target was one-hundred and fifty yards away. Jeep took a deep breath and let it out slowly as he squeezed his finger on the trigger. The report a .270 cal. makes is extremely loud and for a moment he lost sight of his target as the weapon kicked hard against his shoulder. The six point buck jumped once in the air and dropped after three steps.

Jeep thought for a moment. "This old rifle and me are both as good as ever." The Remington had been in the family forty years, Jeep was thirty-one.

James (Jeep) Patrick leaned back against the tree for a moment, pausing in case it wasn't a perfect shot, even though he knew it was. It's a good practice to observe and let the deer bleed a few minutes rather than run right up on it. Deer have been known to bound up and run when startled by an anxious rookie hunter hastening to his kill. He let out a whistle to his friend Petey who would be coming soon. He was only a quarter mile further up the hill and surely he had heard the shot.

Petey and Jeep had been friends since Petey moved into the house next door when they were both six years old. They had been hunting partners since their first rabbit hunt when they were twelve and business partners the last four years. The roadside restaurant they own has been a pleasant success and tonight fresh venison will be featured on the menu as the "House Special."

"Ya miss it or did you get lucky?" Petey asked as he walked up behind Jeep.

"The only thing I missed was your company," Jeep replied.

"Seems a mite small. I think you shot Clete's dog," smiled Petey, looking down range at the fallen deer.

"Small? Why that buck will dress out at about two-hundred pounds." He knew Petey was impressed, but they didn't cut each other much slack.

"Well, Petey, are you going to help me carry him out?" asked Jeep.

"If I was going to shoot him, I would have chased him down closer to my truck," Petey grumbled.

"Why don't you go get that Pennsylvania Porsche and see if you can get up here by using that old loggin' road behind Cooters place? It should bring you one-hundred yards to the right of that buck." Pennsylvania Porsche is the nickname Petey called his pickup truck.

It took twenty minutes before Jeep saw that four wheel drive truck Petey loved so much come crawling over the hill.

After they loaded the deer in the back and started down, Petey said, "On the way up here I saw a weather balloon or something that had fallen down on the rocks. It's just laying there. Do you think we should stop and pick it up? We can drop it off with the sheriff if it's not worth anything, and if it is…well possession is nine-tenths of the law."

They pulled up next to what looked like a deflated weather balloon, which turned out to be a parachute. In its harness was a very sturdy, sealed, twelve by eighteen inch black crate that Jeep loaded in the back of the truck. It was getting dark much earlier since the clocks had been turned back, and he needed to get that buck cleaned and butchered if it was going to make the menu tonight. It was always fun to be able to offer venison to the locals as well as the tourists when you could.

They stopped at Pippins first to drop off the deer. Jeep needed to get a head start on getting it ready for dinner. Pippins was the joint Petey and Jeep owned. A pippin is a small French cooking apple. It was a good name for a restaurant although Jeep and Petey agreed that the real meaning was **P**atrick **I**s **P**etey's **P**artner **I**n **N**othing **S**uccessful. It made them both laugh, but since they hired their new cook, the last two and a half years had been very successful.

Jeep was out back preparing the deer and Petey was sitting at the bar enjoying a cold Iron City.

One of the local guys by the window hollered, "Hey Petey, someone is messing with your Porsche."

Petey walked out the front door shouting, "Get your ugly butt away from my truck!"

A black BMW was parked next to the truck and two guys in suits were trying to take the parachute package out of the truck. Startled by Petey's loud voice, one of them reached inside his jacket and pulled a pistol. Petey saw it just a second before the guy started shooting at him. Scrambling and crawling back to the door Petey roared, "Somebody grab the shotgun from behind the bar!"

Bullets kicked up gravel from the parking lot and splinters from the door jam, but none of them found their mark. Petey crawled, and then ran toward the bar where they kept the equalizer. It was a Winchester Defender twelve gauge pump loaded with double "O" buckshot. When he reached the front door this time he was loaded for bear. He saw the BMW spinning gravel and heading to the highway.

Petey ran for the phone to call the sheriff. "I think it's time we put Sheriff Amos Cottin and his deputies to work."

While waiting for the phone to be answered, he chuckled as he noticed everyone in the bar was lying on the floor.

They spent two hours eating venison and listening as Petey explained to the sheriff what happened in a mere twenty seconds earlier that evening. They were still in possession of the black crate, but Petey had removed it from the truck and for some reason hadn't told Cottin. No one remembered the license number, but Cottin didn't think a black Beamer would be too hard to find in the hills of southwestern Pennsylvania, at least in his county.

Cottin had been the sheriff since Jeep and Petey were teenagers, too young to drink. He had always cut them some slack when they stepped outside of the law with some high school pranks. He said they were good boys and the fact that Petey's dad was a Pennsylvania State Trooper didn't hurt.

It was later when Petey explained to Jeep why he had held out on the sheriff. "I wanted first shot at what was in the box. I didn't want a lot of people involved. Maybe it was bank money, you know like the guy that jumped from the plane in Colorado some years back, D. B. Cooper with all that bank money?"

Jeep suggested, "Let's sleep on it."

"The crate will be too hard to sleep on. I'll put it under my bed," joked Petey with a smile.

Jeep and Petey had been sharing a two-bedroom apartment above Pippins since they built the place four years ago. Although it wasn't luxuriously furnished, it would have made a nice spread in "Redneck Review."

After they made sure the restaurant downstairs was dark and secure, they spent the rest of the evening planning their next step. Jeep was concerned about opening the crate and Petey was already counting the money he was sure it contained. Jeep was trying to think of a place they could get it X-Rayed without calling attention to their secret, maybe the hospital? Jeep knew Milly Boyt, a nurse who worked at the hospital, but she didn't owe Jeep any favors. In fact, he thought he might owe her a few. They knew each other in high school and went to the junior prom together. Jeep knew it wasn't one of Milly's greatest memories, but it still brought a smile to his face.

When they finally retired for the evening, they decided all they had to do was prepare for the return of the BMW. They were sure the men with the guns would be back.

Four days of the week Pippins's was open for lunch. So, on those days Petey and Jeep would normally get downstairs about mid-morning to prepare. Petey would prep the bar and Jeep would prep the kitchen. Lunch was easy—hot dogs, hamburgers, any way you like 'em, egg salad, tuna salad and whatever was left over from the night before. They were maintaining a limited menu until their chef, KC, returned.

When Jeep was cooking the clientele was only interested in getting something in their stomach before the serious drinking began.

Today they were both downstairs by 9:00 a.m. Jeep was on his third coffee waiting for their first customer. It was usually Buck looking for an eye opener that he was willing to pay for by pushing a broom. Buck was a war veteran whose wounds were deep and didn't show. At least they weren't visible to the naked eye. Buck was deeply troubled by all the action he had seen in Southeast Asia. He just never seem to get it all back together when he joined civilian life again. He was a good guy and the boys were good to him. They gave him odd jobs to do and made sure he stayed out of trouble and was well fed.

Nothing extraordinary happened that morning. The sheriff stopped to tell them the BMW must be long gone because his deputies hadn't found it. And if "His boys couldn't find it, it just wasn't in the county."

Jeep suggested, "Maybe they switched cars. People with BMW's could afford more than one car."

"I'm telling you they are long gone," boasted Cottin.

Other than the typical few tourists that came by, things were quite normal and routine for the balance of the day, certainly nothing out of the ordinary happened.

Petey went to the bakery shortly after eleven that night to pick up tomorrow's bread. The bakery would deliver, but that would ruin his excuse to stop by his girlfriend Wanda's for a little sugar. Her house was not that far out of the way.

The only two left in the place were Jeep and Buck, so with no paying customers left in the building, that meant it was closing time. Petey hadn't returned yet, but Jeep expected him shortly. The routine was always the same. Jeep would help Buck out the front door and watch him from the parking lot as he walked down the highway to his trailer. It was only a half a mile and he always made it. As Jeep stood in the chilly evening, he heard someone coming up behind him.

He had just shouted, "Take care!" to Buck, as he turned. There stood the two suits, both with drawn guns, as if one wouldn't be enough. The uglier of the two was also the shortest.

"You know what we want," he spat from a crooked mouth on a face that had no redeeming features.

Jeep nodded, "And you know it's in the back of the pickup truck which isn't here."

"We'll wait!" said ugly number two.

He was larger than his partner and wore an ill fitting wrinkled suit with a stained tie. Jeep couldn't take his eyes off his large, almost comic pock marked nose. *If it was green it would be a pickle,* Jeep thought to himself, almost laughing out loud. *Get hold of yourself,* he thought. *They are pointing real guns at you; this is no time for laughter.*

"Let's go inside," said the shortest and ugliest.

As Jeep pulled the door open, he heard tires on the gravel parking lot and headlights lit the entire front of the restaurant. Jeep slammed the door behind him as he ran for the equalizer. The uglies both turned to face Petey's headlights. Seeing two guys with guns was enough for Petey to find reverse very fast. They froze just for a moment, and then moved toward the lights firing, shots at Petey's truck.

That was enough time for Jeep. He grabbed the shotgun, clicked off the safety and reversed his steps. He exited the front door, and there fifteen feet in front of him were the two of them, silhouetted by the lights and shooting at the truck. Jeep shot the first one in the back of the legs. He cried out and landed on his backside like a ton of bricks. The other spun around just in time to catch a chest full of double O buckshot. He was lifeless before he hit the ground. Jeep's main concern was to see if Petey was alright. When he reached the driver's door he was immediately relieved because Petey was bitchin' about the holes in his windshield.

"What in the Sam-Hill, happened?" he said as he pulled out his cell phone. "I'm calling Cottin."

Jeep turned to check on the first ugly and he saw him place his gun in his mouth and the top of his head vaporized into a red mist. It was a gut-retching sight.

Petey and Jeep just stared at each other, dumbfounded. For a moment they were both stunned, and then Petey said, "Now that is what I call a sore loser."

Sheriff Cottin showed up on the scene rather quickly considering it was almost midnight. He was speechless as he surveyed the results of "The Gunfight at the Pippin Corral." He almost tossed his cookies when he examined what was left of the two uglies. Cottin finally spoke.

"Neither one has any identification, no credit cards, no driver license, not even a library card. This is a very serious mess you two have here," he said.

He ushered them back inside the bar as his boys started yellow taping all around Pippins parking lot. It wasn't long before it seemed like every county official and reporter in the state was there.

Jeep could have done the medical examiner's job. A blind man could have declared them dead. It did however take him a little while to convince the authorities he only killed one of them and that he had done it in self defense. Deputies spent the better part of the next six hours taking photos and asking questions. There was even a TV crew from KDKA Pittsburgh trying to get some film for the morning news and requesting interviews. Jeep had made his one call to his lawyer, and good friend, Robert (Flip) Flockvich. He told Jeep to only talk to Sheriff Cottin, interviews were out of the question.

Cottin announced, "They're not 'mericans."

Jeep asked, "How do you know?"

"They don't look like 'mericans."

"Just what do Americans look like, Cottin?" Jeep inquired.

"I'm not sure, but these two are foreigners. I'm sure of that."

They seemed to have it all worked out as the sun was coming up. The bodies were removed and the area secured. The reporters had left to apply their trade.

Sheriff Cottin told Jeep, "You don't have to come with me, but don't leave town."

"Okay, Cottin, I'll cancel my noon flight to Paris and stay right here," Jeep told him as he rolled his eyes to Petey.

This wasn't the first time Jeep had shot and killed someone. He had spent eight years in the military, ranger training, and sniper school. He became the United States Government's most efficient weapon. During a war, hundreds of thousands of shots are fired for one kill, but for a sniper it's one shot one kill, thus saving the government a lot of money on ammunition. He had spent two tours of duty in the Middle East.

Jeep was still young enough at thirty-one to be in pretty good shape without working out habitually, although he did like to hit the heavy bag and the speed bag, as well as lift weights whenever he found the time.

Everything seemed to be returning to normal. The yellow tape the deputy's had strung up was gone by late morning. They decided to open for lunch.

Petey was having fun with the chalkboard menu. He had listed for lunch:

SCRAMBLED BRAINS
STRANGER STEW
PARKING LOT KIDNEY PIE
WINDSHIELD SALAD
JEEP'S FRESH JAMBALAYA

Jeep finally made him stop because suddenly no one was hungry and he was afraid they'd lose even the drinking crowd.

Petey McDade was Jeep's best friend. Petey was both strong and fast, with the highest pain level in any human being he knew. At six-two he was about two inches taller than Jeep. His sandy blond hair was always in need of a haircut. Jeep always teased him his hair was two inches away from a page boy. Petey would just glare at him with those green eyes and that crazy smile. Petey had been a very good football player in high school. He didn't go to college for the same reason Jeep didn't go, they couldn't afford it. No scholarships were offered to Petey because he played the entire senior year not knowing that he was hurt. Oh, he knew his left shoulder was sore, but didn't know it was damaged beyond repair. Now he can pop it in and out of the socket at will. He also has a stomach made of cast iron. He could, and sometimes would, eat anything that wasn't moving as well as a few things that moved too slowly for their own good. He was fun to be with and always made people smile.

Jeep and Petey were going to join the Army together after high school. Jeep did, but Petey was four F because of his shoulder. It took Petey eight years to talk Jeep into quitting the military and go into partnership in the restaurant business. They built Pippins from scratch. They were both much happier now. Jeep had experienced enough killing. Being a sniper can drain a man. At ranger school the sniper is sometimes referred to as god. He decides who lives and who dies.

Petey was the fun-loving of the two. He had the quicker wit, at least now as they were older. He was prone to be a little more daring. Jeep was worldlier and had traveled more with the Army and maybe was hardened by his military experiences. Of the two Jeep had become the thinker and Petey was still the hip-shooter with plenty of street sense.

Their lawyer Flip had put it best one day when he said, "Jeep was becoming a responsible adult. On the other hand, Petey does whatever his Rice Krispies tell him to do!"

Chapter 2

A week had passed and things were becoming commonplace. Jeep attended a few meetings with his lawyer Flip during the week, and it seemed he was going to be cleared of any wrongdoing.

It was a slow Tuesday afternoon, about two o'clock. Petey was upstairs and Jeep decided to open early out of boredom.

A man in a dark suit and inexpensive tie came in; Jeep immediately knew he was here for business.

"Blyden, Joseph Blyden," he said as he flashed a FBI badge. Jeep was sure this guy thought he was James Bond. He wanted to talk about the shootings last week. He told Jeep, "We still haven't identified the two guys, but we do know they were terrorists."

"That's what Cottin said when he called us yesterday," said Jeep. "I told you they weren't 'mericans," he imitated Cottin. In his attempt at humor he also told Jeep it was alright to go to Paris.

"Don't you guys travel in pairs?" asked Jeep.

"My partner is looking around outside. We want to be sure you're not being watched. Is Petey here?"

"He's upstairs."

"Would you and Petey take us to the site where you found the black crate?"

"What black crate?" Jeep said.

"The agency knows about it and that is why I'm here."

Just then Petey came in from the kitchen. Jeep introduced him to Agent Blyden.

"They know all about the black crate. They want us to show them where we found it. I wasn't quite sure, but I thought you would remember," said Jeep.

"Sure thing," said Petey, giving Jeep an inquisitive look. "I remember exactly, let's go."

Petey placed a sign on the locked front door that read: WILL OPEN FOR DINNER @ 5:30pm.

"Let's take my truck," Petey said. "We won't have to walk so far when we get to the site. Jeep, you ride in the back, Agent Blyden and his partner can ride up front with me. You better get your Woolrich jacket out of my bed box. It might be cool when the sun goes down," laughed Petey as he slipped into the comfortable cab of his Pennsylvania Porsche.

As they started down the highway toward Ohiopyle Jeep opened the bed box. He put on his jacket, took out his hunting fanny pack and his Remington.

Jeep's fanny pack was personalized. He looped it on his belt. It contained a plastic bottle of water, a few glow sticks, some dry soup packs, some of Jeep's homemade jerky as well as some Gorp mix, his own recipe of trail mix. It also had a few soft hand-warmers, the kind hunters and cold weather golfer's use. They stay warm about six hours when shaken and rubbed. There were other handy items such as a needle, some nylon thread, a Bic lighter, a length of cord, the always useful duct tape and a couple of rolls of Lifesavers. Jeep liked sucking on Lifesavers when he hunted. It was a habit he acquired in sniper school. While Jeep was sitting in the back of the truck, he checked to see if he had reloaded his rifle after he cleaned it—he had.

As they turned off Rt. 381, Jeep thought Petey was taking a different route, but then again, he wasn't with him when he came up to get the deer. They drove for quite a while, too long. Jeep sensed something was wrong. He wasn't sure now exactly where they were going. They had been on this dirt road for what seemed like quite a few miles. As they came around a bend in the road, Jeep looked over the cab to see where they were. It was then that he saw five or six guys standing in front of a truck that was blocking the road. They were all armed, some with automatic weapons.

At that exact moment, Blyden stuck a gun in Petey's ribs. Petey screamed, "He's a phony, Jeep, Blyden's pulled a gun on me."

Jeep knew exactly what the situation was and hurdled over the tailgate. Petey had been compromised and Jeep had to remain free if they were going to have a chance. Rifle in hand, and using the truck as interference, he ran like hell back down the road they had just come up. Jeep covered a hundred yards or so before they knew he was gone. Using the bend in the road as his new cover, he scurried left into the woods thick with fall foliage. He continued forty or fifty yards into the dense forest and took another sharp left. Jeep was now heading back toward Petey and his captors. He knew the closer he could get to Petey's truck, the safer he would feel. That would be the last place they would think to look. He could hear them running down the road thinking they were chasing him. The faster they ran, the more distance they were putting between them.

Jeep thought he had covered enough ground to be about even with Petey's truck and the roadblock. He heard the road block truck start.

Someone hollered, "Follow me." as both trucks started moving further up the road.

Jeep thought he could follow from his place in the woods. The trucks weren't going that fast, but the road they were on started turning to the left and declining. Jeep's terrain was inclining and going up rather steeply. After a few hundred yards, the road was at least sixty feet below him. Jeep was on a steep hill that would have to end with a cliff. The truck that had Petey would be below him and long gone.

He had to stop and rest. He was completely out of breath. He covered almost a thousand yards, mostly up hill. Not hearing his pursuers, he sat down facing back down his trail searching and listening for any activity— it was silent. He took a gulp of water and rested for five minutes. Popping a Lifesaver in his mouth, he started walking again. This time at a slower pace so he would be more aware of his surroundings while conserving energy. Jeep perceived the trees to his right were thinning. Walking in that direction, he came upon a high precipice overlooking what appeared to be a small lake or a cove. The land on the other side he estimated to be five- hundred yards. He continued to walk along the cliff, staying out of sight of anyone on the other shore. The land on the other side was getting closer. It was then he noticed a rather large camp with a road leading into it and Petey's truck parked at the guard gate. It was getting dark and he was quickly running out of real estate. He had to hole up for the night, so he found a good spot where he could see and not be seen and started digging a makeshift spider hole in the leaves. Jeep had all he needed to rest comfortably for the night. He knew he had it much better than Petey.

Just before dark his pursuers gave up and returned to the camp. From his position above their camp he could tell they were drinking beer and he was sure they were bragging how they almost had him and they would surely get him tomorrow.

As he lay in the soft leaves thinking, it dawned on him what this camp was all about. He had heard rumors about a bunch of radical skinheads that lived in the woods somewhere on Chestnut Ridge. It was thought their camp might be near the Youghiogheny River or Confluence Dam. According to the newspapers, their leader was an ex-army wacko that called himself Major White. As Jeep remembers hearing, his nickname was Red. Yea, that was it Jeep remembered Petey joking about Red White, a blue blooded American. Made you want to throw up.

Jeep was waiting for the sun to break so he could scope the camp. It must have been about an hour after sunrise when he saw groups gather in the center of the camp. The creep in the white sweatshirt was alias Agent Blyden. Standing next to him was some guy dressed like Gen. Patton. That must be ol' Red White. The third guy, Blyden's partner was leading Petey to the center of the camp. It looked like Petey's hands were tied in front of him with ty-wrap type handcuffs. *You've made a big mistake, boys,* Jeep contemplated to himself. It looked like they were trying to decide what to do with Petey. If he told them where the black crate was, they would have known what to do with him and would already have done it. Jeep was pretty sure Petey would know what to do when Jeep started the fireworks.

He knew the rifle report coming off the walls of the cliff and over the lake would make it hard to know the direction of the shot. .He estimated the shot to be three-hundred and fifty yards downhill. There was a very slight left to right wind, but it was less than five miles an hour, as attested to by the three-inch thread Jeep always had tied on his gun barrel. That meant that the bullet drift from the wind would be less than a half an inch at a shot under four-hundred yards. This was an acceptable drift rate, simply reminding him to aim a fraction to the left of his true target. He made the adjustments and laid the cross hairs right on old Red's head. He squeezed off the shot and Red's head jerked back abruptly and he was on the ground that fast. Chambering the second round, Jeep caught the phony agent square in the back as he spun around to run. It now looked like Petey was holding his captor's hands. The guy had a panicked look on his face as he tried to pull away from Petey. *I must remember to thank Petey for the easy set-up*, Jeep thought. The round caught him in the neck. That's not where Jeep was aiming, but he just wouldn't hold still. Everyone was running to hide. Petey started running for his truck. The last obstacle was the guard standing next to Petey's truck at the gate. Petey was running right at him. At fifty yards away and closing the guard couldn't miss. He raised what looked like an AK47 but never got the chance to fire it. Jeep was four for four. Petey picked up the guard's weapon turned and emptied the entire clip into the center of the camp. Anyone thinking of chasing after Petey quickly changed their mind. The truck was throwing gravel and dirt from all four spinning tires the minute Petey jumped into it. It's amazing what one can do with his hands cuffed in front of him instead of behind him.

It was time for Jeep to set some speed records of his own. He was going to have to hurry to beat Petey to the bend in the road. As it turned out, he broke out of the woods onto the road fifty yards behind Petey and his highballing "Pennsylvania Porsche." His only hope was to keep running after him, confident that Petey would look in his rear view mirror to see if anyone was chasing him. As good fortune would have it, he did. Jeep saw the truck lock its brakes and skid to a stop. Catching up with the truck, he climbed in the cab screaming, "GO, GO, GO!"

Petey's face was cut and battered and his lip was split bad, but the damn fool was laughing.

"Can you cut these ty-wraps? My ass is itching," he said.

They had their story straight by the time they got back to Pippins. It was a good thing too. One of Cottin's deputies was waiting in the parking lot.

"Where have you guys been?" asked Deputy Porter "Cottin put an APB out on you two last night. You never opened up your joint at five-thirty like the sign said."

Shamefully Jeep said, "I'm sorry, Porter, please call in and tell Cottin we're okay, I know he's worried. Petey got into a little shoving match in Pittsburgh yesterday and it took me all night to bail him out. And being in a hurry to help Petey I put the wrong sign on the door. It should have said, 'We'll be open tomorrow as usual.' Tell Cottin I am really sorry and that I owe him a dinner on the house."

Jeep could hear Porter call in as he drove away laughing about Petey's beat up face and saying,

"It must have been a helluva fight."

They had a few hours before lunch, enough time to clean up and think about what to do next. Petey wanted to open the black crate, but Jeep didn't think it was a good idea. They still didn't know if it was safe or not. What they did know was that no report would be filed about their incident on Chestnut Ridge. Those camp folks didn't want to talk to the authorities any more than Jeep did.

Petey's lip needed a stitch or two so Jeep dragged him down to the hospital kicking and screaming that he didn't need any medical attention. One and a half hours and six micro stitches later Petey was sitting at Pippins bar drinking a cold Iron City through a straw. Jeep was just sitting there smiling at him.

Chapter 3

Well, today was going to be a better day. K.C. was coming back from the two week refresher course she just finished at her alma mater.

Kathleen Connelly, "K.C.," is the chef at Pippins as well as the love of Jeep's life. Jeep hired her a little over two years ago and she's the main reason for their success. She had just graduated from cooking school and was looking for a break. Jeep would have hired her even if she couldn't cook. She's the kind of girl you would like to bring home to mom if you could trust dad. They hit it off immediately, and they have been a couple for the last two years. K.C. was the calming effect in Jeep's life. She'd shown up for the interview fresh out of CIA (Cooking Institute of America). She was born in Connecticut, educated in private schools and was supposed to marry a rich lawyer from New Canaan. But she had her own ideas about her future. She wanted to be the owner of a restaurant and her own boss. She didn't look like a typical chef—you know the type. She was five feet five inches tall; her auburn hair was always neatly groomed. She obviously didn't eat much of her own cooking. She was slight of build, but not lacking in any department, and she could match wits with Petey.

A magnificent cook; one of her specialties was a meatloaf, which she cooks in muffin tins. When they were on the menu, along with her garlic mashed potatoes, the dinner wait was forty-five minutes. Her sauces are world class. One is mushroom and reduced balsamic vinegar; another is mustard and Jack Daniels which goes with everything from filet mignon to knockwurst. One of Jeep's favorite sandwiches is a squashed down muffin meatloaf, with a thin slice of red onion on a hamburger roll, chased down with a cold "Rollin Rock."

They have four cottages on a cul de sac behind the restaurant. It was nicely landscaped, creating a vacation atmosphere. Each cottage was eight-hundred square feet. They are single rooms with electricity and indoor plumbing. Each one has a completely new bathroom, as well as a new wood burning stove for heat. Petey and Jeep worked very hard fixing them up—in the big city they would be known as studio apartments. Three of them were rented year round. K.C. lives in one. A trucker named Bo, an old friend of the family's lives in one, and a Korean named Master Lee, a fifth degree black belt Tae Kwon Do instructor, lives in the third one. The fourth one remains empty, but ready for friends that stay more than one day.

B is also coming back from vacation today, she had been visiting her family in Buffalo. Bridget Keely McDade is the head bartender, restaurant manager and all-around keeper of the peace .She is very knowledgeable in the service aspect of the business and the customers appreciate her wit and "can do" attitude. She is a cousin of Petey's and has a smile that would melt the hardest of hearts. She moved down here from Buffalo at Petey's request. They had been searching for reliable help and B was the answer. Although she was only and inch over five feet tall and cute as a button, she is as tough as nails, and don't even think of messing with her! She can take care of herself as well as two or three others at the same time.

Petey and Jeep really needed K.C. and B's help operating Pippins. They can now deal with the problem at hand without letting the business suffer. They were sitting at their favorite corner booth discussing their options.

"Okay," said Petey, "This is what we don't know. What's in the crate? Who wants it? Why? Where was it supposed to go? Who's after us? This is what we do know. There are six people dead. You killed five of them and the cops only know about two of them."

They agreed that they didn't have to tell K.C. and B everything that had happened.

"If they ask about your face, just say that you fell off a dirt bike," Jeep said.

"But, I don't have a dirt bike," Petey replied.

"Then tell them that you fell off of Wanda's."

"She doesn't have a dirt bike either," he explained.

"Then tell them you fell off of Wanda!"

They had not unlocked the front door yet. It was still too early, but someone was unlocking it as they sat there. Other than Petey and Jeep the only people with keys to Pippins were K.C. and B. While they were guessing who it was, B stuck her head in the door.

Looking at them she said, "I think you were both sitting there when I left two weeks ago." They jumped up and hugged her. They were very happy to see her back. All is right with the world when B's around.

"Did you have a good time in Buffalo?" Petey asked.

"Did you eat a beef on a weck?" Jeep wanted to know.

"Yes and yes," B answered. "A very good time and I ate too many wecks."

Roast beef on a Kimmelweck roll with horseradish is native to Buffalo and just about the best sandwich you've ever eaten. If they could get Kimmelweck rolls down here, Petey and Jeep could retire years sooner. When B wanted to know if K.C. had returned, Jeep told her he expected her later that day.

Petey said, "Jeep and I are telling you right now, you and K.C. aren't taking time off at the same time ever again."

"What happened to your face, Petey?" B inquired.

"Awe, I fell off a dirt bike. It's nothing," mumbled Petey.

"You're right, on your face it's nothing." She laughed. She looked around the place.

"Speaking about nothing, have you guys used a broom or a bar rag since I've been gone? Don't answer that, take the fifth for your own good."

B was ready to go to work. She walked behind the bar and picked up a new apron and wrapped it around, tied it off and started cleaning.

Intimidated by her action, Jeep headed into the kitchen to get ready for lunch. Petey started bringing in cases of whisky to restock the bar. They expected Buck to come wandering in soon. Considering all that happened Jeep felt pretty good.

In the slow part of the afternoon Jeep was upstairs alone and thinking no one alive knew they had the black crate. Having it under Petey's bed wasn't accomplishing anything. It would just be replaced by those who were missing it and their plan would go on. He was sure that their intentions were diabolic. It appeared that the crate's destination was that camp, and surely nothing good was being planned there. Assuming all that was true, he and Petey had to take some action.

Maybe Petey could remember something he saw at that camp that would give them some thoughts as to what the camp residents were planning, whoever they were.

K.C.'s arrival led to an impromptu party at Pippins. Jeep thought everyone was overdue to let their hair down and have some fun. It was a great party, and after helping K.C. get settled in her cottage, Jeep didn't get up to his room until after three in the morning. It sure was good to have her back. After breakfast K.C. went to the Farmers' Market for produce and Petey and Jeep went for a ride.

"What do you remember seeing at that camp, Petey?"

Petey smiled and said, "Did you know that you hit that guy Red right in the eye with your first shot? The guy I was holding by the hands started to cry when he realized what was going to happen to him. You weren't aiming for his neck, were you?"

"No," Jeep assured him, "I was aiming for yours." He chuckled. Jeep made a mental note to himself that Red had turned his head at the last second and that aiming at his head was a mistake. The third target was moving too much for a good shot. Overall, his old gunny sergeant would have given him a score of seven on a scale of ten.

Petey remembered a lot of plastic bottles—the kind of water bottles that everyone carries around every day. Some had Dasani labels and others were Aquafina, Crystal Lake, etc. It seemed like a large assortment of sizes and brands. *There was a whole building full of them*, he thought. They agreed they had to get back into that camp, but they both knew Petey couldn't go because they would recognize him unless…Jeep took him back as his prisoner. It was worth thinking about; it was also the only idea they had.

The bottom line was they had to include the law for their own protection. Jeep decided to tell the whole story to his lawyer Flip and see what he might suggest.

Flip sat mesmerized as Jeep related their adventures over the last few days. With Flip asking questions and taking notes, it took two tape cassettes and most of the afternoon to bring him up to date. He said the first thing he would do was contact the ATF. Alcohol, Tobacco, and Firearms is a part of the Federal Government that conducts criminal investigations relating to firearms and explosives. They assist other law enforcement agencies to prevent terrorism. Jeep thought that was a good place to start. Their Pennsylvania office was in Philadelphia.

Flip said, "Don't touch the black crate and keep Petey away from it too. Go back to Pippins and get on with your life as best you can."

"But, Jeep," he warned, "staying alert means staying alive."

Being able to share their secret gave Jeep some peace of mind. Besides, it was Friday and they were going to be busy. The word spread fast about their shootout in the parking lot. It didn't hurt business at all, in fact it helped. Jeep said, "I will never understand the American public. I really think if we told them there would be another shootout tomorrow, the crowds would get larger."

The parking lot was filling up fast. Jeep told K.C. it was obvious the word was out that she was back. He went upstairs to lie down and rest before the peak of the evening hit them. Petey was there cleaning his new Weatherby Mark IV. He asked if Jeep wanted to go shooting tomorrow morning. He said his new scope needed to be sighted in and after that shooting demo Jeep had put on the other day it was obvious he needed some practice. Jeep knew he didn't need the practice, but it might help him get his mind off the incidents surrounding the black crate. He had planned to switch barrels on his 270 so no ballistics could be traced back to it. Over the years he had acquired several different type barrels for his weapon, some were bull barrels for target shooting, other's had the slimmed-down mountain rifles barrel, so tomorrow it was going to need some tweaking itself.

Chapter 4

They arrived at the gun club at seven-thirty Saturday morning. It was located about three miles off the highway up in the hills among the old unused coke ovens. Coke ovens were just brick lined holes in the side of the hills. They were once used to burn coal into coke to be used in the iron and steel foundries. The gun club had a four position shooting shack with right and left hand shooting tables and plenty of small sand bags for support. The front flaps were tied up and Dickey Lee Landy was shooting. He was so focused on his task he didn't even look up when they arrived. Down range you had a choice of targets at one, two or three-hundred yards. They put their ear plugs in and got right to work. It took about an hour and a half of shooting and walking down range examining their targets before they were both happy with their results.

As they started back down the hill Petey was looking in his rear view mirror and he said as if thinking out loud,

"If Dickey Lee was the only other person up there and his truck is red, then who are these guys following us?"

At that moment the rear window of Petey's truck exploded and sent flying glass everywhere.

"Hang on!" Petey shouted.

He cut the wheels hard to the right and floored it. They started up a knoll that was as steep as the third turn on the track at Daytona. It was at least 30 degrees and Jeep didn't know if the Pennsylvania Porsche could make it, but he was pretty sure whoever was behind them wouldn't even try. Their rifles were in the bed box so shooting back wasn't an option.

They had just about reached the peak of a ridge when the truck stopped. The other side of the ridge fell off so fast that the truck would fall out of control if they went over the crest. They both had slid down in the seat far enough so their heads wouldn't be targets. Regrettably, Petey couldn't see over the dashboard so he slammed on the brakes with both feet. The truck was perched dangerously on the top of the ridge. They looked at each other helplessly knowing they were in a mess.

Then Petey smiled and said, "What's our next move Kemo Sabe?"

"Keep the truck right here." Jeep said.

He opened the door and rolled out, desperately looking for cover, but noticing there was no one on the road below. *They must have kept going after they shot at us,* thought Jeep. He then noticed that the front tires of the truck were not touching the ground. It was that close to going over the ridge.

"They are gone, Petey, but so are you if you take your feet off the brake." Jeep informed him. "Put it in reverse and see if you can back down. Don't turn the wheels or you might roll it over as you start back down. I'll wait out here if you don't mind," he confirmed with a big grin on his face.

With the brakes on and sliding most of the way down he got the truck safely back on the dirt road. That was the best jockeying of a vehicle Jeep had ever seen.

"Did you get a look at who the hell was shooting at us, Petey?"

"Yep," Petey said. "It was the same truck that was blocking the road into that camp."

"How could they find us? The remaining people left alive at the camp have no idea who we are," inquired Jeep.

"Maybe they took the number off my license plate and traced it," suggested Petey. "They must have a friend at the Department of Motor Vehicles or in Law Enforcement"

"Get us back to Pippins quick!" Jeep said.

They skidded into the parking lot and headed right around back to the cottages. Jeep knocked on K.C.'s door, Bo's eighteen-wheeler was parked out behind the cottages so they knew Bo was home. Petey was knocking on Bo's door; it wasn't locked and it swung open as Petey hit it.

"SHIT!" Petey shouted. Jeep ran over to Bo's place and saw Petey leaning over Bo's body.

He looked up and said, "He's alive, but I don't know for how long—call an ambulance."

While Petey stayed with Bo, Jeep checked the restaurant. It was still locked up. It was too early for B to have arrived, so he quickly unlocked the place and made the 911 call. It was just nine-thirty and K.C. was nowhere to be found. Jeep was getting that sick feeling in his stomach, the kind you get as you start down the first hill on a roller coaster.

After the ambulance left with its siren screaming, they told Sheriff Cottin what little they knew of K.C.'s disappearance. Jeep went inside for a much needed drink. He sat alone for quite a while. He knew he was mad and scared because his hands were shaking.

It was now eleven a.m. and Jeep was sitting in the corner booth with Petey and B. Jeep was at his wit's end.

He said, "Don't open for lunch."

"Wrong," B stated emphatically. "We must be cool and operate as if everything is okay. We must wait to hear from her kidnappers and be where they expect us to be so we don't miss their call."

It appeared that Jeep was the only one that wasn't making any sense. Petey said, "Where's your car?"

"It's down at Kendal's garage," Jeep said.

Jeep had a 92 Chevy Impala SS with a 350HP Twin turbo charged Corvette engine.

"Good," said Petey. "We are going to need it while my Porsche gets some glass put in it. I'll have Kendal give it the once over to see how bad I tore it up, although I think it s okay. Is your car ready to be picked up?"

"Yes it is," said B. "Kendal called yesterday and said it was ready to run at Indy if you wanted and you could pick it up anytime."

Jeep knew Cottin was going to notify the FBI. He had to in a kidnapping case, and then they were going to have a whole bunch of strangers telling them what was best for K.C.

"This whole mess is about to go downhill rapidly," Jeep said. "Petey, we have to act fast. Do you have any ideas?"

"Yeah," he said, "Let's go up to Chestnut Ridge and kill 'em all. We'll let the devil and God fight over who wants them."

With that remark, the phone rang. B answered it, paused for a few seconds then said, "Wait a minute." She turned to Jeep and Petey with a stunned look on her face and said, "They hung up."

B explained, "All the voice said was don't tell anyone and bring the box, if you want the broad back. Do you know what box they are talking about and where they want you to bring it?"

They both nodded.

As B opened for lunch Flip was one of the first to show up.

"What are you doing here?" Jeep asked.

"I'm hungry."

"For food or information?" inquired Petey.

"Both," he replied.

He had a guy with him that was Government Issue. He introduced Jeep to Agent Jamison Bradley and asked Jeep to join them for lunch. He was the image all agents were designed after. Six foot, athletically built, well dressed, short neatly trimmed hair, no facial hair, and looked like he could run a 4.5 second forty. Agent Bradley told Jeep that Flip had brought him up to date on their adventures and now he wanted to let us know what they knew. He said the camp had been around for about ten years and it was founded and run by Royce (Red) White. There were about twenty-five members and they had many weapons, but nothing illegal as far as ATF knew. They didn't have an alcohol still on the premises and weren't growing anything unusual. They had built two large warehouse type buildings in the last two years and had acquired a few large trucks. There has been increased activity the last six months. They may have been running trunkloads of cigarettes up from the Carolinas, but nothing of any consequence.

"Mr. Bradley," Jeep started to say.

"Call me Jamie," he interrupted.

"Okay, Jamie. Do you have anything on Royce White?"

"Not yet, but he will slip-up sooner or later," stated Jamie.

"I don't think he'll be making any more mistakes," Jeep said, smiling at Flip and thinking to himself, *I guess Flip hasn't told them about Mr. White untimely demise.*

"I would like to pick up the crate while I'm here," Jamie said.

Petey responded, "Where do you want me to put it?"

"In my trunk," he replied.

They left after lunch with Flip promising to call Jeep later.

As soon as Petey walked back in, Jeep screamed at him, "What were you thinking?"

"About what?" he asked.

"Did you just put the crate in the trunk of his car?"

"I put *A* crate in the trunk of his car, but not *THE* crate. Petey smiled. "I figure Bradley won't open that crate until he gets to the ATF lab. And didn't you say that was in Philly?" smiled Petey.

He had used the crate his Weatherby had been shipped in, figuring only the two of them knew what the crate looked like. Now, if they could come up with a plan to get K.C. before the FBI got involved, they just might have a chance of saving her.

Petey's girlfriend Wanda had been nice enough to come in and help them with dinner. The evening dragged, but they finally let the last customer out. B locked up and Petey was taking Wanda home. B told Jeep she was going to stay out back at K.C.'s place. She said she wanted to be close and available if she was needed. Jeep thought it would be safe enough. She told him Master Lee had said he would keep an eye on her. Jeep started packing for their little adventure. He put his 9mm S&W Model 659 in an extra fanny pack he had. He made sure the pistol's 14-round magazine was full and put the remaining box of 9mm's in with a box of 270's. His Remington Model 700 only held four rounds, a disadvantage when you are outnumbered. Their objective was simply to liberate K.C. not to engage the entire camp in a firefight.

They entered the road to the camp at four a.m. Petey was driving Jeep's car. Jeep slipped out at about the same spot they had been stopped by the roadblock. Petey was going to give him fifteen minutes to get settled back at his old shooting spot. He then proceeded down with the lights out to a spot about a hundred yards in front of the guard shack. Taking a crate, this one he had picked up at Kendal's garage, out of the trunk and placing it in the center of the road, he backed up about thirty yards. He turned the headlights on the crate and started tooting the horn. He did this off and on for about an half a hour. Finally two guys appeared at the guard shack and it looked like K.C. was with them. They told Petey once they saw what was in the crate they would let the girl go. Petey said fine, just bring the girl out with them while they examined the crate. Jeep knew they had a gun aimed at K.C. but as long as Petey stayed behind the headlights, they couldn't see him. Jeep scanned the limit of the headlights, mentally thanking Petey for remembering to turn on the high beams. As the two guarding K.C. knelt down to open the crate, Petey calmly told K.C. to start walking toward his voice. As she started for the car, the two of them looked up. Petey had picked up the Colt .45 Combat Commander that was lying conveniently on the hood. Firing quickly, they both were sent spinning to the ground dead or dying shortly. Jeep fired at his dimly lit targets as effectively and as fast as he could. There was no return fire. Meanwhile, Petey and K.C. were in the car. With the lights now out, the car was speeding in reverse back up the dirt road, and as soon as the headlights were turned off it was Jeep's signal to retreat down the hill. They were to meet at the same spot they met early Friday morning. Petey beat Jeep there again, although Jeep arrived by the time he had the car turned around.

"Go.Go.Go!" Jeep said as they both started laughing.

"We have to stop meeting like this," Petey joked.

K.C. was in the back seat trembling with fear, but even she started laughing. She was returning to normal as she looked at Jeep and said, "What took you so long"? She then grabbed his neck and kissed him, her eyes were still wet with tears.

"Are you okay? Did they hurt you?"

"No, they treated me okay," she answered. "One guy said I was a prisoner of war. What did he mean by that?"

"I don't know. He is just some nut that never grew up and is still playing war games. He must think we are trying to capture his flag," Jeep said.

They headed back to Pippins using the turbo most of the way. Jeep put in a call to the sheriff's office. Colleen was on the night desk. Colleen

(Cookie) Wildey was by far the best deputy sheriff Cottin had on his staff. Her nickname came from when she was a kid. Her grandfather used to say; "She was one tough cookie." She had graduated from Western Kentucky with a degree in criminal justice and had plans for a career in law enforcement with one of the government agencies. Jeep told Cookie they had found K.C. and she was fine.

She said, "Jeep, that's great news, I was worried about her." Cookie and K.C. had become great friends. "I was planning to come out to your place when I got off duty this morning." she said. "Would that be okay?"

"That would be fine. Give us a few hours to get some sleep and come on out. We'll tell you everything that has happened," Jeep said. "Just tell Cottin to call off the FBI."

Today was Sunday, and thanks to the Pennsylvania Blue Laws, they were closed on Sundays. They also were closed on Mondays, and they didn't open up until late afternoon on Tuesday. They only served lunch on Wednesday thru Saturday.

B stayed with K.C., Petey and Jeep laid down for a few hours rest. Jeep fell asleep hoping things would calm down, but knowing even normal was a little hectic around here.

It was noon when Jeep awoke and he thought he heard K.C. and B. downstairs in the kitchen. Jeep's bedroom was directly over the Pippins kitchen. When they built the place he was concerned that they only had one set of stairs leading down from Petey's side of the residence into the restaurant area. He thought it would make his side of the apartment building perilous if there was a fire. So, without telling anyone but Petey, Jeep installed a fire pole in the deepest corner of his walk-in closet near the rear wall of the building. The floor lifted up on both sides of the pole. The floor of the closet closed around the pole with half moon cutouts so it fit snugly with the pole. The slide down terminated in the kitchen near the back door between the walk-in freezer and the wall. It was out of sight from anywhere in the kitchen. You could only see it if you looked to your right as you entered the kitchen from the rear door. It would be behind the open door. It looked like a support beam. Although he never used it, it was nice knowing it was there. As time passed B and K.C. had learned of the secret pole.

Jeep took a quick shower, threw on some clothes and went to find the source of the noise. Petey, K.C. and B were standing in the kitchen finishing breakfast.

Jeep folded a napkin over his arm and with the air of a maitre'd announced, "I think I might be able to find you folks a table if you would like."

"Want some eggs?" said B. "I'm cooking!"

"Yea, I'll have some any way you want to make them, some toast, also, if you please." Jeep yawned.

"I couldn't sleep, I was starving. They didn't have any s'mores at that Girl Scout camp I stayed at last night," commented K.C.

"That's right, you haven't eaten since Friday evening!" Jeep exclaimed.

There was a knock at the back door. It was Deputy Wildey.

"Come on in, Cookie, and have some breakfast, Jeep can't charge you because it's Sunday and we're closed," shouted B.

Jeep asked Cookie if she had told Sheriff Cottin to call off the dogs. She commented that the sheriff was out of town and wouldn't be back until sometime Monday afternoon.

"You know, Jeep," she responded, "you just can't tell the FBI not to show up. Once they have been notified, they are like a blue tick hound on a slow rabbit. They just won't quit! I must say, I'm surprised they have not shown up already."

"Petey, we've got to talk," Jeep whispered. "Holler when the eggs are done, B."

Petey and Jeep talked while the girls were in the kitchen. Petey thought he killed both the guys by the crate. Jeep told him he wasn't sure what he hit but he thought he hit two. Jeep thought the FBI would show up today or tomorrow morning at the latest. They did not know how much of the story they should tell them.

"I think we should just tell them K.C. escaped and didn't get a good look at them," said Jeep. "She hid in the woods and worked her way back here this morning. Did K.C. see who shot Bo?" Jeep wanted to know.

"She doesn't even know Bo was hurt," Petey said. "That must have happened after they had her blindfolded and in the car."

Chapter 5

There was no plan today except that everyone was to stay close to home, take it easy and watch some football on TV. The Steelers were playing the Ravens in Baltimore at one o'clock. The four o'clock game was the Packers vs. the Bears. Jeep was looking forward to a lazy afternoon and maybe even a nap some time during the boring part of the games.

Sunday was monotonous, the Steelers won. So did the Packers. Monday was another lethargic fall day. The only excitement was when Agent Bradley called to tell them the crate was empty.

"How could that be?" Jeep responded with mock surprise. "Are you sure you've got the right crate?" he teased.

"It's the one Petey gave me," was Jamie's stern reply.

"How could so much commotion be made over an empty crate?" Jeep inquired.

Jamie said that Jeep should talk to his friend Petey and that he would be back here Tuesday or Wednesday. Just before he hung up, he asked Jeep if Petey was enjoying his new Weatherby.

It was Tuesday morning and Jeep was having breakfast with Master Lee down at Gov's diner. It was owned by Warren (Gov.) Landy. The official name of the diner was Gerry's Diner. Jeep enjoyed Master Lee's company. He was a two-time Korean Army T.K.D. Champion. He had only been in this country for three years and already had his own business. In his spare time, he was learning English, which was already superior to some of the guys that had graduated from high school with Jeep. He always greeted you by saying "Ar-e-ass-i-o." or something that sounded like that. It was a Korean greeting that meant hello, how are you today. At least that's what he had them believing, it was probably his little joke on round eyes. He wanted to know how Bo was doing and to tell them he was sorry he wasn't there that morning.

"It not happen if Lee there," he said.

Jeep believed that was a fact. Jeep told Lee that Bo was still in intensive care and he didn't know any more than that. Master Lee wanted to help in any way he could, as he was presently the official watchdog for Pippins when Jeep and Petey weren't around. Jeep told him he appreciated his friendship very much and would let him know. Jeep asked how B was doing with her Tae Kwon Do training.

"She very good student," he said. "She's going to test for first degree red belt next week."

Jeep noticed Petey pull up in his Pennsylvania Porsche and he had Kendal with him. He was probably going to try to buy Kendal breakfast instead of paying for the repairs. Kendal was much too good a businessman for that to happen.

"Hi, guys," Petey greeted all as he slipped into our booth. "What's ya eating?" Jeep suddenly knew his bill was going to be for two more.

Petey told Jeep he was going to Pittsburgh for the rest of the day. He would be back when Jeep had cleared up the little misunderstanding that Petey had with Agent Bradley. They agreed to turn over the crate to ATF. It had already caused nine or ten deaths, and even Petey agreed it probably didn't contain money.

Later that day, as they were getting ready to open Pippins for dinner, Agent Bradley showed up.

"Hello, Mr. Patrick, is Mr. Mc Dade around?" he asked.

"No, he isn't and I don't know where he is or when he is coming back...he told me to say." Jeep smiled. "But, I think we can fix the problem he created."

Jeep took Jamie up to the apartment. He explained all that happened and he told him why there had been a deliberate mix-up with the crates.

Until K.C. was safe, they just couldn't part with that crate. He was concerned they never heard from the FBI, in fact, they still haven't heard from them, and that made Jeep feel they couldn't trust anybody. He also reminded Agent Bradley that he and Petey were the ones that introduced the ATF to this terrorist plot. He reminded Bradley that without Petey the ATF was clueless.

After Agent Bradley delivered a very strong lecture on the law he said, "Give me the crate and all is absolved." He said he understood their dilemma as Jeep helped him put the crate in his car. He said that he arranged to take it to the FBI lab in Pittsburgh where it would be opened and examined. Jeep thanked him for his understanding, and asked Jamie to let him know what he finds. He said he would call once they determined the contents of the crate. As Agent Bradley was pulling out of the lot, Sheriff Cottin was pulling in, they didn't seem to see each other.

"Hey, Cottin, where you been?" Jeep asked.

"We were up in the hills looking for K.C. I thought we might have a lead on who took her, but it didn't pan out," he said. "I sure am glad to hear that K.C. is okay."

"Did you notify the FBI?" Jeep asked.

"Yep."

"Do they want to talk to me"?

"They don't need to now that your girl is safe."

"Come on in, Cottin, and I'll buy you that dinner I owe you," Jeep said.

Cottin sat at the bar and had a root beer, while Jeep called Petey's cell phone and left him a text message. "Come home. All is forgiven."

He asked Cottin how his investigation was progressing. He didn't have anything new. They had not identified the two uglies and they had not found the BMW. They were clueless as to why any of this had happened, however, Jeep was sure Cottin knew more than he was telling him. His dinner arrived, so Jeep left him alone. Jeep spent the rest of the evening greeting and seating customers. Tuesday nights were slow. Petey showed up about closing time. He told Jeep he had taken Wanda to Pittsburgh to show her the sights. Knowing Petey, all Wanda saw was the inside of a Holiday Inn hotel room. He thanked Jeep for squaring things with the ATF.

"Don't thank me, thank a very understanding Agent Bradley."

Petey and Jeep were going to a restaurant trade show in Washington D.C. for three days. Jeep liked these shows because you could learn a lot and stay on top of the latest trends and gadgets in their business. They stayed at a nice hotel in Silver Springs and got a chance to visit the new War Memorials. D.C. is a great town for tourists.

The show was very informative. It gave them a lot of new ideas to bounce off K.C. and B. They took turns going to trade shows like these. If they all went together they would buy every new gadget and idea that was offered. If K.C. and Jeep went, everyone was sure they would get distracted and forget about the trade show. This way the two that were left at home served as the Devil's advocate and weren't intoxicated by the show and its bright lights and tinsel.

One of the things they learned was that no one drinks tap water anymore. Bottled water sales were through the roof. Even drinking fountains were a thing of the past. You could pick up bottles of water everywhere. The show representatives were suggesting that restaurants shouldn't serve water in pitchers anymore, as even the upscale restaurants with the white gloved water boy was a thing of the past. Back at Pippins they served fresh spring water that they collected right from the spring.

They also learned a lot of recipes for the new martini drinks. Jeep always liked gin drinks, although they didn't always like him. He thought vodka was overrated. Everyone was raving about all the new expensive vodkas. In Jeep's mind vodka was tasteless, therefore he would tell his vodka drinking buddies, "Why don't you just drink water and act stupid? You'll have the same effect for a lot less money."

They were always trying to improve Pippins. With a chef as good as K.C., their goal was to keep improving the quality of food and service until they could get customers to drive down from Pittsburgh for the experience. They had so much to learn, and K.C. was the only one with a formal education in the restaurant business. So far they were doing very well, making a lot of money, and their customer base was growing. Their reputation was good and getting better. Their building was new and built for expansion, they had the latest equipment and they were having fun!

But, two days were enough. They had seen it all and were ready to go home. They were talking about all they had seen as they drove home. They both noticed the security that was in and around D.C.—there were guards everywhere. They saw guards at all the government buildings, at the historical memorials, the train and bus stations. The reservoirs and energy plants, even the dumps and waste areas were under guard.

Jeep was looking forward to an easy ride home. They left D.C. on Rt. 270 north to Frederick, then Rt.70 thru Hagerstown to the Rt. 68 junction.

They would go west on Rt.68 until they reached Pa. Route 40, then just shoot up toward Uniontown, Pa.

When they were alone in the car was when Pippins held their stock holders meeting. The trip was one of the few times Jeep and Petey had to talk.

"Have you ever seen that much security?" asked Petey.

"There were guards everywhere," noted Jeep.

"I didn't know that you couldn't drive by the White House," stated Petey.

"This Homeland Security is taking their job seriously," said Jeep. "I guess they are looking out for us."

They didn't have much family left between them. Jeep's mom had died of breast cancer when he was in the Middle East. She had been alone for eighteen years. His dad had been a long-hauling eighteen-wheel truck driver. He had died in an accident when Jeep was six years old. Their good friend Bo (who was still in intensive care) and Jeep's father had been the best of friends. They had plans of going into business together before the accident. Jeep was told by Bo what had happened that fateful day.

A careless driver had hit a school bus in the hills of Tennessee. The bus was in the middle of the road full of kids when his dad's eighteen-wheeler came barreling around the curve, heading down hill. His dad didn't have enough time to stop, so he took his rig off the side of the mountain rather than hit that bus full of kids broadside. He never had a chance of surviving. As a young man, Jeep often wondered to himself if he could ever have that much courage. Jeep remembered his dad once said to him, "The only difference between a coward and a hero is one step sideways." He also used to say when Jeep hurt himself, "Put your big boy pants on and deal with it."

Jeep wished he could have gotten to know him better, Jeep's mom said they were a lot alike. His name was Tom and his friends called him Truck, so when his son was born, the nickname Jeep just sort of stuck.

Petey had just moved in next door when Jeep's dad died. Petey's dad was very good to Jeep and included him in almost everything he and Petey did together. He even took Jeep to the father and son breakfast at school. Petey's dad still lived in the grove a mile up back of Pippins. Petey's mom was in a home suffering from dementia. She didn't recognize anyone anymore. So, it was just Jeep and Petey, no one ever called them James and Peter, everyone in this part of the country had a nickname. Come to think of it, the only person Jeep knew that didn't have a nick name was Kendal.

"Hey, Petey, let's see if we can get your dad out deer hunting this season," Jeep said. "We'll stick him in a tree blind somewhere. He'll get a kick out of it. We can get him in pretty close with your truck, so he won't have to walk too far. He's still in good enough shape."

"Pop.", as they call him, is a retired Pennsylvania State Trooper.

"Okay, but if he gets the first deer we are going to have to move out of state because we won't hear the end of it," moaned Petey.

It was almost eleven when they pulled into the lot at Pippins. They pulled around back so they could unload the mixer and some cool glasses they had purchased. The glasses were straight sided with a flat bottom. But, on the middle of the bottom was a glass ball. This made it impossible to put the glass down flat. It would lie on an angle sort of like when you laid a brandy snifter on its side. The liquid would come to the edge but not spill out. If the surface wasn't level they even spun around a little. They made great martini glasses or double shot glasses. Jeep was going to try them out and even thought they might make a great logo-trademark.

It looked like business had been good as the kitchen was a mess and the dishwasher and bus boys were working very hard starting to clean up.

Master Lee saw them pull up. He had been sitting outside on the little front porch of his cottage. He walked over to tell them he had been down to the hospital and they were taking Bo out of the ICU. They were overjoyed upon hearing the good news. Jeep started dancing with Lee who thought Jeep was crazy. Jeep thanked him for waiting up this evening to tell them. Master Lee was a good friend and knew how much Bo meant to Jeep.

In the little office off the kitchen, B was getting ready to close. K.C. was still doing the last of the desserts. Jeep kissed her, trying not to disturb her effort of topping bread pudding with whipped cream. His mistake, he caught a face full of very tasty whipped cream from the aerosol container. Everyone was laughing,

"It's great to be loved!" He laughed. He stuck his head into the bar wiping the last of the cream off his face.

Buck said, "Well, look whose back, I'll drink to that."

"On your own tab," Jeep said. "It looks like we have a decent bar crowd," Jeep announced loudly. "I mean in quantity, not quality."

Four of the people at the bar flipped him the bird.

Dickey Lee glanced around at his bar cronies inquiring, "That must be an answer to a question no one asked?"

Jeep chuckled, he was glad to see that everyone was having a good time.

Jeep got to bed late as usual. After making sure K.C. was all tucked in safe and sound, he fell asleep thinking, *I must go see Bo in the morning*

After having breakfast with Gov. and his brother Dickey Lee at Gerry's place, Jeep was going down to the hospital to check on Bo. The pancakes at Gerry's were addictive. The eggs were fresh, the bacon was lean and the coffee would put Dunkin Donuts in second place. Jeep had it all, and headed down to the hospital wondering when visiting hours started.

Jeep asked if Nurse Boyt was on duty. She knew how close Jeep was with Bo and would make sure he got the right answers. Milly took Jeep up to Bo's room and said she would get the doctor on duty to explain everything.

"I'm going to tell the doctor that you are family," Milly confided.

Bo had tubes stuck in him all over the place, his nose, his mouth, his arms and a couple that went under the covers, and Jeep didn't want to know where they were stuck.

Dr. Hudacek explained that Bo was going to make it, but it was going to be a long recovery. He had been hit by three bullets, one in upper leg, one in the stomach and the third one in the upper chest. They didn't know how mobile he would be when he recovered. They would just take it a day at a time.

"You know, Mr. Patrick," the doc said. "He was shot by two different guns—a .38 and a .44. I turned the bullets over to the FBI."

Jeep was driving back out to Pippins when a siren went off right behind him, just one loud blast. He looked back and saw Deputy Wildey. He pulled over and Cookie walked up to his driver's door.

"Sheriff Cottin is looking for you," she said. "He's got some ATF guy with him. We called out to your place, but they said you were out and about. Sheriff radioed if any of us saw you to send you to his office."

"Thank you, Cookie, I thought I was getting a ticket until I saw it was you," Jeep said. "Tell the sheriff I'm on my way."

Agent Jamison Bradley and Sheriff Amos Cottin were having coffee in the conference room. You could sense tension, and it looked like they were waiting for him. Agent Bradley said, "I'm glad you could make it, I got some things to say. First of all, the crate had anthrax in it. The largest amount the agency had ever seen. The production of which had to have been manufactured off shore. This amount was overkill, pardon the pun, but enough to wipe out North America."

"Holy mackerel!" gasped Jeep. "That crate was under Petey's bed and he wanted to open it. We could have exposed hundreds of people."

"This is extremely dangerous stuff. It only takes a dusting, a wisp, a very small amount to kill," stated Jamie.

Jamie wanted to know if Jeep was sure it was intended for Royce White's camp. Jeep told him he was sure the crate's intended destination was the camp. Cottin said he wasn't sure it was. He said that he had stopped out to the camp the other day just to check up on those boys.

"I didn't find anything unusual. Just a bunch of good ol' boys trying to hang on to the fighting edge they had when they were defenders of liberty. Doesn't seem to be as many of them as there were six months ago," Cottin said. Jeep bit his tongue, trying to remain composed.

"Didn't you see anything suspicious? Did they let you look around?" Jeep inquired.

"Nobody stops ol' Cottin from nosing around when I'm doing my duty," he answered indignantly. "It's my job. I think those boys are harmless."

Jamie nodded his head. "What do you think, Jeep?"

"I don't know. I'm just a restaurant guy that found a crate," Jeep said. "If that's all guys, I got to get going."

Jeep started for the door, and then paused with an afterthought. "Oh, Jamie, I was just curious—what kind of gun do you ATF guys carry?" Jeep asked.

"We have an abundance of weapons available to us," he said. "However, our sidearm is a personal choice and most of the agents carry .380 cal. Model 85 Berettas. A few of the guy's will spring for the 9mm. Glock Model 17. Why do you ask?" Jamie said

"Oh, Petey and I had a bet. It looks like we were both wrong. What about the sheriff's department, Cottin?" Jeep asked.

"Well, most of the boys carry 9mm, a few carry big bore stuff .357, .44, .45," he said, "but I can't stand the weight of those guns pulling my pants down. Although I own a lot of guns, I carry the old reliable Colt Diamondback .38 special."

Jeep told Jamie to stop by when he was off duty and he would buy him a drink and he could stay in the empty cottage and head back tomorrow.

"That sounds like a great offer I just may see you later but it depends when I finish my work today," said Jamie.

"I'll see you law enforcers later," Jeep said as he exited the room. "Hey,

Cookie, you going to stop out later?" Jeep called to her as he walked to the front door.

"Yea, now that I'm back on days for a while I can get some of K.C.'s first-class cooking. I'll see you later," she yelled after him.

Jeep was very confused. Cottin was not telling the truth, but he didn't know why. Maybe he was keeping information from Jamie for a reason. Jeep knew for certain that he wasn't going to share any information with Cottin. He also knew that if he was going to find out about these attacks, he was going to have to do it himself.

Later that evening Jamie stopped by for dinner. "I thought I would take you up on that offer, but let the government buy the drinks."

"Okay," Jeep said, "but either way I think I'm still paying."

Jamie said that he wanted to talk to Jeep alone. They went to the corner booth so they wouldn't be disturbed. Jamie told him while he was in the Pittsburgh FBI office waiting for the results of the crate, he asked around and they had no report of a kidnapping from this county. Jeep was puzzled, but it did explain why there hadn't been any FBI agents snooping around. Jamie also explained about the three different ways anthrax could make you sick. One was inhaling it; another one was touching it, or getting it on your skin, both took a while to detect. In either case it could make you quite sick, but the fatality rate was low. The third one was the deadliest, if it was consumed it caused a gastrointestinal infection that had a fatality rate of over fifty percent.

Jeep and Jamie enjoyed a nice dinner in spite of the conversation. They had stuffed sole with a blueberry and cream sauce. It was outstanding. Jamie decided to spend the evening, staying in the available cabin. Jeep thought he had really enjoyed himself. Jeep thanked him for taking the time to keep him informed and educating him about anthrax. They had a few after dinner B&B's and then Jeep showed him to his cottage out back. The rest of the evening went smoothly and they locked up after midnight.

Ever since they found that crate Jeep hadn't been sleeping well. He awoke after three in the morning and checked to see if Petey was home, he wasn't. He was just getting back into bed when he thought he heard something in the kitchen. He knew that was not likely, this place was as secure as Fort Knox. He then heard some shouts followed by a few gunshots. He leaped from the bed and into his pants and slipped on some shoes and a sweatshirt. He decided to use the fire pole in his closet. He threw open the trap doors and slid down. The back door was open and he pushed it partially closed to go around it. Jeep observed a lit candle in the middle of the kitchen floor. Watchfully he scanned the entire kitchen for any movement as he approached it. There appeared to be a half-filled water balloon lying next to the candle. Puzzled he picked up the candle and blew it out. The kitchen lost what little light the candle had provided. Hearing what sounded like talking outside, he turned his attention to the back door. As he exited the rear of the building he saw Master Lee standing over a moaning body on the ground.

He said, "I see this fellow shoot at someone in front of Cabin Four. He try to run away. He not make it. Poor fellow not see me." Cabin four was where Jamie was staying. Jeep saw the light from K.C.'s cabin as her front door opened.

He shouted, "Its Jeep, honey. I'm okay. Call the sheriff.

She disappeared back inside the cabin. It was then that he saw Jamie lying in front of cabin four. He wasn't moving. Jeep checked for a heartbeat—he found nothing. He'd been hit in the chest and there was very little blood, which meant the heart wasn't pumping. Vainly checking his wrist, neck and even his breath for vital signs, he found nothing. Jamie laid on his back lifeless. Jeep was certain he was dead. Crossing back across the lot to Lee, he saw his victim for the first time. He wasn't going anywhere soon. He was semi-conscious and it looked like most of his limbs were broken.

"This man need help," said Lee. "Him not feel well"

As a sheriff's car approached the rear of the building, *Here we go again,* thought Jeep.

Jeep walked back into the kitchen remembering the water balloon. As he picked it up, he smelled gasoline, suddenly realizing he had stumbled across a makeshift incendiary bomb and someone was trying to blow-up Pippins.

It appeared Jamie had seen the intruder leaving the back door of the restaurant and startled him. The perp (as the deputy calls him) shot Jamie, and in running away didn't see Master Lee in the shadows. He would have been luckier if he had run in front of a bus. Jamie died saving Jeep's life, had he not seen the guy leaving Pippins, Jeep would surly be dead.

Petey showed up sometime during the commotion. It helped having him around because Jeep was starting to lose it.

"Jesus, Petey, I was safer in the Middle East," Jeep snapped. "There is no reason to blow up Pippins or try to kill me. We don't have the crate."

They didn't know who the bad guys were and Bo hadn't told them who shot him. The only reason Jeep could think of was revenge. They had killed a few camp residents and somebody was really pissed. But, thanks to Master Lee they had a suspect. Someone to tell them what was going on, even though it was going to take "all the Kings Men" to put this guy back together again.

Chapter 6

The next few days all ran together. The FBI was no longer among the missing. They were coming out of the woodwork. A Federal agent had been killed in the line of duty. The bomber was under federal protection; even Cottin didn't know where he was being held.

ATF had a new agent assigned to the case; her name was Agent Meghan Williams. She had known Agent Bradley very well. They had worked together often; needless to say she was focused. Agent Williams was very pleasant and made a good first impression. They had spent the last few days together almost 24-7. She had been thoroughly briefed and knew everything Jamie and Jeep had talked about. It was obvious she wasn't going anywhere until this whole mess was wrapped up. B took a liking to her and that was very helpful. Soon Agent Williams became comfortable with everyone at Pippins. They were even calling her by her first name. Meghan was a very attractive five foot nine inch field agent. She had shoulder length blond hair that she kept up in a bun or ponytail during the on duty hours. In the evening she would let her hair down. (literally).They got used to having her around, especially Petey. All of a sudden Petey was very helpful and seemed to be around more than usual.

Meghan and Jeep had the same theory; someone at the camp was trying to even the score with him. It was just revenge; it had nothing to do with the crate, or any plot that involved the crate. Jeep had told her about shooting a few camp dwellers in his effort to rescue Petey. She knew the camp had not reported the incident. She appreciated that Petey and Jeep were honest and straightforward with her; they had a friend in Meghan.

They had been more forthcoming with information than Cottin. Things were once more just starting to slow down, when suddenly we got the phone call from Nurse Boyt that Bo had died.

Jeep told Petey to take care of the arrangements. He had to talk to Doctor Hudacek. Jeep requested an autopsy and the doctor agreed, although he doubted it would show them anything. He told Jeep, Bo was doing too well to have a dramatic setback, although it appeared he had a massive coronary. He had never regained consciousness to tell them who shot him. It was another convenient break for the bad guys, whoever they were.

Meghan reminded Jeep his safety was not her primary assignment. Finding the people responsible for Jamie's killing and how the anthrax was intended to be used were her number one priorities.

"If you feel a need to have a peace pow-wow with members of the camp, be my guest." She smiled.

Jeep thanked her for the hunting license.

She said, "Just keep me informed and I will cover your back."

They both knew of the camp's involvement, but if Jeep did it on his own she wouldn't have to notify the FBI. This was a bright lady.

The autopsy didn't prove any foul play, but Dr. Hudacek wasn't convinced. Petey and Jeep decided that we couldn't just wait around doing nothing. So, at Bo's wake they made a plan. They decided that after the funeral they would take a letter up to the camp and leave it on a pole stuck in the middle of the road where they would surely see it. The letter would request a meeting in a safe place. It would have to be a safe place for both parties.

Bo's funeral had been well attended. Bo was a private man that traveled a lot, so Jeep was pleased to see so many people in attendance. He suspected Petey had threatened a few people into attending, but his heart was in the right place. All they had to do was wait until someone from the camp got in touch with them.

They had a late dinner at Pippins. As the evening wore down and things slowed, K.C. and B found time to sit with Petey, Jeep and Meghan.

It was a good quality gathering with friends, an infrequent occurrence in recent times. Petey was in a good mood although he had broken up with Wanda, coincidently coinciding with Meghan's arrival on the scene.

When asked why he and Wanda split, he joked, "She was a cold fish. In fact, when she dies I'm going to put on her tombstone: HERE LIES WANDA COLD AS EVER."

B said that Wanda told her what she was going to put on Petey's tombstone: "HERE LIES PETEY STIFF AT LAST"

They all laughed hard, B was funny, she was real good for business and the customers loved her. If the truth were known K.C. and B were the reason Pippins was doing so well. They had a lot of fun laughing and telling jokes, Meghan fit right in. Cookie stopped in and Petey was now bragging that the prettiest women in the county were at his table. Jeep was thinking, *Six people in the corner booth and four of them were packing heat.* What a peaceful place this was.

It was Wednesday and they had just opened for lunch. B told Jeep there was a phone call for him; he took it behind the bar. The letter had been read, the guy on the phone said they would meet per the instruction. The note hadn't stated a time, so the caller suggested this afternoon. Jeep said that would be fine. After Jeep hung up, he called Meghan's cell phone. He left her a text message that the meeting was going down at three this afternoon at St. Bernard's church. She called back and said she felt a need to pray and was going to church at two-thirty. Jeep was sure no one at the camp knew her so it would be okay.

Petey and Jeep entered the church at three and they sat in the last pew observing a few people spread throughout the church praying. Most of them were women, and they knew one of them was Meghan. Two guys entered from the vestibule. They must have been in the shadows when Jeep and Petey entered. Jeep suggested they go up to the choir loft.

They were sort of scruffy and said their names were Bone and Heck. Jeep asked, "How do we put an end to this war?"

"What war?" said Heck. He seemed like the spokesman.

"Okay, end of meeting!" Petey announced sharply. "It was our

51

mistake, we have the wrong guys. Just think about one thing, Bone! When we get off of the church property, I'm going to kill you. I remember your face from when I was a guest up at the camp."

Bone stared at Petey, Jeep could smell the fear.

"Slow down, cowboy," Heck pleaded.

"Okay, let's start over," Jeep said softly, reminding the others they were in a church.

"You killed my brother," Bone mumbled.

"Would you like to meet up with him before the day is over?" snarled Petey.

They finally got things settled down. It was obvious they weren't the brains behind the scene—they were just messengers. Jeep told them he would leave them alone if they would do the same with him. He told them he didn't care what they did at the camp as long as he wasn't part of it. Heck understood. Jeep also said they should be very careful, they were being watched by the government.

"In a month there won't be anybody to watch us," Bone threatened.

"Shut up!" snapped Heck.

Jeep could see that this meeting was over. Jeep offered his hand to Heck to seal the deal. He shook it quickly and they both started down the stairs.

"Remember, I have your word!" Jeep shouted after Heck. Petey and Jeep followed them down the stairs. At the bottom of the stairs in the last pew was a blond, kneeling, hands folded, head bowed and a babushka wrapped around her head. She looked deep in prayer. Jeep knelt alongside her

"Something big is going down in the next thirty days, Meghan," he whispered. "I wish I knew what it was, but I think I can make an educated guess."

Petey and Jeep needed to get away.

"We need to get our minds off all this sorrow and death," Jeep said.

"Okay, let's go kill some deer," laughed Petey.

Maybe Jeep wasn't the only one that needed to get away, although Jeep knew that was Petey's way of dealing with our problems. What a breath of fresh air he was, and going hunting was a good idea, they could take Pop with them. Talking things out with him might help—Pop always had good advice. Petey and Jeep should have listened to him more often when they were young; life would have been easier, but probably not as much fun.

They had a good deer blind stuck up in a tree behind Cooter's place. It would be a good spot to put Pop but the problem was it's closer to that camp than they wanted to get.

Petey said, "We can't spend the rest of our lives avoiding our best hunting ground just because of some wackos." Jeep knew he was right, so they told Pop to get ready.

"We are going to give you a hunting lesson tomorrow," Petey told him. Pop laughed for some time over what he called, "The funniest thing he heard this year."

They left about three-thirty in the morning. They wanted to get Pop in that blind before sun-up. The plan was Petey and Jeep would walk around the crest of the mountain about three quarters of the way up. The theory was this should move the deer around the mountain back to Pop's blind. It's worked before. Pop got up in the tree blind without their help. The rig was quite high and they made sure he was settled. The deer blind was a very comfortably constructed platform strapped securely to the trunk of a large tree, similar to a child's tree house, but smaller and less elaborate. The surrounding branches were cut away allowing for visibility, and the platform was cleverly camouflaged. It had all the comforts—food, water, camouflaged sleeping bag and pillows. Petey told him they should be back around in about three hours.

"Now don't fall asleep," Petey warned. "If we spook a deer back to you and you miss it, I'll cut your shirttail off like just like I'd do a rookie."

"We'll try to come in high to your right, uphill, so only shoot straight ahead or down to your left. Okay, Pop?" Jeep instructed.

They started out behind Pop and in three hours they should be walking toward him, moving deer in front of them.

It was mid morning and Petey and Jeep were walking softly. They knew they were moving a few deer out in front. Jeep figured they were only three or four-hundred yards from Pop's blind. They suddenly heard a shot and they were sure Pop got his deer. As they got closer to Pop's blind they saw two hunters that were standing over a downed deer.

As they walked up on them, one shouted, "You shot my buck!"

Jeep couldn't believe his eyes, it was Bones. He knew neither he or Petey had shot the deer. The strange thing was they were standing only about thirty yards from the tree that Pop was in. When Bones saw it was Petey and Jeep he aimed his rifle at them.

"Look what I found," he bragged. "Don't either of you move or I'll kill ya."

He explained to his companion, "This is the SOB that killed my brother Clive, and it's my turn to get even."

"DROP YOUR GUNS AND DROP TO YOUR KNEES," a very loud deep voice came from above. "THIS IS GOD."

They froze; they didn't know where to look. The companion lowered his gun. Petey started walking right at Bones.

"Keep the other one covered, God. Me and the Devil have an issue to settle."

Petey laid his Weatherby down gently, it was the last gentle thing he did.

This wasn't going to be pretty, thought Jeep.

He hit Bones with a crushing right. Bones head snapped to his right, he staggered but remained standing. A left and another right caught him before he hit the ground, and just as quickly Petey picked him up and hit him twice more. He was trying to prop him up against a tree to hit him again when God said, "REPENT SINNER," and Jeep started laughing because the other guy was about to faint. Petey hit Bones once more right on the nose as he was falling to the ground. Petey looked up into the tree and started laughing. It was the only thing that prevented manslaughter that day. Jeep told the companion to get what was left of Bones and get off this mountain fast.

With the buck in the back of Petey's truck, they headed home. No one could stop laughing. Petey had cooled off. Jeep didn't like to see Petey get that upset. Pop had told them, while gasping for air between laughs, what had happened.

As he was sighting in on the deer the boys had flushed, he heard a noise coming from downhill. So did the deer, it took off running right at Pop's tree. He hit him on the dead run. It was a shot of less than 40 yards. Then, suddenly running up the hill appeared those two idiots wondering who shot their deer.

"I sat silent in the blind knowing you two were going to be walking up any minute. When I saw the one point his gun at you two, I thought I would have some fun. They had no idea I was in the tree," explained Pop

This was a day to remember. Jeep hadn't laughed so hard since he was a kid and Petey thought camphor would be good for jock itch.

Chapter 7

Even praying wasn't helping Meghan with her investigation, although Jeep's information in church had put a time frame on it. Something was going down in the next 30 days.

What Meghan knew was the radicals in the camp had a plan that included using anthrax. What was holding up a raid on the camp was there wasn't anything in the camp that would be incriminating. They were pretty sure the radicals hadn't had time to replace the anthrax. With the new information Jeep had gotten her, it sounded like they were going ahead with the plan, maybe using something other than anthrax. She had informed the FBI of her latest information. The FBI's primary focus was the action at the camp. Her primary case was finding who was behind the murder of Jamison Bradley. Oh, they had the shooter, what they needed was the motive. She was even sure she had the motive also, but no proof. Both the FBI and Meghan felt sure that their investigation would lead to a mutual conclusion.

Meghan had spent hours in Pittsburgh questioning the shooter. Who told you to plant the bomb? Were you acting on your own? Why did you shoot Agent Bradley? The shooters name was Harley Ingram. He didn't have much of a rap sheet. His story was he didn't plant any bomb and he shot the guy in self defense, the guy had a gun. He didn't work for anyone. He said he was looking for a place to sleep and in the morning he was going to apply for a job as a dishwasher. He intended to sue the guy that attacked him and broke his arms and leg. He was still in the hospital and would be for a while. He didn't have any known address, although he did slip one time, leading Meghan to believe he lived at the camp. What they didn't know was who the leader at the camp now that they had found Royce White buried in the cemetery at the camp. Someone had to be in charge? It certainly wasn't the two Jeep met in the church, it also wasn't Harley Ingram.

Meghan tried to arrange a meeting with Sheriff Cottin. She was told he was out at the shooting range with some of his deputy's qualifying. Once a quarter the sheriff's department deputies had to qualify with their pistols. Meghan got directions and drove out to the range. There were five of them shooting.

"Hi, Sheriff," she said. "Do you mind if I do some practicing? I have to qualify myself next month."

"Come on," said Cottin. "Do you want us to move the targets closer for you?" He laughed.

"I think I can see them from here." She winked. Going to her trunk, she removed a Feather AT-9, walked over next to Cottin and with a long burst of fire destroyed all their existing targets.

"What the hell…is that?" shouted Cottin.

Meghan smiled and said, "It's a 9mm, 25 rounds, 5 pound, folding stock, fully automatic attention getter. It is also known as a Feather AT-9." She took it back to the trunk, removed the empty clip, inserted a fully loaded new clip and placed it back in the trunk. She walked back to Cottin and calmly requested, "Do you have any more targets? I would like to do some pistol practicing. Oh. and by the way, Sheriff, when we're through here we need to talk." Meghan's sidearm of choice was a Colt Mustang Plus II .380ACP, it was fairly light at 20oz.

Sitting down with Cottin and taking the plugs out of her ears, she said, "Most of your deputies are shooting big bore pistols with heavy or mag. loads."

"Boys will be boys," smiled Cottin.

"Are you expecting a war to break out?"

"You never know what to expect in these hills," said Cottin.

"What have you found out about the goings on at the camp?" Meg inquired.

Cottin said, "I've been up there a few times, but haven't seen anything unusual. I saw one of the boys that were beat-up pretty bad. He said that Petey had attacked him. I asked him if he wanted to press charges and he said he would take care of it himself. I told him not in my county, either press charges or drop it. There seems to be some action up there, people seem busy, but nothing that looks illegal."

"I talked to the shooter, Harley Ingram, but I didn't get anything."

"Tell me where he is and I will make him talk"

"I'm sorry, Cottin, but that won't happen," stated Meghan. "Do you suspect any wrongdoing in Bo's death?"

"Yep," Cottin said, "but we can't prove anything. Nobody unusual visited Bo. In fact, I was up at the hospital that night. Deputy Porter's wife had a baby boy and I took time to stop by with some chocolates. I didn't see anything."

"Tell me about yourself, Cottin, I'd like to get to know you better." inquired Meghan

. "Not much to tell," Cottin said. "I'm fifty-nine years old. I was born in Huntsville, Alabama. I'm an only child and I came into this area in '85. I had been a lawman in a few southern states, but I always wanted to be a sheriff. I went to work as a deputy in this county. I worked hard, and when old Sheriff Murtha retired, I got myself elected. That was in '92 and I just got elected to my fourth term. I think they like me."

"That's quite a success story," Meghan said, "but you and I better solve some of these cases or this will be your last term."

Jeep was sitting in the corner booth with K.C. They were taking a break between the lunch clean-up and getting ready for dinner. Jeep was saying they should take a trip to D.C. It would be good to get away, just the two of them. "We could leave Friday morning after Thanksgiving. Petey and B could run the place Friday and Saturday, we would be back to open for dinner on Tuesday." Jeep was saying how much he enjoyed the trip he and Petey took, and how much more fun it would be with her. K.C. liked the idea. All Jeep had to do was bounce it off B and Petey. He knew they would be fine with it.

Master Lee came in and Jeep called him over to the booth. He had been in a funk since Bo had died.

"They find who kill Bo?" he wanted to know. He also was sure Bo was assisted in death.

"Not yet, but they will," K.C. said.

Jeep said, "That fellow you caught that killed Jamie is still in the hospital, Lee,"

"He lucky, we will always know him by his limp." He smiled.

Jeep just laughed and said, "Can I get you some tea?"

Deputy Wildey walked in the front door. She was smiling. "Wait until you hear this," she said. "You know there have been some threats on Master Lee's life? We think it's from friends and family of Harley Ingram. Well, Sheriff Cottin has assigned me to guard Master Lee, make sure no harm comes to him was the way he put it. So, Master Lee, you can consider yourself protected, I'm on the case." She laughed. Everyone saw the humor in her statement.

"The people that are going to need protection are the ones that come after him," Jeep said.

Deputy Wildey sat down with them and had some coffee.

"I have to go to your classes with you, so I might as well sign up and have you teach me Tae Kwon Do while I'm hanging around"

"That would be fine." Lee nodded.

K.C. headed for the kitchen

"Meatloaf on the menu tonight!" she shouted back to B. "Put it on the chalkboard."

"Make enough for leftovers," Jeep pleaded.

The drinking crowd was starting to drift in. Master Lee got a ride to his classes in a deputy sheriff's car. Jeep was starting to wonder where Petey was when he and Meghan walked in the front door. Petey said he had been showing Meghan around the countryside, helping her get her bearings so she would know her way around.

"You're lucky you are armed, riding into the boondocks with Petey." Jeep laughed

. Jeep told Petey that he and K.C. were thinking of going to D.C. the day after Thanksgiving. Petey was fine with that and he thought it was a good idea. Jeep walked behind the bar and bought drinks "on the house" for the early patrons.

Pop had just entered and said, "I heard that, and count me in." Daniel (Pop) McDade was coming in for his "Early Bird Special." He somehow sensed when meatloaf was on the menu.

It seemed like the deal they made at the church with Heck and Bones was being upheld, although Jeep thought Bones would just want to stay in the camp for a while. He wasn't foolish enough to think they were safe. It would just be a matter of time before camp followers started seeking their own form of justice. As Pop would say, "You'll have a bumpy road if you keep looking over your shoulder and forget about what lies ahead."

Jeep said, "I guess I will just put on my big boy pants and deal with it."

Tomorrow was Thanksgiving and Jeep had to help prep some turkeys. Petey told him everything would be in good hands Friday and Saturday night while he and K.C. were gone. He was going to do the cooking. The menu was as follows:

LEFTOVER TURKEY & ANYTHING THAT WILL FIT IN A GLASS

They had a few customers that would love that menu. Jeep thinks a good time will be had by all those two nights. He didn't think they would make a lot of money, but with Petey in charge you never knew.

It was Friday morning and K.C. and Jeep were trying to get an early start for their trip to Washington. As they finally pulled out of the parking lot, they saw a sign that Petey had put out front of Pippins, his last attempt to make them worry, "CLOSED UNTIL FURTHER NOTICE."

Jeep thought to himself, *My partner is a sick dude.*

Petey enjoyed working the bar. He worked well with B and was looking forward to the next two days. The day after thanksgiving would be slow; everyone stayed home and ate leftovers. Their lawyer, Flip, stopped by looking for Jeep. When Petey told him Jeep was on his way to D.C., he said, "Okay, nothing important." He ordered a Gentleman Jack on the rocks so the trip would not be a total waste.

The bar was quite full by eight thirty. It hadn't been much of a dinner crowd, as expected, but the bar crowd was a pleasant surprise. Petey and B were kept very busy. The evening flew by, it was now eleven o'clock and the crowd was lessening. It was then that Petey noticed the four guys standing at the end of the bar near the door. They looked like they could be camp residents. They weren't causing any trouble. They were laughing and having a good time. Petey looked at B and nodded his head toward them, silently asking if they were trouble. She shook her head and shrugged. He took that to mean they were okay. It was shortly after Petey noticed them that they put their bottles on the bar with a tip and left. Petey quietly slipped the equalizer from under the bar and disappeared through the door into the kitchen. He thought he should check the grounds out back. He walked to the back door and exited the building. He moved to his right into the shadows away from the back porch light. It was only a minute or two before he heard some people coming down the road toward the back of the building. It was the same four guys. One of them seemed to have fire in his hand. It was a bottle firebomb, a "Molotov cocktail."

"Hold it right there!" Petey demanded.

He did not see that they all had guns in their hands. The peaceful night exploded with gunfire, Petey got off two rounds of double O buckshot. He heard someone screaming, and then he was knocked to his knees. The pain in his gut doubled him over and Petey's world went silent. B rushed thru the back door—it took a moment for her eyes to adjust. She then saw Petey lying on the ground and the front of Master Lee's cottage was ablaze. She heard some screaming and an engine roar out front. Running back inside, B called the fire department. Going back to help Petey, she saw that Master Lee was already at his side putting pressure on Petey's midsection.

"Is he...is he?" stuttered B.

Master Lee shook his head. "I don't know. Doctor must hurry"

Some people were coming around back to see it they could help. B told the first two, "Keep everybody up front, this is a crime scene."

B rode in the ambulance to the hospital. They took Petey directly into surgery. B tried to get a grasp of everything that had just happened. The sheriff told B his people would lock up Pippins. Lee's cottage was severely damaged. B told Master Lee to use the empty cottage. She knew she had to get in touch with Jeep and Pop. Her head was spinning. The hospital called Pop and they told B he was on his way down. She couldn't remember the name of the hotel Jeep and K.C. were staying. K.C. had joked about leaving her cell phone home so no one would bother them. Petey knew the name of the hotel, a lot of good that would do.

Deputy Wildey walked into the waiting room. She had brought Master Lee into the emergency room. After the ambulance left with Petey, she noticed that he had burns on his arms

"How's Petey?"

B shook her head. "He's in surgery, I don't know if he's alive or dead." She wept.

"Take it easy B, Petey's tough, he'll make it," said the deputy.

"Cookie, I need your help. Jeep is in D.C. with K.C. and I can't remember where they are staying."

"Don't worry B. I'll get in touch with them."

Knowing that K.C. must have made the reservations Wednesday or Thursday, she would get a list of all the outgoing phone calls made from Pippins on those two days. The one to Washington D.C. would be the phone number of the hotel where they were staying. Being a deputy made this a very easy task.

When Cookie returned to the waiting room, Pop had arrived and was comforting B. She gave the phone number to Pop and said that he should be the one to call Jeep. It was one-fifteen in the morning when Pop reached Jeep. Jeep said he would be here before six. There was nothing to do but wait. Cookie said she was going to call Meghan and tell her all that had happened.

When Jeep came running through the waiting room door with K.C. in tow, the room was full of familiar faces. Master Lee with bandages on his arms, B, Pop, Meghan, Cookie, Flip, Cottin and a FBI agent whose name he couldn't remember.

"Where do we stand?" was all he wanted to know.

Pop said, "He's still in surgery"

"What the hell happened?" he directed at Cottin.

"Somebody tried to burn out Lee," Cottin said. "Petey surprised them in the act. A shootout erupted and Petey took one in the stomach. There were four of them; we know he hit one of them, maybe two. There was blood in the driveway."

"Were they from the camp?"

"We don't know," stated Cottin.

"Bullshit," said Jeep. "I know, you know, everybody knows they were from the camp." Jeep turned to the agent. "Sorry, I can't remember your name."

"Grabowski, Agent Danny Grabowski," he said.

"What is the agency doing?" snapped Jeep.

"Officially, I can't say what our plans are," stated Danny. Pulling Jeep aside he said softly in his ear, "Unofficially, we will be in that camp, in force, this afternoon. We are sure we will find the shooters if we move fast."

Jeep sighed. "Thanks, Danny."

With that the door to the operating rooms swung open. It was Dr. Hudacek. He told Pop that the operation was a success. They had stopped the bleeding. The bullet had missed his stomach—that was good news. The bullet hit him in the left side of his abdomen. They had to remove eight to ten inches of his descending colon. It had also hit his kidney and there was a lot of bleeding. The next twenty-four to forty-eight hours would tell. If no infection sets in, he has a good chance of making it. If Pop insisted, the doctor would let him in to see Petey for a few minutes, but he recommended they just let him rest, he was still unconscious. Pop and Jeep agreed. Jeep was completely worn out.

"Let's all of us get some rest," suggested Pop. "We can take shifts staying here."

K.C. thought that was a good idea.

"Pop, you take the first shift, I'll take these three," pointing to Jeep and B and Lee, "home for some rest. I'll be back this afternoon," she said.

Jeep asked Agent Grabowski it he would stop by later and tell him the results of the raid. He nodded he would.

When Jeep awoke it was three in the afternoon. He needed a shower to clear the cobwebs. K.C. was in the living room when he walked in.

"I heard you get in the shower," she said. "I made you some coffee."

Taking the coffee, he sat down in his lounge chair. K.C. said that B was sleeping in Petey's room; it didn't make sense for her to go to her place. K.C. had gone over to B's and gotten some fresh clothes for her while we were sleeping. Lee had gotten some of his things that weren't damaged from his place. He was now staying in the spare cottage. She had also made a few turkey sandwiches.

"What a gal, how would I manage without you?" Jeep said. "I didn't even know that I was hungry." He smiled. He told her that the FBI was going to raid the camp this afternoon, they obviously had just cause. He was sure they would find the wounded felon there.

Cookie came up the stairs. "You know your front door is open, even though the sign says CLOSED?"

"I must have forgotten to lock it," said K.C. "I'll get it now," she said.

"That's what I came over to talk about," said Cookie.

"The lock on the front door?" Jeep said.

"Yep." She nodded. "The sheriff wants the place locked up for a few days. He says it's a crime scene. He sent me over because he was afraid to tell you himself." She laughed.

"He's right," Jeep agreed. "Besides, we should consider the safety of our customers. There has been a lot of shooting around here recently."

Cookie was surprised Jeep agreed, but knew the sheriff was right.

"Yea," Cookie said, "it puts a whole new meaning to 'a shot and a beer.'"

Jeep got to the hospital about four in the afternoon. Pop was sleeping on the couch. He woke him and asked if there was any news. There wasn't, and Pop agreed to go home and freshen up while Jeep stayed. He went to the cafeteria to get some coffee before it closed. Meghan walked in while Jeep was sitting at the table. He told her there was nothing new on Petey's condition. She told him the FBI had pulled off a successful raid on "Camp Hades." They had arrested fifteen people. (nine men and six women) Two of the men were wounded—one was hurt enough to require hospital attention. She was sure they had enough information to close the camp for good. She also told him that the DNA in the driveway would surely match the two wounded. They would be held on arson and attempted murder charges. The FBI had numerous other charges for the camp residents, unlawful gathering, intent to commit treason, terrorism and other overt acts against the government. She said Agent Grabowski told her he would stop by Jeep's place the first chance he had.

Meghan said we still had Jamie's murder to solve. She was sure the camp had some involvement in it. This shooting was going to be harder to prove. Sheriff Cottin was helping, if you could call it that. Jeep asked Meghan if it would be okay for them to drive up to the camp tomorrow. She said that would be fine. Jeep went home at about eleven that night. B and Cookie were going to stay the night and then Pop and K.C. were to relieve them in the morning. Jeep went back to Pippins and sat at the bar alone in the dark thinking about Petey, about all the good times and what Petey meant to him. The Jack Daniels was going down very smooth and doing the job for him. He went to bed after about an hour.

Chapter 8

The first thing Jeep did was call the hospital. He was talking to B. She told him that Petey had rested through the night and there was no change. He was still unconscious. She said K.C. and Pop had just arrived and she was going to come out to Pippins. He told her his plans. He then spoke to K.C. She said Pop was doing well and that he should not worry. He told her he loved her and they would finish their trip first chance they got.

Meghan picked Jeep up at nine in the morning. He made her stop at Gerry's diner. Gov wanted to know how Petey was doing. Jeep told him everyone was still praying, and Petey was resting. He gobbled down on Gov's pancakes like a starved wolf. He must have had a little hangover. They drove out to the camp and discovered that the FBI had it locked up very tight. They had a guard at the gate and a few investigators poking around. Jeep couldn't have gotten close to the place without Meghan. One of the agents told Meghan they think they have found a burial ground behind one of the buildings. Jeep thought to himself, *With my .270 slugs in a few of them.* The warehouses had stacks of empty plastic drinking bottles. This must have been the place they kept Petey. Meghan asked if they had figured out what was going on here. They said talk to Danny, he had it just about figured out, it was pretty cut and dry. One of the agents said they had caught two more residents last night. They must have been away and didn't know about the raid. The FBI were concerned that a few cell phone calls had been made during the raid, thus warning the people off campus about the arrest of the camp residents. They suspected that they had lost a few that were now on the run.

Meghan's phone rang. She said it was for Jeep. It was K.C. She joyfully told him that Petey had regained consciousness. The doctor said he was alert and aware of what happened to him. He wanted to know if Pop and Jeep knew he had been shot. Jeep asked her if the doctors would let him see Petey. She said she thought so—Pop was going in to see him now. Jeep told her we would be right there.

He said to Meghan, "Petey's conscious. Let's hurry." As they were running to Meghan's car Jeep asked, "Do you have a siren on your car?"

"No," she said.

"You'll get a ticket."

"Only if they can catch us." She smiled.

Pop had only spent five minutes with Petey, so the doctors would allow Jeep some time with him also. Jeep rushed right into the ICU. There was Petey looking similar to his memory of Bo except Petey was awake.

"How was D.C?" Petey whispered with a faint smile.

"I don't remember, it was a lifetime ago," Jeep replied. "You're going to be fine."

Petey said, "Jeep, take care of Pop, he looked old today."

Jeep said, "You worried some life out of quite a few of your friends the last forty-eight hours and I'm going to kick your butt when you get better."

"You better do it now while you can," he whispered. That made Jeep smile. Petey was going to be just fine. Jeep told him he would see him tomorrow and to get some rest.

Jeep was back at Pippins in the dark. He was starting to enjoy this place dark and quiet. He knew they were going to have to open again. The sheriff had told K.C. it was okay to open up. He figured one more night of peace and quiet wouldn't hurt business. He was sitting at the bar reflecting on all that had come to pass. All they did was find a parachute in the woods. Now eleven people had been shot and nine of them were dead. Seventeen or so had been arrested. Two murders, one unsolved (one a Federal agent) and a terrorist plot was still in question. Jeep thought, *There are only 26 shopping days till Christmas. I think I'll have another*

Black Jack on the rocks.

Agent Grabowski had left word last night that he would stop by this morning. Jeep heard the front bell ring at eight-thirty. He was watching cable news, and their little episode was the feature story on every cable channel but the Weather Channel and ESPN. He brought Danny upstairs for some coffee.

"Do you want any breakfast?" he asked.

"Yea, some toast or a muffin if you have it," Danny replied.

"I'll see what I can do," Jeep said. He toasted three stale English muffins and they sat at their small kitchen table. Danny started to explain the plot that Petey and Jeep had stumbled upon.

"The anthrax had been intended for the camp, but the drop had missed its target. When the terrorist saw you and Petey pick it up, they followed you to Pippins. They had to get it back or face failure. Petey scared them away on their first attempt. They tried again that night and you stopped their second attempt. These two were fanatics, and when they failed the second attempt, the wounded one took his life rather than being disgraced by failure.

"Now, enters the phony agent," Danny explained. "You said he called himself Blyden? We think he was Royce White's right hand man. If so, his name was Yough, Fredrick Yough. When the attempt to kidnap you and Petey failed, their plan was falling apart. Without the anthrax they could not execute their plan. They developed a real hatred for you and Petey. They tried to kidnap K.C., killing your friend Bo in the process. We believe he tried to stop them. We suspect Bo might have recognized them. They were hoping to negotiate with you; they would have traded K.C. for the anthrax. When that failed, they were pissed, and out of frustration they decided to blow up Pippins. That's when Agent Bradley was in the wrong place at the wrong time. He saw Ingram come out of the back door and it cost him his life. At that point we felt we had enough information to move on the camp. Looking for the arsonists and the person that shot Petey was enough for our people to move in and search the camp. Their plan was diabolical."

"Jeep, you are a hero," Danny said. "Unfortunately, no one but us will ever know."

"That's fine," Jeep said. "Let's keep it that way."

"They planned to fill all those bottles with water contaminated with anthrax," Danny explained. "They had capping equipment at the camp and their intention was to take the entire shipment to D.C."

"You know, Danny, when Petey and I were in Washington we noticed everything was under heavy guard. You couldn't get near a reservoir," Jeep said.

"Most everything," smiled Danny. "No one is guarding the convenience stores and bodegas. Their pawns, people…whatever you want to call them, were going to carry bottles into the stores and bodegas. Leave them behind in the coolers, even in the cafeterias in the congressional buildings. No one is suspicious of someone carrying water. Everyone is carrying water these days. If someone saw them putting water in the coolers, they would just say they were putting it back, that they had changed their mind, the water was too expensive or some other excuse. Jeep, had they been successful, the damage to America is beyond our imagination," he said.

"Wow!" It was all Jeep could say.

"It's not over," continued Danny. The leader, he explained was still on the loose. "The agency has no idea who was the mastermind behind the plan. It wasn't Royce (Red) White."

"Do you mean that the lead wacko is unknown and still planning?" Jeep asked.

"Yes, for all we know he could be anyone, living anywhere," sighed Danny.

Later that morning Jeep picked up K.C. at the cottage and they went to see Petey. He was resting. Dr. Hudacek said he was doing well. At this rate of recovery, he thought that Petey could be home for Christmas.

"Will he have time to go shopping and buy me a present?" Jeep joked.

"No, Jeep, no Christmas shopping for Petey this year," said Dr Hudacek.

Doctors don't laugh much, Jeep thought.

When they peeked in on Petey, he opened his eyes and smiled. No talking, but he knew they were there. Jeep asked Pop to come down to the cafeteria with him. He swore Pop to secrecy and then related Agent

Grabowski's story to him. He thought Pop would be proud of Petey's part in saving America. He watched Pop's chest swell up with pride and his eyes moisten just a little as he related Petey's part. He thought somehow that it made Pop feel better, somehow justifying his son lying in a hospital fighting for his life.

Oh well, I am not a shrink, but somehow to a guy like Pop I think it helps, Jeep said to himself.

Pop told Jeep he had heard from a long lost friend—Tom McLaughlin, a high school classmate from Peoria, Illinois. Pop had moved to Pennsylvania when he was in high school.

Mac had heard Petey's name on the news and wondered if he could possibly be the son of his old buddy that had moved to Pa., forty-eight years ago. Pop was very excited. He told Jeep there was going to be a reunion of his old high school classmates and he was thinking of going if Petey was better by then. Mac asked why he had never come back for a reunion. Pop said he had moved away the end of his sophomore year. I never graduated from the Institute, so I never thought I would be invited back for a reunion.

Mac said, "Hell, Dano, a lot of us escaped and didn't graduate. Some of us got asked to leave. But we still get together for the memories."

Pop was laughing as he told Jeep the story. "What a guy and what great memories he stirred in me." Pop was doing just fine

They had opened Pippins again. They were hoping that their customers would be brave and come back. B was doing a good lunch when they got back from the hospital. She said Meghan was looking for Jeep and a contractor Jeep had called to fix the damaged cottage had called. Jeep told B when he called back to tell him to get started, we would talk about the money later.

That evening Meghan stopped in, you could tell she was irritated. She sat at the bar with Jeep and had a bourbon and water. She was out of leads on Bo's murder and frustrated. They were going to convict Harley Ingram of Jamie's murder she was sure. But she was still assigned to Bo's case because of the tie in with the camp. She was sure someone from the camp had killed Bo, but it wasn't going to be easy to prove. She also said that she missed having Petey around.

"Hmmm!" Jeep said. "Absences makes the heart grow fonder?"

"Hey, Dear Abby, get me another bourbon and water, and shut up!" she snapped.

B was smiling as she walked up to the bar.

"What's so funny?" Jeep said.

"Oh, this customer was asking one of our waitresses 'How do you prepare your chicken?'" I walked over and said, "Nothing special, we just tell them straight out that they're going to die!" That made even Meghan smile.

It was three days until Christmas and Petey was coming home. This was the best present for everyone. Jeep had put a tree up in the apartment. K.C. and B had done a great job of decorating Pippins and all was well with the world. At least the little world they lived in today.

They had Petey's bedroom all set up with a TV. They brought him home in an ambulance. He got a standing ovation from the customers when they brought him in the front door of Pippins and then upstairs to the apartment. It was great having him home. He was starting to act like old Petey. The doctors told Jeep they wanted him up and walking around the apartment twice a day. Jeep said that would be great, Petey could make him breakfast and lunch.

Pippins was closed for Christmas day. They had a great party planned in the apartment. Christmas morning they opened presents early as was family tradition. It was K.C., B, Master Lee, Petey, Pop and Jeep. Petey got a much needed cane. Master Lee got a gift certificate to Kaufmann's Department store.

"I need this—all my clothes are same charcoal color and smell like smoke ever since fire," He smiled. "Thank you, Santa Claus."

B got some great looking slacks, although they had to be shortened about three inches. "I guess Santa doesn't know about petite sizes," she said.

Pop got a round-trip plane ticket to Peoria, Ill.

K.C. got a gold chain and a jacket, and Jeep got some nice sweaters. It was a great Christmas. Petey was feeling better every day. This afternoon they were having a larger private party. It usually spills over to Pippins downstairs where there is a larger selection of booze. They invited Meghan, Cookie, Danny Grabowski, Gov, Dickey Lee, Flip and his secretary Sally, Kendal, Sheriff Cottin and Buck. Jeep insisted that K.C. and B do nothing. He would take care of the food. He cooked some frozen pizza and made all the snacks at the bar available for free.

Petey said, "What a guy."

The days were going fast; Petey was almost back to normal. Pop was getting ready for his trip to the reunion. The snow was starting to melt, although another snowfall or two before the winter was officially over was expected. Meghan was back in Philly working from her office. Danny Grabowski was back in Pittsburgh working on another assignment. Master Lee was back in his cottage and business was better than ever. Jeep started working out at the YMCA again. He thought he was getting soft. They had only gone hunting twice this year. It seemed like he had spent an unusual amount of time indoors. Jeep spent a lot of time sitting with Petey keeping him company, but he thought Petey was getting sick of him. He was longing for some female company. Wanda had been over a few times to visit with him during his rehab. She really was a nice girl.

Jeep was taking Pop to the Pittsburgh airport. His flight was at nine-forty in the morning. With the new security, they had to get there two hours before the flight, so they intended to get there by eight. It was a little over an hour drive so they had to leave by seven. Jeep dropped him off a few minutes after eight. He had called Danny Grabowski earlier in the week to see if he was available. He said he would make himself available. Jeep got to his office about nine.

"Am I in time for breakfast?" Jeep asked.

Danny said, "Lets go down to the cafeteria and see if they have any stale English muffins."

It didn't take long to tell Jeep they had nothing new. He had talked to Meghan, and she was being pulled off the case. Other than knowing that there had been two shooters they had nothing to go on. Jeep asked Danny what information they needed to continue the case. He said other than an eye witness, matching the bullets they had taken out of Bo's body with the guns was about their only hope. Jeep visited with Danny for about an hour. Danny asked how B was doing.

Jeep said she was fine. "She is going for her second degree red belt with Master Lee. I'll tell her you asked," he said. *Hmm, I should have paid more attention at the Christmas party,* Jeep thought to himself.

Jeep asked, "Would you like to come down some weekend? You could stay free at our extra cottage."

Danny said, "I would love to and I will let you know as soon as I can break away from here."

While driving home, Jeep was thinking how he was going to find bullets that matched the ones the FBI had. *Where do bullets go after they have been used? This was silly.* He was looking for a .38 and a .44mag. He might have a chance with the .44mag, it was not as common as a .38cal. He could not go around checking all the .44mag's in the world. He had no idea where the shooters were today. *Wait a minute,* he thought. *Did they find any .44mags at the camp? That would be a good place to start. Surely Meghan or Danny had pursued this line of thinking already.* When he got home he called Danny and asked his question. Yes, he said, they had thought of that. They didn't find any .44mag's at the camp.

B was getting ready to open and Petey was sitting at the bar.

"Well, look at you," Jeep said. "It looks like old times with you sitting there"

"I'm feeling pretty good," Petey said.

That made Jeep very happy. "Good, then we can expect you to start pulling your weight around here, huh?" Grabbing Petey around the neck he winked at B and it was obvious that Jeep was pleased to see Petey in good health.

Jeep told B that he had invited Danny down for a weekend and asked if it was okay with her.

She just got this big old smile on her face and said, "Sure."

"Are you planning on getting in trouble with the FBI?" Petey asked.

"Yea," she said, "handcuffs and all, and don't either one of you think of bailing me out."

They were all laughing when Jeep called the sheriff's office looking for Cookie and he left word for her to stop by Pippins

It was about dinnertime when Cookie walked in. She sat down with Petey and Jeep in the corner booth and said, "What's up"?

"We want to bounce some ideas off you," Jeep said. He explained what was needed to continue the investigation of Bo's murder. The ATF and FBI were moving on and if they wanted it solved it was up to them. "We need the gun," Jeep said.

"How do we find a .44mag in this county?" Cookie said. "That is, if it's still in this county? I'll go over the list of all registered handguns that are .44mags, but my guess is only about twenty-five percent are registered."

"This isn't going to get us anywhere," Jeep said.

"Do you think a matching slug might be at the pistol range?" suggested Petey.

"How would we find it?" Jeep said. "That would really be the needle in the haystack."

"Well, it's a soft sand bank behind the targets," said Petey.

"We could dig out about six wheelbarrows full of sand and sift it thru a screen," said Cookie.

"You two are crazy," Jeep declared.

"If we ended up with a thousand slugs, how many would you guess would be 44 magnums?" asked Petey.

"Less than a hundred," said Cookie.

"Stop the madness," Jeep said. He left the two lunatics in the booth and went to help in the kitchen slamming the swinging doors. He was very frustrated. He knew they were trying to help, but they were just making him realize how impossible it's going to be solving Bo's murder.

Four days have passed and it's time for Pop's return. His flight was arriving at three. Petey said he would like to ride to the airport with Jeep.

They left at two. It gave Jeep a chance to spend some time with Petey. A lot had happened in their lives the last few months. Petey was saying that he thought he would be a hundred percent healthy in another month. He was actually feeling pretty good, nothing was hurting, although the incision was a little numb in spots, but that was it. He told Jeep that he really liked Meghan and that he missed her. Jeep asked what he was going to do about it. He said there wasn't any future for the two of them. She was a college graduate with a career and a future, and that he was a co-owner of a bar who lived five hours away. Being the other co-owner Jeep was offended and he told Petey he was wrong, that he had a lot to offer. Jeep suggested that maybe he should take a trip to Philly.

"I don't want it to look like I'm chasing her," he said.

"Why not? You are." Jeep smiled. "Tell her we are thinking of opening a Pippins East in Philly and you're scouting out the area if the truth bothers you." Jeep asked, "Since you are feeling better, could K.C. and I continue our trip to Washington?"

Petey said, "Yea, I'm okay with that."

Chapter 9

Pop's plane was on time. He was smiling from ear to ear. He said he had a great time and he didn't stop talking the entire ride home. He had a lot of stories to tell us. It was good seeing Pop so happy. One of the stories he mentioned was about a friend's wife. "I was talking to Mac's wife, Irma, and she mentions in passing that she was from Huntsville, Alabama," Pop said. "I told her I knew someone from Huntsville although he was younger than her. Did she know a family named Cottin? She said she did and they were nice folks. They had two boys. She went to high school with the older one, his name was Amos. She said he died in Vietnam."

"That can't be the same family!" exclaimed Petey. "Although, it sure is weird that there were two families in Huntsville named Cottin and both had a boy named Amos. What a small world," he said.

"Are you sure you got the story straight, Pop, or were you knocking down *tee many martoonies?*" Jeep asked.

"I was doing that too, but I got the story right," smiled Pop.

"Well," Jeep said, "Cottin must be a little older than he say's he is and she is wrong about Vietnam."

"Maybe he lied because he didn't want people to think he was too old to be sheriff," said Pop.

That must be it we agreed.

When we got back to Pippins, K.C. said that Danny had called and asked if it would be okay to come on down this weekend. She had said that would be great. He then asked to talk to B. When B came walking out of the kitchen, Jeep said, "K.C. told me Danny's coming down this weekend."

"That's great. We'll have a party."

"He is coming this weekend, and we will have a party, except you're not invited, Jeep." She smiled.

"You didn't have to hit me with a sledgehammer," Jeep said. "I guess you want to be alone."

It was Friday night and business was booming. The wait to be seated was a half hour, the bar was packed and B was working hard. We had two bartenders plus her working, and at times even Jeep would try to help. He was better on the stool side of the bar.

Jeep was sitting in the corner booth with Pop and Petey—they had just finished eating. Jeep had Dean Martin music playing in the dining room and it was a splendid Friday night. About ten o'clock Sheriff Cottin stopped by to check the place out and Pop waved him over.

"Hey, Cottin, I met someone that knew you from Huntsville," Pop said. This got Cottin's attention as his head snapped around to face Pop.

"Who was it?" he inquired.

"Did you know a girl named Irma, oh what was her maiden name? Fisher...or..."

"Fishell," said Cottin. "Yea, I knew a girl name Irma Fishell. She was older than me."

"Well," said Pop, "she said you were killed in Vietnam."

"She's wrong," he answered decisively. Then he smiled and said, "I'm too fat to be a ghost." He chuckled and said, "How is old Irma doing?"

"Fine," said Pop. "She married a classmate of mine from Illinois." Cottin wanted to know where she was living now. Pop told him she and Mac were living in Huntington, Indiana, just southwest of Fort Wayne. "Her married name is McLaughlin."

Danny showed up at ten-thirty and Jeep told B she was through for the night. The supper crowd had left and the bar was manageable. "I will do the receipts tonight," said Jeep

B thanked him and said to Danny, "Come on, I will help you get settled in your cottage."

K.C. had sat down with them. She was tired. "That's the last we will see of them tonight," smiled K.C.

"Danny will be safe," said Petey. "He's armed."

Cottin had given Pop a ride home. It was K.C., Petey and Jeep enjoying the crowd.

Jeep had rented Bo's cottage. The cottage area was quite nice, once you got used to the fire bombing and shootings. The new tenant was also a truck driver by the name of Mike Austin. He had bought Bo's rig from the estate. Flip was the executor of Bo's estate. The truck and trailer brought the estate sixty thousand dollars. The money paid for Bo's funeral and the remainder would go to a niece. Mike was a fellow Petey and Jeep knew from school, his class graduated two years before they did. Jeep thought he might want to tend bar for them when he's not on the road. He also was a fine piano player with a pleasing voice. Jeep told him he could play at Pippins Piano Bar if they had a piano.

Petey was getting itchy; he wanted to go to Philly, so Jeep told him one morning they would flip a coin to see who would take the first trip.

Petey said, "What do you mean, take a trip?"

"I thought you might want to go to Philly," Jeep said.

"No way, why would I want to do that"?

"Okay," Jeep said. "K.C. and I are going to D.C."

"TAILS," said Petey.

Petey called Meghan and told her he was coming to Philly, Friday and asked would she be available for dinner. She said by all means, she would love to see him. He asked her if she knew of a good place to stay and she said she would make the reservations for him. She would get him the government rate. She told him her address and said pick her up at six o'clock. She would tell him where he was staying when he got here. Petey told her that would be great. He thanked her for all the help and said he would see her at six on Friday. He was higher than a kite when he hung up the phone. It was two days until Friday, which meant Jeep was going to have to put up with a silly teenager until then. The last time Petey acted like this was the junior prom. He wanted to know if he could borrow Jeep's car because he didn't think his Pennsylvania Porsche was a Philadelphia type of vehicle. Jeep told him that would be okay.

Petey waved goodbye at eight in the morning, he couldn't wait to get started. It was a great day he thought as he drove up three mile hill to the Donagal entrance to the turnpike. Petey was remembering when there used to be seven tunnels on the Pennsylvania turnpike now there were only three. *I guess that's progress,* he thought. He pulled into Philly at three after a very leisurely trip, and bought a map of the town. He found Meghan's address and had two hours to kill. She actually lived in Cherry Hill, New Jersey. He drove around for a while and was sitting in the car in front of her place at five-thirty when Meghan came home. He saw her pull into the lot and he jumped out of the car and went over to greet her. He hugged her and then he kissed her. She was pleased to see him.

"Get your suitcase, every hotel in town was booked. You are going to have to stay with me." She smiled sheepishly.

Petey said, "Just my luck! I think I like the government rate."

They had a great dinner that Meghan cooked. She made tilapia and fettuccine alfredo. She said it was too crowded to go out on Friday night. After dinner they drank some wine and talked. Petey couldn't stop smiling—he thought he had died and gone to heaven.

Meghan said, "Petey, you look great. You would never know that you've been shot. You look like you are in superb condition," she said. "How is your stamina?"

"Not bad for a lonely country boy," he boasted with a coy grin.

'You'll have to show me," she cooed.

He did, several times that weekend.

Agent Grabowski called to give Jeep some new information, so he said. He told him that the leader of the camp was named Joshua. He said one of the wounded prisoners was trying to make a deal. He then divulged the real reason for the call by asking if B was available. Jeep wanted to tell him that B had joined the Peace Corps and had gone to Bosnia, but he behaved himself and called B to the phone.

Petey got back about one in the afternoon on Monday. He said he had a great time and that Meghan said she misses all of us. "She said she was coming to visit us the first chance she got." Jeep told Petey that Danny had called and they are now looking for a guy name Joshua.

Petey and Jeep were standing outside in the parking lot of Pippins. They were trying to decide if the place needed paint or a spring wash. Cookie pulled up in her deputy sheriff's car.

She said, "Hey, Petey, I have a job for you." Walking around to the back of the car, she opened the trunk.

"What have you got?" inquired Petey.

"I have about eight-hundred slugs I dug out of the pistol range," she said.

"What?" Jeep exclaimed.

"Yep," she said. "Petey and I had a deal. If I would dig them out, he would separate the .44mags from the rest."

"Yea," said Petey. "I can't wait to get started, it shouldn't be hard to do."

"What do you plan to do with them after you separate them?" Jeep asked.

"Danny has agreed to go through them and try to get a match. All I have to do is take them down to Pittsburgh. Do you want to take a ride with me? If not, will you lend me your car?" Petey smiled.

"You two are insane, what will this prove?" Jeep asked

"That our killer uses the range," Cookie said.

The next five days were uneventful. B wanted to know when she could have a weekend off. Jeep told her she could have the sixth weekend of any month off. He asked her if Danny was getting tired of the drive from Pittsburgh. Don't be silly, she told me, he'd walk down from Pittsburgh if he had to. Petey told her they were going down to see Danny Monday, did she want to come with them. She said she would love to if it was okay with us. It was fine with us—we looked forward to B's company.

It was a good ride with Petey and B. They were both fun to be with and very funny. We arrived at Danny's office mid-morning. Jeep asked Danny why he was humoring Petey with this bullet sham.

"How many spent bullets did you bring me, Petey?"

"Eighty-nine," said Petey.

"This isn't a sham, Jeep!" Danny said. "This is the unglamorous part of police work. If we find a matching slug, we will have something to go on. Maybe the gun owner will continue to practice at the range. The next .44mag shooter at your pistol range becomes a suspect, so let's hope we find a match. The downside is this will take a while."

The ride home was without incident. They got back in time for Petey to take a nap. This coming Friday K.C. and Jeep were going to try again to enjoy Washington D.C.

K.C. went shopping with Cookie since they both had the day off. K.C. told Jeep she had bought a few things for the trip to D.C. She and Cookie put on a fashion show for B and Jeep.

How did this happen? I was trapped! thought Jeep as he sat there with a frozen smile on his face and nodding approval.

They finally left for D.C. They stopped at Nemacolin Woodlands Resort for breakfast. What a great spot. Jeep would love to stay here sometime, but it's just too close to home. They have great golf, skeet and trap shooting, horseback riding and a few fine restaurants. You just can't go on vacation to a resort so close to home. The weather was pleasant and there was no traffic congestion. They made excellent time to D.C.

Jeep has always enjoyed the sights in Washington. There is so much to do—just the Smithsonian can keep you busy for a week. They stayed very busy because they didn't have much time. They took as many tours as they could, but they were time-consuming. They looked at all the war memorials. K.C. wanted to get a pencil rubbing from the "Vietnam Wall." Her uncle (her father's older brother) had died in Vietnam. They searched for Ed Connelly. When they found it, Jeep helped her lean over to make a pencil rubbing of his name. His eyes wandered below Ed Connelly's name and stopped in shock. There it was as big as life—AMOS COTTIN—he gasped!

Back in the hotel bar, K.C. and Jeep pondered what they should do. Could there be two Amos Cottins? No, they didn't think that would be possible. Could the military records be messed up? Maybe! But they didn't think so. Could our sheriff be someone other than Amos Cottin? Possibly! What they knew for certain was, they had to be careful with their information. They agreed to tell no one, not even Petey. When they got home Jeep would call Meghan or Danny. The balance of their visit in Washington was spent in a fog—they couldn't focus on anything. As much as they tried to see the sights, their thoughts were on their discovery. They left Monday for their trip home. In spite of the newly acquired information, they had a good time. They got to enjoy each other's company relaxing together, instead of working together. They just didn't get enough time to themselves. However, their most enjoyable conversation always ended up being about making Pippins bigger and better. It was their mutual hobby, as well as their passion. The fact of the matter was, it was there life and their careers. The beauty of it was they enjoyed doing it and that made them happy.

They arrived back at Pippins Monday evening and no one was around, so they did get to spend the last few hours of their mini-vacation alone. Pippins seemed very large when it was dark and empty. K.C. and Jeep were in her cottage eating pizza when Jeep saw the lights come on in his apartment.

"Petey must be home," he said to K.C. "I guess it's time for me to go and see what's shakin' with him." He told K.C. he would see her tomorrow. "Sleep in if you can." He went in the back door and upstairs to see Petey.

Petey had been playing cards with the boy's. Jeep asked him who was playing.

He said, "Dickey Lee, Mike Austin and some of the sheriff's boys, Rufus Porter, Coon Dog Campbell, and Tiny Hayes. I was sniffing around about who owns a .44 mag," he said. "They said quite a few people. It used to be a very popular gun back in the seventies and eighties. The only deputy that carries one is Rufus Porter. They said the same thing that Cookie said. Not many people around here bother to register their handguns." He wanted to know if we had a good time in D.C. Jeep told him it was an interesting trip. He asked Petey if he had Meghan's phone number.

He said, "That may be the dumbest question you have asked this year."

Jeep said he wanted to call her in the morning. Petey wanted to know why. Jeep said he wanted to invite her down for a weekend. He thought it would be nice if he did it, instead of some horny country boy breathing hard into the phone.

"Ha, ha, ha," said Petey. "I'm going to bed."

Jeep called Meghan and told her what he had seen on the Vietnam Wall. She was very interested, and said she would check with the veteran's administration. "There has to be a mixup," she said. "Either it's a mixup or you have a ringer as a county sheriff."

Jeep said, "Cottin has lived around here for quite a while."

. Meghan said, "Since '85, that's what he told me."

"I would guess that's about right," Jeep said.

She said, "I'll get back to you when I get to the bottom of this mystery, but for the meantime don't turn your back on Cottin."

Chapter 10

They were getting ready for Tuesday night dinner. K.C. had Steak Oscar on the menu, also cat fish, stuffed pork chops and her killer lasagna. The people in this county were eating well. Jeep got a call from Agent Grabowski,

"Jeep," he said, "we've got a match."

"Are you kidding me, Danny?" Jeep said.

"No, we have a positive match. Bo's killer has used your range. What's really interesting was almost all the spent bullets matched. This was not a very hard task of looking for a match. It almost looks like our shooter is the only one using a .44mag at that range. This is a huge break. Petey and Cookie are geniuses. Tell Cookie, but warn her to keep it a secret. I will be there in two days to formulate a plan. I think we are going to catch one of the shooters."

"Well, Danny, I have some news for you," Jeep said. He told him about their findings at the Vietnam wall, and that Meghan was checking it out. Danny was surprised and said he would catch up with Meghan and they could share information." Things were getting exciting.

Jeep told Petey that Danny had called. When he told Petey the news, he thought he was going to jump out of his skin. Jeep told him to inform Cookie, tell her not to breathe a word of it to anyone. Jeep expected to hear from Danny and Meghan very soon.

Petey was so excited. "Jeep, remember what I said last night. Rufus Porter carries a 44. He spends a lot of time at the pistol range!" exclaimed Petey.

"Let's not jump to any conclusions," Jeep said.

Meghan called to tell Jeep she was on her way to Alabama. A town called Union Grove. She had checked with the veteran's administration and Amos Cottin had indeed died in Vietnam. He was a young man of twenty-one. She also found out that he had been married for a year before he was sent overseas. She had located the widow who was living in Union Grove. The woman was willing to talk with Meghan. She had remarried, but was now a widow again. The second marriage lasted thirty-four years. She had three children and five grandchildren. She didn't have any children with Amos. Meghan said she would call after her meeting with the widow.

It was after the dinner crowd and business was slowing down. Jeep was sitting in his corner booth when Cookie walked thru the front door. He waved her over—she was not in uniform.

"Hey, Jeep, I want to bounce an idea off you," she said as she sat down.

"Shoot, deputy." Jeep smiled. "It's only a figure of speech," he joked.

"I was thinking of asking Deputy Porter if he wanted to qualify at the range with me tomorrow," said Cookie.

"Can you manage to get a bullet sample?" Jeep asked.

"I'm sure I can, although I haven't figured out just how I'll do it," said Cookie.

"Ask him if you can try his pistol, and then miss the target," Jeep suggested. "Just remember what part of the sand bank you hit."

"Yea," said Cookie, "I'll make a mental note, then go back and dig it out."

"It works for me," Jeep said. "Go for it. You know, Cookie, you and Petey were right, Agent Grabowski said you two were geniuses. You should be very proud, that was excellent police work. The hardest part now is keeping quiet. If Porter is guilty, I'd like to take him out back for some county justice, if you know what I mean," Jeep said.

"Why don't I just shoot him while we're up at the range?" She smiled.

K.C. came out of the kitchen for her first break of the evening. "What evil are you two planning?" she asked.

"It's not that evil, but we are planning," said Cookie. They told K.C. of their plan; she agreed with them that the shooting range was a good idea.

That night when everyone went home, Petey and Jeep were up in the apartment. Jeep told him about Amos Cottin's name on the Vietnam wall. He swore him to secrecy, but Petey wanted to go get Cottin right now. That was an emotion that Jeep understood, but they couldn't act on just yet. Petey also knew that, but he wanted dibs on Cottin. They talked quite a while about Bo and how Jeep had lost the last connection to his father when Bo was murdered. Jeep really used to appreciate it when Bo would tell stories about when he and Jeep's dad were young. Before they turned in they agreed to find out what time Cookie was going to the range with Porter. They thought they would make sure they just happened to be there at the same time. Jeep fell asleep thinking they had assumed the person that shot Bo was the same person that made sure he didn't get better in the hospital and assisted in his demise. He didn't think they would be able to prove Bo's murder, but he thought they would be able to prove attempted murder.

Petey said Cookie was going up to the range with Porter during their lunch break. Petey and Jeep decided to be there when they arrived. Jeep needed some practice with his pistol. Shooting a handgun was not his strength, and the truth was Petey is a much better pistol marksman. Cookie and Porter pulled up shortly after noon. Petey and Jeep acted surprised to see them. Cookie joked that Porter had challenged her to a shooting contest. Cookie was very good with a handgun. Porter walked to the line and started shooting right away. The report the .44 mag made was deafening and they all scrambled for their earplugs.

"Christ, Porter!" Petey screamed, "give us a little warning." The deputy just smiled.

"Do you have to hit anything with that cannon or does the concussion knock them out?" Jeep said. He did hit the target a few times.

Cookie said, "Let me try that mule."

"Hang on tight, honey," smiled Porter. Cookie missed the target three times to the right.

Porter laughed. "Missed!"

Jeep knew better, all three bullets landed in the same spot, right where she was aiming. *Good going, Cookie,* he thought.

The next hour the two deputies qualified. Petey was shooting at a further distance of about a hundred feet. Jeep, on the other hand, was frightening the target with near misses at fifty feet. They said their goodbye's as Cookie and Porter went back to work. Petey and Jeep went to work digging for spent .44mag bullets. They found all three within five inches of each other. Their mission accomplished, they headed back to Pippins. Petey said he was going to take the slugs to Agent Grabowski first thing in the morning.

Jeep rolled out of bed around seven-thirty and Petey was walking out the door, heading for Pittsburgh.

He said, "The quicker I get these slugs to Danny the sooner we will know about Deputy Porter. See you later, Jeep," he sang out as he ran down the stairs. Jeep showered and walked out back where Mike Austin and Master Lee were talking.

"Who's buying breakfast?" Jeep asked.

Master Lee said, "I flip you for it. If you land on your head I buy, if you land on your feet you buy! Ha, Ha, Ha!"

"Let's go Dutch treat," said Mike.

"Okay by me," Jeep said. They went down to Gerry's diner.

Gov was pouring out coffee and asking, "Do you think they will ever catch the guy that shot Bo?"

Jeep told him, "I hope so, but I don't think they have any suspects."

Mike said, "I get questions all the time from the truckers wanting to know how the investigation is going."

Jeep told them, "The FBI runs a tight ship. They don't say much about the case."

After another great feed at Gerry's, they went back to Pippins. Jeep had a few odd jobs that he had put off for too long. He was fixing a wobbly table when Meghan called. She said she was flying from Alabama direct to Pittsburgh, could he pick her up? Jeep asked her when, and she said her U.S. Air flight arrived at one-thirty that afternoon. He said either he or Petey would pick her up. He explained that Petey was in Pittsburgh and if he could get in touch with him, Petey would be there. Jeep called the FBI office in Pittsburgh and asked for Danny. They said he had a visitor and was away from his desk. He left word for Danny to call him as soon as he returned to his desk. Meghan had given Jeep her cell phone number so he could let her know if they could pick her up. She would rent a car if she had to, but this stop in Pittsburgh was not official. Petey called back shortly and Jeep explained what he needed from him and he could feel the smile over the telephone. He would pick up Meghan if he had to, but it was out of his way, Petey mugged.

Jeep asked, "Do you have Meghan's cell phone nu….OH! I know that's the dumbest question I have asked this year, and I just asked it again." He went into the kitchen to see if K.C. needed the help of a dummy.

It was a little after three when Petey and Meghan arrived. K.C. B and Jeep had just sat down to rest after the lunch crowd and they joined them in the corner booth. Petey said he had not talked to Meghan about her trip to Alabama, so she wouldn't have to repeat it.

Meghan explained what she had learned on her trip. She had flown to Union Grove, Alabama, to interview a woman who was married to Amos Cottin thirty-eight years ago. Her name was Lilly Ogilvie and her maiden name was Findley. She had known the Cottin family for as long as she could remember. She and Amos were high school sweethearts. When she married Amos she was Lilly Findley. She was married to Amos for just a year when he was shipped to Vietnam. It was two days before their first anniversary. A few months later she was notified he had been killed in action. She was all alone. She has always regretted they didn't have any children. The body was shipped home a few weeks later and there was a memorial service and that was it. She had to get on with her life. Four years later she married Homer Ogilvy. She raised three children and had five grandchildren. Homer died a year ago and she was now widowed again.

The Cottin family had two boys; the younger boy took Amos's death very hard. He had idolized his older brother and he was never the same after his brother died. He got into trouble and became very embittered. He hated the United States for killing his brother. He withdrew from everyone and she lost track of him. She heard he had moved up north and some people said he moved to Europe. His name was Joshua, Joshua Cottin. The four of them sat listening to Meghan's story and they were mesmerized.

Petey was the first to speak. "Joshua is the leader of the camp!" he exclaimed. "What does this mean?"

"I'm not too sure," said Meghan, "but I suspect that Amos and Joshua are the same person."

What she asked of them, was to keep an eye on things around here so she could sort things out at the agency. "I'm going to Philly to get the warrants I will require," she said. "We will try to gather some evidence and then we will talk to Sheriff Cottin. Keep your eyes open and your mouth shut. If Cottin has a hint that we are investigating him he will cover his tracks and disappear, or worst case he will strike back and someone will get hurt. Either way we lose our advantage." They all agreed.

Early next morning Jeep went down to Flip's office. He was lucky to catch him. He was just finishing a brief that had to be delivered to the courthouse. Jeep gave him an envelope that contained everything he knew about this whole mess. It started with finding the parachute right up until the meeting last night.

Jeep said, "Put this with my will, and only open it in case of my departure from this world."

"You expecting that to be anytime soon?" smiled Flip.

"Not if I can help it," Jeep said. "I just thought it would be a good idea if someone else knew what I knew, just in case, and you drew short straw." Jeep smiled.

"Okay Jeep, consider it done. I plan to hand this back to you on your ninetieth birthday," Flip said.

"That would be fine with me," Jeep said.

Jeep left Flip's office and headed back out to Pippins, making a coffee stop at Gerry's diner. As he pulled into the lot he saw Cottin coming out of the diner—he was dressed in civilian clothes.

"Hey, Cottin, who's protecting me today?" Jeep said. "You look like you are goofing off."

"My boys can take good care of you if the situation arises. I am just on my day off. I have to clean my uniform once in a while." He smiled.

"You are entitled to a day off, I was just kidding," Jeep said.

"If I have a good time today, I might just take two off," he said.

"Did you ever take a couple of weeks?" Jeep asked.

"No," he said, "I have traveled for a few days, but it's mostly associated with a business trip."

"Did you ever take a trip back home to Alabama?" Jeep asked.

"Nope," he said, "I never wanted to go back home."

"I'll see you later," Jeep said as he went into the diner to have a cup of coffee with Gov.

"Hey, Jeep, what happened to that good looking federal agent?" asked Gov.

"You mean Meghan?" Jeep asked.

"Yea," said Gov.

"Why do you ask?" Jeep said.

"Oh, I don't know, Cottin just reminded me of her. He asked me if I had seen her around lately."

Jeep got back to Pippins in time to help get ready for lunch.

Petey was cleaning the bar.

"Have you heard from Danny?"

"Be patient, we will hear from him the second he knows something," Jeep said.

Petey said, "I'm keeping my eye on Deputy Porter."

"Do it from a distant, Petey. We don't want to spook him."

"I can watch the Easter Bunny without him knowing it," said Petey.

"That's what you think! I didn't get a basket last Easter," Jeep said. "He probably knew you were watching!"

"What am I, flypaper for bad comedians?" asked Petey.

Jeep thought he would call Cottin's office and ask him if he was looking for Meghan. He would be happy to give him her number if he wanted it, just to see how he reacted. Then Jeep remembered Cottin had taken the day off. *I will call his secretary in the morning,* Jeep said to himself. Lunch went smooth, and in the afternoon Petey and Jeep did some spring yard work, just picking up branches and raking a little. This place could get ahead of you real fast if you did not stay on top of it.

That evening Pippins had a brisk dinner crowd. About midway through dinner, Jeep noticed Sheriff Cottin's secretary having dinner with her husband. Jeep stopped at their table to say hello.

"How are you doing tonight, Rosemary?" asked Jeep.

"Fine" she said. "Do you know my husband, Claude?" she asked.

"Sure, I remember Claude," said Jeep. "You work out at the feed plant don't you, Claude?"

"Yep," said Claude. "I've been out there fourteen years this year."

"Say, Rosemary, will you have the sheriff call me in the morning?" asked Jeep.

"I can't do that," she said. "The sheriff won't be in tomorrow."

"Oh, he took another day, did he?" asked Jeep.

"Took a whole week," said Rosemary.

"Where did he go?" asked Jeep.

"He had me buy him a plane ticket to Indiana," she said. "Fort Wayne, Indiana."

Jeep didn't know how to reach Danny in the evening, so he called Meghan in Philly. He told her that Cottin had flown to Fort Wayne this morning. He explained to her that Fort Wayne was where Pop's friend Tom McLaughlin lived. His wife, Irma Fishell McLaughlin was the woman that knew the Cottin family back in Huntsville. She was the one that first told us that Amos Cottin had died in Vietnam. Meghan asked did the McLaughlin's live in Fort Wayne proper or a suburb. Jeep couldn't remember, he said he would call her right back. He called Pop. Pop said he thought it was Huntington, Indiana. Jeep asked if Pop had a phone number. Pop said he did and gave it to Jeep. He called Meghan back with the information. She said she would get in touch with the authorities and let them know.

Jeep said, "I will stay near the phone, please hurry." He hung up the phone and started pacing. It was nine o'clock.

Jeep and Petey had locked up Pippins after Buck left. It was close to one o'clock. They still had not heard back from Meghan.

Petey said, "Let's call her."

Jeep thought it was better to wait and not tie up Meghan's line, or their line. The two of them sat in Jeep's room and stared at the telephone. Finallym at quarter to two the phone rang, it was Meghan. Petey got on the extension in his room.

"Sorry I took so long, but we had to get an agent in touch with the police in Huntington, Indiana," she said. "The FBI agent just got there less than an hour ago. There has been a fire at the McLaughlin residence. I don't know if there have been any casualties. The home has been gutted."

"What can we do?" Petey asked.

"We have to wait," she said. "I have reached Agent Grabowski in Pittsburgh and he is on his way to Indiana. Just so you boys know, this case belongs to the FBI, the ATF is only assisting. They have promised to keep me in the loop, I am sure Danny will keep his word."

"We are not very good at sitting around," said Petey. "Is there anything we can do?"

"Nothing that I can think of that you can do right now," Meghan said. "But stay available."

"Well, Jeep, what do we do?" asked Petey. "I don't like sitting around. I would like to know if Pop's old friend is alive or dead."

They left a note for K.C.

Chapter 11

They picked up route 70 just south of Donora, and headed west through "Little Washington" and were on their way to Wheeling, West Virginia. From Wheeling to the Ohio-Indiana border was about 250 miles. A straight shot across Ohio, thru Columbus to Richmond Indiana, then north about ninety-five miles to Huntington. It was ten-thirty in the morning when they pulled into the center of town.

"There's the police station," Petey said. "Let's go find out what we can."

They walked into the station and the sergeant on the desk said, "May I help you?"

"Yes," said Jeep. "We are looking for FBI Agent Dan Grabowski. He told us to meet him here."

"Are you with the bureau?" the sergeant asked.

"We're from the field. We work with Danny," Petey said. "Can we get some coffee? We've been driving all night."

"Sure thing," said the sergeant. "We have an office set up for you guys. It's the second door on the right, down that hallway," he said pointing down the hallway to his left. Petey led the way.

As they entered the room, Jeep said, "It's a federal offense impersonating a federal officer."

"Then stop doing it," said Petey. "All I did was ask for coffee." There was a fresh pot of coffee on the credenza in the corner.

The sergeant stuck his head in the door, "Agent Grabowski is expected shortly. Should I tell him you're here?"

"No," said Petey, "we want to surprise him. What you can tell us is what you have on the McLaughlin residence." Jeep poured two coffees and sat down at the conference table next to Petey.

"Well, the sergeant said it looks like an explosion. We have found two bodies, we haven't identified them yet. We expect that it's Irma and Mac. The entire house was gutted. It looks like some kind of a bomb went off."

"Yea," said Petey, "it was probably the candle and gas filled balloon bomb. It gives the arsonist an hour or so to get away before the candle burns down and explodes the balloon."

"Do you guys think it was intentional?" the sergeant asked. "That would make it murder!" he said.

"That's why we're here," said Petey.

"What time did the fire department get the alarm?" Jeep asked.

"I think it was ten o'clock last evening," the sergeant said.

"What the hell?" said Danny as he walked thru the door.

"Sergeant, this is Agent Grabowski, Danny this is…excuse me, Sarge, I didn't get your name," said Petey.

"Cushing, Jerry Cushing," the sergeant said.

"Okay, Jerry that will be all," said Petey. "We will call if we need anything. Close the door on the way out."

As the door closed Jeep said, "We can explain."

"Start," said Danny.

It took about a half an hour to tell Danny what they had done. They convinced Danny to take them to the site with him. They took Danny's rented car to the crime scene. A police cruiser led them so they wouldn't get lost.

On the way to the house, Danny said, "How many speeding tickets did you guys get on the way out here?"

"Not a one," said Petey, "but there are a few Ohio troopers banging on their radar guns, wondering why they don't work properly."

Danny said it was clever of Jeep to put together Pop's friends and Cottin's trip to Fort Wayne.

"But it didn't help," replied Jeep

Arriving at the house, or what was left of it, Danny said, "Stay out here. I don't want to explain you guys to my people. Let me find out who is here first. It should be some local fire inspector, maybe a medical examiner and our agents from Fort Wayne."

Jeep and Petey stayed in the car as Danny crossed the yellow tape and entered the crime scene. He was only gone about twenty minutes. "They have it all wrapped up here," Danny said as he returned to the car.

At lunch at a local fast food place Danny explained what they thought had happened. Someone had tied Mac and Irma to their beds with ty-wraps, the kind the police use for handcuffs, then poured gasoline all over the place and set it on fire. Petey suggested how it was done using the candle and balloon. Danny agreed that could have been how it happened. The one thing they all agreed on was Cottin was involved. Danny was going to put out an internal arrest notice. He wanted the notice to stay within the bureau. He didn't want the state or local police getting any information. He was afraid it would get back to the Sheriff's department in Pennsylvania. A description of Amos Cottin wanted for murder, with a warning that he was armed and considered dangerous was distributed within the bureau.

Back at the police station, Danny said, "I'm going to call Meghan and let her know what has happened."

Petey said the he and Jeep were going to head back to Pennsylvania. They had to give Pop the bad news about his friend Mac.

They drove as far as Richmond, Indiana, and then found a motel. They both needed a bed and a few good hours sleep.

The ride back was a lot slower, relaxed and uneventful. They pulled into Pippins parking lot at four-thirty the next day. K.C. and B were getting ready for the dinner crowd. They explained to the girls what the emergency in Indiana was and why the had left so suddenly.

K.C. asked, "What's your next step?"

"We have to go tell Pop," said Petey. "This news is going to hurt him."

"Let's go," said Jeep. "Putting this off is not doing any of us any good. I know Pop is going to blame himself for telling Cottin where Mac lived."

"Let's be selective on the information we give him," suggested Petey

Pop was sitting on the front porch when Petey and Jeep pulled up.

"Welcome, boys," Pop said. "I was just thinking of coming down to

Pippins for an early dinner. Do you know if K.C. has meatloaf on the menu?"

"I don't think you are going to be hungry when you hear what we have to tell you," Jeep said. "We just got word that your friend Mac and his wife Irma from Indiana have died in a fire."

"What!" gasped Pop. "How? When?"

"The fire was of a suspicious nature, it could have been arson," said Petey.

"Who wanted to kill Mac and Irma?" asked Pop.

"We are not sure, it might be tied into the trouble we are having here," said Jeep.

"I don't understand," Pop said.

"We are not too clear about it either," said Petey.

"All we know for sure is their house burned down late last night and they didn't get out. We will just have to wait for more information," said Jeep.

"Let's go down to Pippins and get a drink," said Petey. "I won't even charge you for the first one, Dad," smiled Petey.

This made Pop smile and he told them he would follow them back to Pippins in a few minutes.

That night after dinner, Jeep called a meeting at the apartment to explain to everyone what had transpired in Indiana. He had asked K.C. Lee, B, Cookie and Flip to attend. Jeep didn't know who in the sheriff's department was involved, but he knew that Deputy Colleen (Cookie) Wildey was one of the good guys.

The plan was as follows; K.C. and B were to keep their ears open around Pippins for any information they might hear. They also had to make sure everything and everybody looked and acted normal. Flip was to make sure their backsides were covered legally. Cookie was to be their eyes and ears in the sheriff's department and Master Lee was the guardian of their precious assets at Pippins. He was to be the homeland security.

"Has anyone at the sheriff's department heard from Cottin?" Petey asked.

"No, everything seems normal, he is still on vacation," said Cookie. "I asked his secretary Rosemary when he was coming back and she said he was expected back next Monday."

"I can't believe that he will just show up Monday as if nothing has happened," said Flip.

"I agree," said K.C. "Something is about to explode"

"All we can do is wait," said B. "No one has a clue as to what is going to happen next."

"Well, early to bed, early to rise makes one healthy, wealthy and boring," said Petey. "So let's have a closer." Everyone agreed.

The next morning Jeep and Petey were up earlier than usually. They had landscaping to do around the grounds. There were flowers to be planted, weeds to be pulled, earth to be turned.

After a few hours, Petey said, "I've been thinking Jeep. Here we are two restaurateurs doing landscaping work. How many landscapers do you think are running restaurants."?

"What's your point?" asked Jeep.

"If they are not taking work away from us by competing in the restaurant business, why are we stealing work from them?"

"I think I know where you are going with this," said Jeep.

"Let's call some landscapers and let them do this work," smiled Petey.

"And we feed them while they're out here?" asked Jeep.

"You're catching on, and we could barter with them," said Petey. "Food for flowers, hedges for hamburgers, mulch for munchies, raking for baking etc, you get the idea."

"I like it," laughed Jeep. "Get on the phone and start wheeling and dealing. I'll make up a sign—YARD TOOLS FOR SALE—slightly used." They both went in Pippins laughing with their arms around each other. Petey went to the corner booth with the phone book and Jeep went to the cooler and got two cold ones, an Iron City and a Rollin Rock. As Petey started making calls with his cell phone, the restaurant phone rang and Jeep answered it.

"It's Cookie," she said. "Cottin just called Rosemary and she switched the call to Porter. He has just hung up the phone and he looks nervous."

Jeep said, "If he leaves, can you follow him without being seen?"

"Not in a deputy car, he'd spot it in a heartbeat," she said.

"Nose around see if you can get an idea where he's going," urged Jeep.

"I'll let you know," Cookie whispered as she hung up.

Jeep called Danny's office and Danny was on another call. Jeep was put on hold for a few minutes. "Grabowski here," said Danny

"Danny, it's Jeep. Cottin just called his office!" exclaimed Jeep

"Yes, Jeep, I know, that's what my call was about. He was calling from Wheeling, West Virginia. He spoke to Deputy Porter. We don't know where Porter is meeting him. He told Porter to call him later from the road."

"You've got the sheriff's office bugged?" inquired Jeep with surprise.

"We've got their phones tapped," explained Danny. "Cottin suspects something or he wouldn't be so cautious. At least we know he is in the area. Tell Deputy Wildey to be careful. They might suspect her."

Jeep called Cookie back. "The sheriff called from Wheeling," Jeep said.

"What? How in the heck do you know that?" Cookie asked.

"I'll tell you later. The first thing I want you to do is leave the office and call me on your cell phone," said Jeep.

She said, "Okay," and hung up.

Petey said, "What's going on?"

Jeep told Petey while he was waiting for Cookie's call.

The phone rang only once and Jeep grabbed it before the second ring.

"Okay, clue me in," said Cookie.

"The FBI has the sheriff's office phones tapped," Jeep told her. "I don't know if the sheriff has bugs in his own office, but that's why I asked you to leave the building and not talk in the office or on a land line."

"So that's how you knew Cottin was in Wheeling."

"Where is your personal car?" asked Jeep

"It's in the lot right here," said Cookie.

"Could you follow Porter in your car when he leaves the building? He will lead us to Cottin I am sure."

"I'll try, but he will catch on eventually," Cookie responded.

Jeep told her to hang up and call Petey's cell phone. He then told Petey to get in his "Pennsylvania Porsche' and try to intercept Cookie and Porter using Cookie's directions on the phone. If this works Petey might be able to follow Porter a little further than Cookie could.

B overheard the conversation and threw Petey her keys. "Here, use my car. Porter won't recognize it. It might help you stay unnoticed."

"That's what I like, teamwork!" shouted Jeep. "What a team! I hope this works. Let us know as soon as you can, Petey."

"Will do!" yelled Petey as he ran for the door while answering his cell, "Hello, Cookie baby, what's your 10-40?" Now all Jeep could do was wait.

About twenty minutes later Cookie walked in the front door at Pippins.

"What's happening? Did Petey catch up with you?" asked Jeep

"Petey picked me up on Rt.119. He's following Porter and he just told me Porter went home. Petey said he has been sitting down the street from Porter's house for the last ten minutes."

"Porter isn't going anywhere," Petey said over the phone. "I'm coming back to Pippins, we have been tricked."

Cookie explained that Deputy Porter had left the sheriff's office and after driving around for a while went home.

"It looks like he was a decoy," said Cookie.

"A decoy for who?" inquired Jeep.

"Unless I miss my guess, we have more than one dirty deputy," said Cookie.

"Who did Porter talk to before he left the office?" asked Jeep.

"It seemed like everyone. Let me check in and see if anyone is missing or has taken the balance of the day off. If so, then that's the person that's on their way to meet with Cottin," said Cookie.

Cookie called Rosemary at the sheriff's office. After talking for a few minutes, she hung up smiling.

"Well, it looks like Tiny Hayes got sick right after he talked to Porter. He left shortly after Porter left and said he didn't know when he would be back," said Cookie. "I bet he is on his way to meet with Cottin."

B was standing behind the bar, she said, "I think we should call Danny."

Jeep had called the FBI office in Pittsburgh and they said that Danny would call back. Petey had returned and he was visibly upset.

"I don't like being made a fool of by Deputy Dawg," he grumbled.

"Did he know you were following him?" asked Jeep.

"Nope, he was heading home right from the start. They were making sure they played it safe. They must suspect that we are on to them."

The phone rang and K.C. answered it as she was coming from the kitchen. "It's Danny," she said as she handed the phone to Jeep. Jeep told Danny tailing Porter was a dead end, but now he thought that Deputy Hayes was involved. Danny said he was on his way to Pippins.

"It's time we pick up Porter, I think he's about to make a run for it," said Danny.

As Jeep was talking to Danny he saw a look of fear develop on K.C.'s face as she looked toward the front door. Turning his head to the front door he saw Porter standing there with his 44mag in his right hand.

"Oh, hi, Porter," Jeep said into the phone. "Why the gun?"

Porter snapped to Cookie, "Drop the gun belt on the floor." Turning toward Jeep, he said, "Don't even think of going for that shotgun. Come out from behind the bar and get into the corner booth with the rest of them."

Jeep hung up the phone and walked around the bar toward the corner booth. Petey was sitting in the booth with K.C. Cookie was standing next to the booth with B. Cookie's gun belt lay at her feet.

Porter said, "Who were you on the phone with, Jeep?"

"Nobody, I was just about to call a landscaping company," said Jeep.

Gathering everyone in the corner, Porter walked toward them grinning "Well, isn't this a motley crew?" he asked.

"What's the problem, Porter? Why are you pointing a gun at us?" Jeep said with as much innocence as he could muster.

"Cut the act, sniper, you've caused us enough trouble," Porter growled.

"So what are you planning to do? Shoot all of us because Jeep caused you some trouble?" asked Petey. "He's caused me a lot of trouble over the years and all I ever did was punch him once or twice. I would never shoot him!"

"Knock off the funny stuff, Petey," said Porter.

Porter took his Nextel two-way phone off his belt and spoke into it, "I got the whole crowd corralled at Pippins. What's our next move?"

"Bring me Jeep and Petey," commanded a scratchy voice from the phone. It sounded like Cottin's.

"What about the rest of them?" asked Porter.

"Collateral damage," responded the familiar voice. "Make it look like an accident if you can."

"You must be kidding," said Petey He was trying to keep Porter's attention. He had noticed a head peeking in the front window off Porter's left shoulder. He wasn't sure who it was, it could have been Buck or Mike Austin, or maybe with any luck it was Master Lee.

Suddenly the front door burst open and in a flash Master Lee dove across the fifteen feet to the bar. He disappeared behind the bar in a tuck and roll. Porter turned and fired instinctively. That was all the diversion that B required. All five feet one inch of her moved swiftly leaping into the back of Porter's knees with both feet. His head snapped back and he crashed face first on the floor. Temporarily stunned, he raised his head to see Master Lee standing a few feet in front of him with a smile. "Do you want this over quickly or do you want the deputy to suffer before he loses consciousness?" Lee asked the stunned group in the corner.

"Take your time," said Petey. "I'll get you a beer."

Lee moved in a blur, his one foot landing on Porter's right wrist with a crunch as his other foot lashed out at Porter's jaw. Porter let out a groan as his head snapped back. In the next nanosecond Porter was on his back as Lee smashed a fist into his sternum. Porter's eyes bulged as he gasped for air and his face started turning red. Master Lee turned and extended his hand to B who was still on the floor. "You do very good, B, but try to stay on feet next time." Lee smiled.

Jeep picked up the deputy's gun that lay next to his useless right hand. Cookie strapped her gun belt back on and K.C. said, "Someone pour me a double scotch."

Master Lee turned his attention back to Porter. "Someone get some duct tape. We can't use handcuffs on crushed wrist." B got some tape from behind the bar and taped Porter's elbows together behind his back using a broom between the crook of his elbows.

"This is the way the V.C. restrained our soldiers," Master Lee said.

They sat Porter on a bar stool. It was obvious he was in a great deal of pain. He was having a difficult time breathing. Jeep sat beside him. "The

FBI will be here shortly," said Jeep, "so if you want our support you had better start talking."

"About what?" coughed Porter.

"Let me lay it on the line for you, deputy," stated Jeep. "We have matched your pistol to Bo's shooting. We suspect the other shooter to be Cottin. We know your involvement in the terrorist activities at the camp and we will connect you to the kidnapping of Petey and K.C."

"I don't know what yoOOWW!" Porter screamed as Master Lee squeezed his wrist.

"I think it broken," said Lee. "You want me to make other wrist match it?"

"NO!" whined Porter.

"Okay, talk to Mr. Jeep." Lee smiled.

"It was all Cottin's doing, I just followed orders," cried Porter.

"Where is Cottin now?" asked Jeep.

"I don't know," said Porter.

"Mmmm, let me look at wrist," said Lee.

"No, I was supposed to call him when I finished here." Porter flinched.

"Make the call. You're finished here," said Petey sarcastically.

"Let's wait for Danny; we are going to need some help," said B.

"Who else is involved?" asked Jeep.

"Noone err...Tiny Hayes," Porter said glancing at Master Lee. "Just Tiny, that's all."

"Where is Tiny now?" inquired Jeep.

"I think he is meeting with Cottin," said Porter.

About three quarters of an hour later Danny arrived—he had two agents with him. He introduced them as agents Al Daula and Jake Darcy. They said they would take Deputy Porter to the hospital for treatment and then Darcy would take him to a secure location for safe keeping. Agent Daula would return to assist Agent Grabowski.

Danny said he expected Meghan sometime this evening. Before they left for the hospital they had Porter call Cottin.

"It's all wrapped up here, Cottin," Porter said into his phone. "I have Patrick and McDade. Where do you want me to deliver them?"

"The same place we agreed upon earlier," mumbled Cottin.

"Okay, Chief, see you soon," said Porter, and hung up the phone.

"And you didn't know where he was," said Petey mockingly. "Master Lee, see if he can touch his right elbow with his right thumb."

"He's at the camp!" shouted Porter. "Get me away from these madmen."

"How long will he be there now," asked Danny, "after that little coded message you just gave him?"

"What—(looking at Petey and Lee) Okay, Okay! He will only wait one hour and he will be on alert, then he will take off for places unknown."

"That little indiscretion will cost you in court," said Danny.

They were lucky it was Monday and Pippins was closed. It made a good command post. Danny knew he couldn't get an assault team to the camp within an hour. He and Agent Daula would have to go to the camp without backup. He told his Pittsburgh office what his plan was and they said they could have a team on site to support him in three hours. Petey and Jeep volunteered to go with them, but Danny had to officially turn them down. He told them to wait for Meghan and maybe the ATF would need directions to the camp to support the FBI. The bottom line was he couldn't wait, Cottin would be long gone. Danny and Daula had to take priority over procedure and go now

It seemed like they waited forever for Meghan to arrive. In the meantime, Jeep and Petey prepared for a human hunting trip. It was getting dark and Jeep was thinking how he wished he had a night scope. They had K.C. lay out some of her hiking gear for Meghan.

It was after seven when Meghan arrived and they answered her questions while she changed clothes.

K.C. kissed Jeep and whispered, "Take care of Petey and Meghan, I know you can take care of yourself."

Jeep smiled, "I'll do my best."

Master Lee said he would be "Homeland Security" and take care of Pippins and all its residents.

Cookie stayed to be our center of communication. She also needed to go into the sheriff's office tomorrow morning.

"Let's take the Pennsylvania Porsche!" hollered Petey as he headed out the door.

"Let me get something out of my car, I'll be right with you," said Meghan. She opened her trunk and removed her Feather AT-9

"What's that?" asked Jeep.

"It's my 9mm attention getter," smiled Meghan.

"It got my attention," said Jeep.

"I sure hope Danny and the other agent are okay," said Meghan.

"Agent Daula looked like he would do just fine," said Petey. "He had the look of a veteran."

"I was afraid to call on Danny's cell phone not knowing how he had the ring set. I was hoping he would have called us by now," said Jeep.

They arrived on the dirt road leading to the camp in short order. Petey slowed when they got to the now famous turn in the road where they first met the roadblock. Petey pulled over to one side of the road and backed his truck into the woods far enough so it was not visible from the road. Struggling to get the doors open amongst the trees, they started out for the camp on foot.

"It's too quiet," whispered Petey.

"No sense going up to my shooting spot," said Jeep. "It will be too dark in a few minutes to be effective from up there."

"Let's proceed down the road as quietly as possible," said Meghan.

Petey had his Weatherby Mark IV and his Colt Commander, and Jeep had his Remington 700 and his S&W 659. Meghan had her attention getter; they were a force to be reckoned with. After a few hundred yards they were getting concerned, it was deathly quiet. Meghan took a few of her business cards and placed them on the road. Petey gave her a puzzled look.

"I want the FBI assault team to know that there are some friendlies in front of them," she whispered.

They were now at the spot where Petey had made the switch, the black crate for K.C.

"It looks like we are the only one's here," said Petey.

"Danny has to be here somewhere." said Jeep

"Have you guys noticed that there are no vehicles?" said Meghan.

"Yep, what's happened to Danny and Daula?" asked Jeep.

"Call Cookie and let her know what's happening," said Petey.

"She needs to call the FBI and let them know they have two agents missing," said Jeep.

Meghan called Cookie while Jeep and Petey crept closer and closer into the camps center. It was chilling; a camp where there had been so much action and gunfire the last few times they visited was now quiet.

"It's as quiet as a church on a Tuesday," whispered Petey. "Where the hell is Danny?"

"Let's check out all these buildings," suggested Jeep.

They made a slow search of every building. Two of them were locked, the warehouse where they had kept Petey and one that looked like the kitchen. The rest of the buildings were wide open. They quickly concluded they were the only two people in the camp. They decided to wait for back-up before they tried to enter either of the locked buildings. When Meghan caught up to them, the three probed and rummaged around between the buildings. She said she had talked to Cookie and that the FBI was being notified. Jeep wondered if it was only Cottin and Tiny that were here, how they got rid of at least two agents and three cars.

Suddenly the silence was broken by a megaphone.

"Attention Agent Williams, if you can hear me, walk toward the guard shack at the entrance of the camp," the voice said. "This is Agent Darcy of the FBI." Jeep and Petey slipped quickly into the shadow of the closest building.

"I hear you, and I am complying," shouted Meghan as she started walking toward the guard shack.

Petey and Jeep watched from the shadows. Jeep was sure it was Agent Darcy, but he wanted to err on the side of caution. They watched Meghan meet with a person at the guard shack.

"Its okay, boys, it's the good guys," shouted Meghan.

"Cover me," said Petey as he laid down his Weatherby and walked toward the shack. "If it's a trap, take out the guy talking to Meghan first."

Petey got to within ten feet of Meghan and recognized Darcy.

"It's alright, Jeep, we are surrounded by good guys," shouted Petey.

They gathered at the crossroads of the community. The FBI had pulled a Humvee into the center and supplied some portable lighting. The assault team was conducting a complete search of the area. Darcy suggested that he keep the team at the camp until dawn. They would conduct a more thorough search at daylight. Meghan and the boys should go back to Pippins and wait for an update. If Cottin did have Danny and Daula, maybe he would be calling Pippins. One of the team asked Darcy if he was ready to enter one of the two locked buildings. They snapped the lock on the warehouse building and executed an armed entry procedure with precision. When all clear was called, Meghan, Petey and Jeep entered to investigate. Petey said it looked the same; nothing had changed as far as he could remember

The building was about one-hundred and fifty feet long and about ninety feet wide. It had two garage doors at the back end that served as ground level loading docks. The rear half of the building had a dirt floor. The front half was a wooden floor over what was probably a concrete slab. Cardboard boxes and plastic bottles covered the left side of the covered floor. In the front left hand side of the building was a wood burning stove that looked brand new. It didn't appear to have ever been used. The furnishing was sparse, a desk, a few chairs and a beat up sofa. There were two vehicles near the rear, one was Danny's car. The other was a deputy sheriff's car.

Taking Darcy's advice, Meghan, Jeep, and Petey decided to head back to Pippins. They started up the road toward Petey's truck

"Hey, Petey pull the truck out of the woods," said Meghan. "Those saplings scratched me getting out before. Jeep and I will wait here for valet service." The three were contemplating the events on the silent ride back to Pippins.

Chapter 12

They sat in the corner booth at Pippins thoroughly confused. Jeep, Petey, Meghan, Cookie, Lee, B and K.C. didn't have a thought between them. The only suggestion that made any sense was Jeep's when he said, "Let's get some sleep and things might be clearer tomorrow." But that was over ruled by Petey's suggestion of "another round of drinks for all." The meeting of the minds broke up around midnight.

It was early Tuesday morning. K.C. and Jeep were eating cereal and toast in K.C.'s cottage. They had finally had some quality time together. Jeep was wishing out loud, "If I could stop time I would do it right now, just the two of us in this cottage."

"Now that I've taken nourishment, let's continue," teased K.C. as she slipped off her nightgown and jumped back in bed.

"Continue hell! Let's start from the very beginning," chuckled Jeep as he dove for her naked body.

It was midmorning when Jeep stopped into Gerry's diner for coffee.

"Petey just left," said Guv. "He told me he had a few stops and he was going back to Pippins."

"Have you seen Agent Williams this morning?" asked Jeep.

"Yep, she was here with Petey, that's a fine looking cop," said Guv.

"How's your car running?" asked Kendal as Jeep sat down for a cup of coffee.

"You've got it in tip-top shape Kendal. It's been to Philadelphia once and few trips to Pittsburgh. It probably needs a quick tune-up," said Jeep thinking there was no need to mention the Indiana trip.

"Bring it down to the garage anytime you can. I love working on that car."

No one seemed to be aware of the FBI activity, although there were some questions as to Cottin's whereabouts. People were just curious because he had never taken a vacation before.

Jeep finished his coffee with the boys and headed back to Pippins.

Petey was sitting in the corner booth when Jeep walked through the front door. Jeep joined him and the two of them sat silently in thought.

"People don't just disappear you know," said Petey finally.

"That's what I used to think, but now I'm not sure," replied Jeep.

"Dang it, Jeep, I feel so helpless, Danny is in trouble and there is nothing I can do about it," complained Petey.

Cookie called to tell Jeep and Petey that the FBI was all over the sheriff's office. "There are about six or seven people from the justice department here," said Cookie. "They are questioning everyone. I spent an hour talking to a big shot named Itzie, Anthony Itzie. I'm not suspected of anything, he just wanted my version of what happened. He told me to give you guys a call and ask you to not go anyplace. They want to talk to you both."

"Tell them we will be right here, we've no place to go," said Jeep.

"They have brought in special police to run the office. The sheriff's department as we know it is out of business," said Cookie.

"What about you?" said Jeep.

"I'm suspended with pay during the investigation," said Cookie.

"That stinks," said Jeep.

"Standard procedure, nothing to worry about," said Cookie.

That afternoon Special Investigator Itzie stopped by to talk to Meghan and the boys. They invited him to the corner booth and he introduced himself.

"My name is Anthony Itzie, you can call me Tony."

"My name is Petey and the ugly one here is called Jeep," said Petey.

"Agent Williams, ATF," said Meghan.

"It's a pleasure to meet you. I must commend you, Agent Williams, on your cooperation with the FBI. Danny told us numerous times how helpful you have been."

"Agent Grabowski is one of your best in my opinion. I have the authority to offer you total ATF support in finding your agents."

"Thank you, that will be helpful."

"Pippins is at your disposal, anything you need, just ask," said Jeep.

"Here is what we have learned," said Tony. "The two deputies, Hayes and Porter were henchmen for Cottin. The rest of the department appears clean and above board. Deputy Wildey will be back on duty in a day or two."

"That's the first good news we have had in a while," said Petey.

"The land the camp is on belongs to a holding company in South Carolina. We are checking into their activities," informed Tony.

"Can I get you guys something to drink?" asked B from the bar. "We aren't officially opened until five o'clock, so anything you want is free. Agent Williams has informed me that I can't charge ATF for any alcohol. It's un-American, so her drinks are free all the time."

"The same holds true for the FBI," smiled Tony.

"Do you have any idea what's happened to Grabowski and Daula?" Jeep asked.

"No, we have searched the hills and we don't have any leads. We will search the entire mountain range foot by foot if necessary. The only car that's missing is Cottin's private automobile and we have an all-points bulletin out on it. I think that will show up rather quickly."

"Would it be okay if Petey and I snooped around and helped look?" asked Jeep.

"We could use your help, but it would have to be unofficially and unarmed," replied Tony.

"But, I don't think either agency would stop you if you wanted to go squirrel hunting. Would we, Tony?" smiled Meghan.

"We wouldn't stop a citizen foraging for food," laughed Tony.

"Let's meet back here when someone has something," said Meghan.

They all agreed that would be the best plan.

B put a tray of cold beer on the table, smiled and walked away.

Jeep went into the kitchen to help K.C. get ready for the dinner crowd and Petey pitched in behind the bar with B.

Petey and Jeep agreed to get an early start on some squirrel hunting in the morning.

The next morning they left Pippins about six a.m.

"This is the first time I ever went squirrel hunting with a .300 mag," said Petey.

"If the FBI is still up there, do you think they will be suspicious of anything?" asked Jeep.

"Hunting little bitty squirrels with high caliber rifles? Nah"

They got to the guard house of the camp and there was only one agent there. He identified himself as Agent Sobolsky. He had been told about the "squirrel hunters." Petey said they would be hanging around the camp, just snooping.

They went to the kitchen building and it was pretty much cleaned out. It contained a large refrigerator, an industrial six burner stove top with a grill, and several built in ovens. The large fuse box was near the corner, it was obvious their power came from the West Penn power plant. *They must have had a big electric bill every month*, thought Jeep. *Their kitchen could support Pippins.*

"Let's try the other building," said Petey.

"The warehouse intrigues me," said Jeep.

"I have the same feeling," responded Petey.

They walked into the warehouse and looked around at the old furniture and the new wood burning stove.

"This stove has never been used and we have just completed a cold winter. Why have a stove put here if you are not going to use it?" asked Petey.

"Petey, some of those bottles have been moved."

"The FBI must have moved them."

Jeep motioned to Petey to be quiet, and come closer to the stove.

"Follow my lead," whispered Jeep and then loudly stated, "Come on, let's get out of here. The FBI are about to shut this place down and pull out. We're the last people here."

They left the warehouse building. Petey had a puzzled look on his face, although he knew Jeep was up to something. As they walked toward the agent at the guard shack Jeep was writing on a piece of paper he had taken from his fanny pack.

As he approached Sobolsky, he said, "Well, I guess it's time to lock this place up." Winking at the agent, he handed him the note he was writing. The note read; SAY NOTHING—WE ARE BEING WATCHED! "Do you want us to help you shut this place down?" asked Jeep.

"Sure, if you would like to help," smiled Sobolsky.

"Petey, bring your truck to the center of camp," Jeep said. "We'll start locking up the main buildings."

Sobolsky and Jeep started walking back toward the warehouse.

As they reached the center of the camp, Jeep said, "Wait here. I'll get the power in the kitchen." Jeep entered the kitchen and went directly to the fuse box. He turned off the main power switch and hurried back out the front door. Petey had arrived with his truck and Sobolsky and he were standing next to it with puzzled looks on their faces. Jeep ran to them and said, "Someone has been watching and listening to us. I just turned off the power for the entire camp. I don't think they have any backup power or we would hear a generator, so I assume it's safe to talk."

"What did you see?" asked Sobolsky.

"I think I heard a noise coming from the new stove in the warehouse. It dawned on me they might be using it as a fresh air vent. If so, there is a room below the floor of the warehouse. I also thought I saw a security camera move while we were in the warehouse. By shutting down the power I think they are now deaf and blind. My guess is whoever is down there will wait a while, and then come up for a look see. If they bought our act ,they think we are closing down the camp and leaving. I believe there are microphones and cameras all over this camp."

"What's our next move?" asked Petey.

"Take the truck and drive out of here. When you get out of sight, block the road with the truck and then walk back far enough so you can scope the overhead garage doors with your Weatherby. Don't let anyone come out of those doors. Sobolsky and I will cover the front door."

"Did you see a trap door in the floor?" asked Petey.

"No, but I suspect it to be behind those cases of plastic bottles."

"Who do you think is in there?" asked Sobolsky.

"I'm hoping all four, Danny and Daula, along with Hayes and Cottin," said Jeep. "We have to wait for them to come out. There is no way we could break in without putting the hostages in harm's way. This way I don't think whoever is down there suspects anything."

"Okay, I'm going," said Petey.

"Try to make it look like we are all in the truck, Petey, just in case they have a periscope or some other mechanical device for spying," said Jeep.

"Okay, let me use some jackets and hats I have in my bed box. Making a dummy look like you should be easy," smiled Petey.

Using some empty boxes he got from the kitchen, Petey placed them on the seat of the truck draped with a couple of jackets.

As Petey's truck pulled out, Agent Sobolsky positioned himself at the corner of the kitchen building across from the front door of the warehouse. Jeep ducked around the corner of the warehouse. He would have a perfect shot at anyone coming out the front door. At this range the S&W 9mm was the weapon of choice.

They were all in position within five minutes with nothing to do but wait.

One hour later and Jeep was starting to second guess himself. Did the camera really move, had he imagined the noise in the stove? And then the door of the warehouse started opening very slowly. It was Tiny Hayes that was peeking out from behind the door. He slipped out alongside of the building and closed the door behind him. Jeep was lying at the corner of the building with just his head peeking around the building amongst the weeds. As Tiny started walking away from Jeep, Agent Sobolsky hollered, "FBI, don't move!" Tiny started to move back toward Jeep. "Don't even think about it, Tiny," said Jeep.

"Put you hands on the wall and spread your feet," shouted Sobolsky. Tiny's pistol was still in his holster. Jeep jumped to his feet and ran up next to Tiny. He hoped that Cottin wasn't just behind the closed door. He removed Tiny's pistol and handcuffs.

Knowing at that precise moment that Jeep's hand were full of pistols and handcuffs, Tiny swung back with his left elbow as he turned to his left. Jeep had sensed the move and had dropped Tiny's pistol and handcuffs as he ducked. Tiny was now facing Jeep with his back to the building having missed him completely. Jeep rose from his crouch with his pistol jammed under Tiny's neck.

"Your next move will be the last one you make. Aw, hell, I'm going to shoot you anyway, so go ahead and move, dance if you want," snarled Jeep. Tiny froze and didn't even take a breath. Other than blinking he was motionless. Agent Sobolsky came up alongside of Jeep and placed handcuffs on Tiny.

"Are you the only one in the building?" asked Sobolsky.

"Yes," said Tiny.

"That better be the truth, the whole truth, and nothing but the truth," growled Jeep.

"Where are the two agents?" asked Sobolsky.

"I don't know," said Tiny.

"I'm going to kick you in the balls once for every lie you tell. I know I have two kicks coming already. Do you want to reconsider either one of your answers?" said Jeep.

"No. Yes. No!"cried Tiny.

Jeep took a half a step back and kicked Tiny in the crotch. Tiny doubled over with a groan and fell to the ground gasping for air and rolling around. He threw up as he moaned.

"Where are the two agents?" asked Sobolsky.

"In the cellar!" screamed Tiny.

"Is Cottin there also?" asked Jeep.

"NO!" coughed Tiny. Jeep stepped to the front of Tiny

"NO! He left yesterday morning. I haven't heard from him," pleaded Tiny. "I was supposed to wait for his call."

Jeep looked to the front door, it was partly open. He went in and looked around. A few of the boxes had been moved. Walking to his left toward the boxes that have been moved, Jeep noticed a space behind them. He saw a trap door that was open and approached the opening with caution. There were stairs leading steeply down along the wall of the foundation. It was dark below the opening. Jeep called Agent Sobolsky. He entered the building pushing Tiny in front of him.

"Is there anyone down there?" Jeep asked Tiny.

"Yes, the two prisoners," said Tiny.

"Are they the only ones down there?"

"Yep," groaned Tiny.

"Do you have a light?" Jeep asked Sobolsky.

"Do you smoke?"

"A flashlight!" Jeep said as he turned and gave Sobolsky a look.

"NO," groaned Sobolsky sheepishly. "Is my Polish showing?"

"I'm going down, If you hear a gunshot, the first thing I want you to do is shoot Tiny, got that?" asked Jeep.

"Wait. Why don't you go back to the kitchen and turn the power on?" said Sobolsky.

"Duh, why didn't I think of that?" asked Jeep. "Is my Irish showing?"

"Push him down the hole if he even thinks of giving you trouble," Jeep said over his shoulder as he exited the warehouse. Wen he got outside he whistled for Petey. He then went into the kitchen and turned the power back on.

When he got back outside he started down the road toward the guard shack and whistled again for Petey. That's when he saw the Pennsylvania Porsche heading back toward the center of camp. He told Petey they had found Tiny as they went back inside.

The cellar was now lit up pretty well. Jeep lay down on the floor and peeked into the cellar. Lying on two of eight beds were Danny and Daula. Jeep jumped to his feet and ran down the stairs. Petey was very close behind him. They each went to an agent and started to untie them. Taking their gags off Danny was the first to speak.

"Thanks, guys, somehow I knew it would be you two who would rescue us!" exclaimed Danny.

"B would never forgive us if we didn't find you," said Petey.

"They are both okay!" Jeep shouted up to Sobolsky. "Call Itzie and let him know."

"How did you get into this mess?" said Petey.

"It was simple," said Daula. "We walked into a trap. They saw our every move. There are cameras all over the place. Cottin just walked up behind us and had the drop on us. Nobody can sneak up on this camp." Jeep looked around the room and saw that one wall was covered with a bank of monitors. This was a command post that overlooked the entire camp.

"Let's get out of here," said Danny. "We can send a crime scene squad back here to investigate."

They climbed up to the main floor of the warehouse. Jeep told Petey to take Daula back in his truck. Jeep would take Danny's car that was in the warehouse and drive Danny and Tiny back. Agent Sobolsky would stay at the guard house until help arrived.

Danny said to Sobolsky, "Call Itzie and tell him Daula and I are bringing in Tiny Hayes."

Jeep brought Danny's car around from the warehouse. They put Tiny in the back seat and Jeep and Danny followed Petey and Daula back to Pippins.

"It's a great day, Jeep, thanks to you and Petey!" exclaimed Danny. "I can't wait to get back on this case and find Cottin—I've got a few things to settle with him."

They arrived at Pippins in short order. It was almost lunch time. Daula took Tiny Hayes straight upstairs. He was going to wait in the apartment until transportation arrived. B was sitting in the corner booth with Meghan. She jumped up and screamed with delight when she saw Danny, then she immediately composed herself. Meghan and Jeep couldn't help but laugh. Danny was happy to see B, but started blushing as Jeep and Meghan tried to control their laughter.

"It looks like you boys had a very successful hunting trip," said Meghan.

"That's a nice looking trophy squirrel you got there, Jeep," smiled B as she nodded toward Danny.

"Yea, we found him up there in the woods trying to save his nuts," said Petey, grinning as his eyes glanced around the room.

The groan from the room was unanimous

"Sorry, sometimes I just can't help myself." Petey laughed.

"What do you need from ATF?" asked Meghan.

"I think we need to meet with Itzie," said Jeep.

"He'll be here within the hour," said Meghan.

"Let's go upstairs," said Jeep. "B, could you have K.C. make a few sandwiches and bring them up? Okay?"

"I'm on it," said B.

They were eating sandwiches when Itzie came up the stairs. Danny and B were eating together, Meghan and Jeep were talking as they ate and Petey and Daula were taking turns feeding Tiny a ham sandwich.

Itzie was very happy. "Great job, boys," he said to Jeep and Petey. "Anytime you want to get out of the restaurant business I think I can find you work." He told AgentDaula that his transportation was waiting for him downstairs.

"Tiny is in your custody—take him to the safe house," said Itzie.

"Okay," responded Daula. "Jeep, Petey, I don't know how to thank you guys. I will be forever indebted to the both of you."

"Can the FBI fix traffic tickets?" asked Petey. "If not, there isn't much you can do for us. Maybe, sometime when you are on a business trip you can stop by and let us overcharge you for dinner." Petey hugged Daula and wished him good luck.

Jeep said, "We will see you real soon, I'm sure."

Daula left with Tiny Hayes in tow.

Itzie sat down at the table with Danny, Jeep, Petey, and Meghan, and said, "Here's what we've got! We have a warrant to search Cottin's house and we are still in the process of doing that. We also believe there is at least one more camp in North Carolina up along the Virginia border. From what we found in Cottin's records both of these camps are making money. Cottin is a real Vito Corleone, the Godfather of the hill country. These camps are involved in drugs, moonshine, illegal gun and cigarette trafficking, as well as prostitution, money laundering, grand theft and their latest attempt at terrorism. Cottin is in for anything that will turn a buck."

"Where is he now?" asked Danny.

"We haven't a clue. We found his car at the Pittsburgh airport, but that doesn't mean he got on a plane."

"I already have my orders. I'm to report to Raleigh A.S.A.P.," said Meghan. "I will still be liaison between ATF and FBI."

"Danny, you will stay here working out of the Pittsburgh office," said Itzie, "and I'm on my way to North Carolina!"

"Have you searched Porter's or Tiny's houses yet?" asked Jeep.

"We may be doing that as we talk," said Itzie.

Itzie left before the dinner crowd. Meghan said she was leaving first thing in the morning.

"You can stay in cottage four," said Petey and smiled like the Cheshire cat.

The rest of the evening went smoothly. Petey and Meghan disappeared early. B and Danny played goo-goo eyes all evening. Jeep and K.C. went out to K.C.'s cottage and told Mike Austin to lock-up.

Chapter 13

The next morning K.C. slept in and Jeep went down to have breakfast at Gerry's Diner. The same crowd was there, but now the talk was about the sheriff's office.

"Hey, Jeep, what's going on?" asked Dickey Lee. "The word is out that you had Tiny Hayes at your place in handcuffs. And the FBI is all over the sheriff's office and Cottin has disappeared."

"You have more information than the *Courier*," said Jeep.

"Aw, that newspaper can't even get the funnies right," said Gov.

"C'mon, Jeep, spill the beans," said Kendal.

"There's not much that I can tell you, The FBI is investigating the sheriff's office. Tiny was involved is some unlawful activity and Cottin isn't back from vacation yet."

"What happened to Porter?"

"He was seen down at the hospital getting patched up," said Dickey Lee.

"He got into a fight and came in second," said Jeep.

"Or third," said Gov.

"Look, guys, there are some things I can't tell you because there isn't any proof. Just take my word for it, everything will be okay. As far as the FBI hanging around, that Danny Grabowski has his eye on B and she doesn't mind one bit." Jeep finished his breakfast and headed back to Pippins.

Meghan left first thing in the morning. Danny left for Pittsburgh at nine o'clock. Petey was aimlessly cleaning the bar area when Jeep got back.

"Missing her already? Did she say when she would be back?" asked Jeep.

"No, she didn't know what was waiting for her in Raleigh," said Petey.

"She said she would let us know as soon as she had a handle on it."

"I asked if we could help, officially she couldn't involve us. Unofficially, she said she would keep us informed and involved. She knows that you and I have a dog in this fight."

B showed up for work a little early. She was beaming from ear to ear and obviously in high spirits. She went into the kitchen looking for K.C.

Petey and Jeep were sitting in the corner booth when B and K.C. came out of the kitchen and sat down with the boys.

B said, "Danny and I would like to go to Buffalo this weekend. Can I get the time off?"

"Why would you want to go to Buffalo?" asked Petey.

"Danny wants to meet my parents."

"That's great, I'm thrilled for you," said K.C.

"What's so great about it?" inquired Petey.

"Men," groaned K.C.

"Do you think he's going to pop the question?" asked Jeep.

"Maybe," smiled B.

"What question?" said Petey.

"Petey, Petey, Petey, what color is the sky in your world?" snapped K.C. "Maybe Danny is going to ask for B's hand in marriage."

"Oh, that question!" said Petey.

Everyone was overjoyed. B was hugged and kissed by all

"Whoa, slow down, he hasn't asked me anything yet," said B.

"He better, if he knows what's good for him. I would hate to see my little cousin disappointed," stated Petey.

"You could have your reception right here. The price would be right," smiled Jeep.

"So I guess the answer to the question is, yes, I can have the time off?" said B.

This put everyone in a very good mood as they started to prepare for the lunch crowd. Danny was a good guy that everyone liked and he had a solid future. It was obvious that he cared for B and would make a first-rate partner.

It suddenly dawned on Jeep that they might lose B as an employee.

"Hey, K.C., where do you think B and Danny will live after they get married?" asked Jeep.

"Slow down, Jeep, Danny hasn't proposed yet," said K.C.

Cookie stopped in at three, she was in uniform and appeared to be in a good mood.

"I'm back on duty," she smiled. "I even have supplementary responsibility. The department answers to me and I report to the special investigator in charge, which is Itzie, just until things can be worked out. I'm excited about the whole arrangement."

"It will be good on the job training," said Jeep, "even if the responsibility is only temporary."

"I can only hope that Cottin comes back into the county." She smiled. "I would love to get my hands on him."

"What's going on with the search for Cottin?" asked Petey.

"Itzie is heading up the search; Danny is covering this area out of Pittsburgh. Agent Darcy is in N.C. working out of the Raleigh office. Agent Daula is following up all the current leads."

When the weekend rolled around, Danny and B left for Buffalo. Jeep and Petey worked the bar side of the restaurant. It was just like old times. K.C. was working her miracles in the kitchen. Tonight's special was beef rollatini with her special gravy, along with Steak Diane, sea bass with a strawberry and a cream sauce and chicken cordon bleu. The wait for a table tonight was almost an hour. They never took reservations at Pippins, the boys always felt they could keep people entertained at the bar spending money for at least an hour.

Mike Austin was pulling more than his load as a fill-in bartender and Jeep started thinking maybe they should put in a piano. Could Pippins be ready for a cocktail lounge with a sing-a-long piano player?

Danny and B left for Buffalo from Danny's place in Monroeville Saturday morning. It took them less than six hours to get to Buffalo. B's parents lived just off the Youngman Highway in Tonawanda. They had a very nice home that backed up to the Brighton golf course. John and Joan McDade were empty nesters, B was the last to leave home and she had been gone for almost two years. John McDade was Pop's younger brother. He had just retired from Dunlap where he was a sales manager. He and Joan were thinking of moving to Florida or some warmer climate.

B was almost giddy introducing her mom and dad to Danny.

"I have your old room all fixed up for you B," said Joan.

"Where is Danny sleeping?" asked B.

"I won the argument with your mother, Danny gets to sleep in the same house," smiled John. Everyone laughed and Danny said he could sleep anywhere.

"We have a very nice guest room for you, Danny," said Joan.

"Yea," John joked, "with the lock on the outside of the door."

They had a wonderful spaghetti and meatball dinner after which B spent the rest of the evening bringing her parents up to date to all that had happened.

"Your Uncle Dano has been telling me about all the activity at Pippins. I even heard you have continued your Tae Kwon Do training, and it came in very handy recently. Your mom and I are very proud of you, B."

The next morning Danny and B went sight seeing. The McDade house was only about twenty miles from Niagara Falls. They had a wonderful day laughing and forgetting all the trouble and danger they had been involved in recently.

Danny said, "Your folks are very nice. Your dad and I had a nice talk after you and your mom went to bed."

They were standing on Goat Island right between the American Falls and the Canadian Falls. They were actually standing right next to the Bridal Falls.

"Your father said it was okay to give you this." Danny smiled as he handed B a velvet ring box.

B opened the box and saw a beautiful diamond ring.

"B, will you marry me?" Danny asked.

"Yes, I will. I love you, Daniel Grabowski!"

There were some people standing close by that saw what was going on. One woman smiled and her husband said to those standing around, "He just proposed to her."

One guy said, "Jump," and then took a punch in the arm from his wife. Another person said, "How wonderful." Soon there were twenty people standing around Danny and B and they started applauding. "Give her a kiss," someone shouted.

"Let's hurry back to Pennsylvania so I can tell the world," said B.

"It looks like the world is finding out pretty fast," said Danny as he kissed B.

"How are Jeep and Petey going to take this? I worry about those two more than I did your father."

"Oh, they are just softies, their bark is worse than their bite," said B.

"No, I've seen their bite, believe me nothing is worse than that."

Cottin was very successful in avoiding the law. He drove his car to the Pittsburgh airport and purchased a ticket to Chicago with his credit card. He then took a cab to the train station and paid cash for a ticket to Harrisburg. Upon arrival in Harrisburg he rented a U-haul truck with a stolen credit card and made arrangements to drop the truck in Philadelphia, he then drove it to Baltimore. He rented a car in Baltimore with another bogus credit card, and drove to the camp in N.C. using mostly back roads.

The land in Carolina was north of Raleigh-Durham off Route 158. It appeared to be just a farm. The house sat back off the road a quarter of a mile. There were a few outbuildings and a large barn that gave the appearance of a dairy farm. Further back behind the farm were woods that according to the land office were not part of the farm. The farm was one-hundred acres according to the county tax office.

The FBI had determined that the South Carolina holding company also held land in Tennessee and Georgia. The name of the company was Attwood Ltd. and appeared to be a legitimate British land holding company. The FBI was watching the properties and so far had not seen anything unusual or suspicious. None of the field offices had reported any sighting of Joshua, aka Amos Cottin.

Meghan arrived in Raleigh on Friday. She checked into the FBI field office, and they had a desk ready for her. Agent Darcy was happy to see her.

"Hey, Darcy, where is a good place to stay?" asked Meghan.

"Since we will be working together you can call me by my first name. It's Jake."

"Okay Jake, where is a good place to stay?"

"There's a couple of motels north on U S. 1 in Wake Forest that might be convenient. A Hampton Inn and a Sleep Inn, I think the Sleep Inn has an indoor pool," said Jake.

"Sounds Jake to me, Jake." Meghan smiled.

"Not the first time I heard that," moaned Jake. "There is also a golf course. Do you play?"

"I'm a fourteen handicap, but I didn't bring my clubs," said Meghan.

"I'm a twenty-two and I'm glad you didn't," laughed Jake.

"When can I see the camp?"

"Tomorrow or Sunday, whatever is convenient. It's a farm, not a camp, at least that's what it looks like," said Jake.

Meghan checked into the Sleep Inn. She went to Target and bought a bathing suit. She then grabbed a bite to eat at a Mexican restaurant across the street and took a late evening swim. She was going to meet Jake in the morning and check out the farm.

It was after ten when she decided to call Pippins to see what was new and to see if Petey was missing her.

"Pippins," the familiar voice said.

"Hi, Petey, how are you doing? It's Meghan."

"Hi, gorgeous, I miss you already," said Petey.

I guess that answers my question, thought Meghan. That's what she liked about Petey. He was honest and straightforward and expected you to be the same. He was also very funny and she liked to be in his company.

"That's why I'm calling, I like to hear that I'm being missed," she laughed.

"It's Friday night and we're busy as can be, but I still have time to think about you," sighed Petey. "Hey, Meghan, guess what? B took Danny to meet her parents in Buffalo. We all think he is going to pop the big question. Isn't that great?"

"Yes, I am very happy for them. They make a great couple."

"When will I see you again?"

"I shouldn't be here for more than a couple of weeks," said Meghan.

"I've got to go, we're very busy. Call again soon. Okay?" said Petey.

"Okay, take care of yourself and keep missing me," laughed Meghan.

It took both Jeep and Petey to do B's job at Pippins. That's why they hated it when she took time off. Friday and Saturday had both been very busy. Today was Sunday and a time for rest. Petey had successfully lined up a landscaper so they didn't have to work on the grounds. K.C. had been working very hard in the kitchen and all three of them were looking forward to doing nothing today.

Jeep was the first one up. He put the coffee on and went downstairs for the paper. The *Pittsburgh Press* was delivered on Sunday and it was usually somewhere near the front door. Jeep noticed the paper was in the middle of the parking lot. Little Freddy had never missed the front door by that much. He started out the front door thinking that the paper looked like bait in the middle of the parking lot. He froze in his tracks. What did he just think? He went back behind the bar and picked up the shotgun. *Easy, Jeep,* he thought, *your nerves are shot. Oh well, better safe than sorry.* He held the shotgun behind his back. Safety off, finger on the trigger, barrel pointed up. He strolled out to the parking lot very casually, noticing a car parked on the shoulder of the highway. As he got to the middle of the lot, the car started to accelerate toward him. Jeep swung the gun around, holding it cocked and ready waist high as the car closed the distance between them. The driver, seeing Jeep in the ready position swerved hard to his left continuing to accelerate, but now trying to get away. Jeep stared at the passenger who was frozen wide eyed, staring directly at the barrel of the shotgun. If he had any intentions of shooting Jeep they were forgotten in that moment, he made no attempt to move. The tires started to grab and the direction of the car was now moving away from Jeep back toward the highway. Jeep was no longer in danger as the car sped away. He took note of the North Carolina "First in Flight" license plates as he lowered the shotgun. Jeep swore to himself, *Enough, I've had enough,* as he picked up the paper and started back toward Pippins.

"Petey!" Jeep shouted as he entered the apartment.

"What?" said Petey as he walked out of his bedroom scratching his head

"Someone just made a feeble attempt at killing me."

"How?"

Jeep explained to Petey what had happened.

"Why didn't you shoot the S.O.B.?" exclaimed Petey.

"I don't know how many more shootings we can get away with. Besides, he would just send more, and I wouldn't know what they would look like. These two I'll remember."

"By saying he, do you mean Cottin?"

"None other," said Jeep.

"I have a plan that I have been giving some serious thought. Tell me what you think."

"Let's hear it," said Petey as he poured himself some coffee.

"It involves you lending your Pennsylvania Porsche to me," smiled Jeep.

Chapter 14

They spent all morning formulating and refining the plan. The newspaper remained unread K.C. noticed as she came wandering up the stairs shortly before noon.

"I'm just checking to see if you people are alive up here. I thought you would be out and about by now and you haven't even read the paper."

"We've been working on a plan to get our lives back and ensure our safety," said Jeep.

"I'm all for that," she said. " I just want to build this business and have a nice normal life instead I'm part of the Hole in the Wall Gang. I'm working for Butch Cassidy and the Sundance Kid and I'm in love with one of them."

"Which one are you in love with?" smiled Petey.

"Which one are you?" she asked.

"Sundance," said Petey!

"Butch," replied K.C. laughing at their banter.

They introduced K.C. to the plan. They all agreed it was risky and they had some small disagreements with parts of it, but overall they knew it had to be done.

Jeep said, "I'll start growing my beard this morning."

Petey said, "Let me get my truck down to Kendal. It's going to take some explaining to him. He's going to think I'm crazy when I tell him I want the Porsche to look like the loser of a demolition derby."

They had agreed that no one else should know unless a need to know situation arose. The first part of the plan was for Jeep to change his appearance as much as possible, and for Kendal to change the appearance of Petey's truck as much as possible.

"I figure it's going to take about ten days to put this plan in motion, so let's remember, staying alert means staying alive," said Jeep.

"What's going to be your reason for growing a beard?" asked Petey.

"I'll tell people K.C. wanted me to try it. Everyone knows I try to do everything she says."

"Right," moaned K.C. as she started to set up the Rummikube game. "How about playing a game? Low man wins when the first player reaches one-hundred."

It was Monday morning and Petey arrived early at Kendal's garage explaining to Kendal what he wanted done to his Pennsylvania Porsche.

"You want what?" Kendal exclaimed.

"Calm down, this will be fun. I don't want the truck ruined. I just want it to look that way. Let's remove the fenders and the interior seat. Maybe we can even replace the bed if we can find a beatup one. Also the doors and my good rims have to come off. But, I want it in good running order. I want good rubber on it, but it shouldn't look good."

"It's finally happened. You've lost your mind!" shouted Kendal.

"Come on, let's go to the junk yard and find the parts we are going to need," said Petey. "We need a couple of fenders that are banged up; it doesn't make any difference what model or year as long as they fit. Remind me to put a few bullet holes in the doors we get."

"Yep, you've snapped," said Kendal.

By the end of the day Kendal was catching on to what Petey needed. In fact, he was starting to enjoy the task.

"I can put a cutaway on the exhaust. It will make it sound like you have blown your muffler when you pull the knob," laughed Kendal.

"Can you rent me a car for the week?" asked Petey.

"Yea, take that van over there," smiled Kendal.

"No thanks, I would rather walk," growled Petey.

"Okay, take my town car, but be careful," said Kendal.

"How much do you charge to rent it?"

"That auto will cost you lunch, dinner, three drinks and dessert a day.

And return it with a full tank of gas. That's a better deal than Hertz will give you," laughed Kendal.

"See you in a day or two. Let me know if you need anything," said Petey.

B arrived at four o'clock; she had dropped Danny off at his condo in Monroeville. She couldn't wait to show the girls her engagement ring and tell them how Danny had proposed. She had called ahead to say when she would be arriving and Cookie and K.C. were all excited. Even Master Lee and Mike Austin were happy for her. They were having a little party out back by the cottages. Lawn chairs and a cooler made it a party. Jeep was cooking hot dogs and hamburgers. Flip stopped by after church for a dog and a brew.

"You plan to shave anytime soon?" said Flip.

"Now that you mention it, I was thinking of growing a beard," said Jeep.

"It was K.C.'s idea," smiled Petey.

"That figures," laughed Flip. "Wuss," he mumbled under his breath to Jeep.

Jeep told Cookie about the incident he had yesterday morning. He underplayed his concern. She still wanted to know why he hadn't reported it.

"I didn't think that much about it," he lied.

"I'll have the deputies drive by Pippins more often on each shift. It can't hurt," suggested Cookie.

Sunday morning Meghan and Jake Darcy had taken a ride out to the farm. There wasn't much to learn looking from the highway. It appeared to be a working farm that employed a half of dozen day laborers depending on the seasons. It was getting close to harvesting and baling the early hay soon. They probably had at least six laborers reporting each day and Meghan was betting that not one of them was legal.

"Where do these migrant workers live?" asked Meghan.

"They have a trailer parked down the road," said Jake." I don't know how many people live, or should I say, exist in it?"

"No one has observed Cottin or anyone that looks like him?" inquired Meghan.

"There hasn't been anyone coming or going other than the guy that runs the farm," reported Jake, "and believe me he isn't Cottin. He's of average build about five feet eight inches and I believe Cottin is six foot three inches and about fifty pounds heavier."

"You know, waiting is the part that I hate," said Meghan. "The time seems to drag, but I guess that's all we can do for now."

"That's what my orders say, observe and report," moaned Jake. "I believe Cottin and his bunch are lying low and will be very cautious. I think we might be on a rather long assignment."

"I suppose we could whip things up if nothing happens in the next few days," smiled Meghan. "I am sure INA would help us verify the citizenship of a few of the workers and arrange for their trip back to their point of origin. That would at least get us into the farm to look around."

"We might be forced to arrange that," said Jake.

Petey got to Kendal's garage just as Kendal was opening up shop.

"How's the Porsche coming?" asked Petey.

"It's not your pride and joy anymore," said Kendal. "But honestly, Petey, it's been a ball working on it. Just wait until you see the changes we've made."

"Let have a look," said Petey as they walked into the rear of the shop.

There sat junk—it certainly wasn't Petey's truck. The fenders didn't match in either shape or color, one was green the other brown. The rear bed was more rust than steel. The passenger side door didn't close properly, perhaps the three bullet holes in the side had something to do with it. The rims were rusted to the core and were without hub covers. The center of the hood was scorched as if a fire roared beneath its surface.

"Oh my poor truck!" cried Petey. "What have you done to it?"

"Nothing that we can't put back together in a day," Kendal proudly proclaimed. "And when you give it back to us we are giving it a custom paint job, courtesy of your friend Jeep."

"Wow, that's great," said Petey. "I hope Jeep gives it back to me in one piece."

Jeep's plan was simple, he was going to grow a full beard and let his hair grow, and he already needed a haircut. He hoped to change his appearance completely. He realized he couldn't accomplish this in ten days but he was hoping to get a good start. Just before leaving he was going to color his hair, beard and all. The major problem was to stay out of sight so as few people as possible would see him. He was going to head to North Carolina in Petey's well disguised Pennsylvania Porsche. His plan was to snoop around the farm and find out what he could about Cottin's whereabouts.

Jeep and K.C. talked of his plan to disappear.

"Where are you going to go to lay low?" asked K.C.

"I don't know. Maybe the FBI will let me live in the hidden room under the warehouse at the camp," joked Jeep.

"I don't think that's a good idea."

"No, then I would have to let them in on my plans. Actually, I'm going to stay in cottage four."

"What are we going to tell people when they ask about you?" said K.C.

"I haven't thought of a good reply, I guess we will just tell them I went to a restaurant show in Chicago. Or maybe I found a long lost relative in Ohio that I went to visit. Petey's's truck is done. I can leave anytime. What do you think?"

"I don't want to see you go, but let's get this over with. The sooner you find that rat, Cottin, the sooner I get you and my life back."

"Okay, I will leave in two or three days," Jeep said. "Do you want to start saying your good byes tonight?" He smiled as he hugged and kissed her.

Jeep told Petey that he would be in touch every night. "I will call you on your cell phone. I bought one for myself, but it's only for outgoing calls. You are the only person that will have my number. Don't ever call me unless it's life and death. I don't want it ringing or buzzing when I'm trying to be quiet."

"You with a cell phone, what's the world coming too?" said Petey.

"Hey, Petey, help me with this problem. How do I get one of the sheriff's guns?" asked Jeep.

"Why do you need one of those?"

"In case there is any shooting. Let's make sure the bad guys get the blame. If my plan works, no one will know we were involved."

"I guess I could slip by Cottin's house tonight and find one lying around," said Petey.

"Is the FBI watching his house?"

"Probably, but that shouldn't present a problem," smiled Petey.

"Check with Cookie, she will know," said Jeep. "Have you talked to Meghan recently?"

"She called last night," said Petey. "I sure do miss her. She said she missed me too."

"Did she say when she might have a chance to visit us?"

"I don't recall her saying that she missed you," laughed Petey as he headed out the door.

When Petey entered the sheriff's headquarters he asked for Cookie.

"She is in her office. Go right in," said Deputy Quigley.

Acting Sheriff Wildey was sitting at her computer.

"What's crumbling, Cookie?" asked Petey.

"I was inquiring with the FBI if they had any news about Cottin's whereabouts, and they don't," said Cookie without taking her eyes off the screen.

"I need your help, Sheriff," said Petey.

Cookie spun around in her chair and said, "You must be in trouble!"

"Not this time, I need to get into Cottin's house. Jeep had lent him one of his guns and we don't want it to get hung up in probate if something happens to Cottin. But I suspect the FBI is watching his house."

"We are sharing that duty with them. I don't think I can let you in alone."

"Oh no, they can escort me in and out, I'd let them get it for me if they knew what it looked like," said Petey.

"When do you want to do this?"

"Whenever we can."

"Let's go right now," said Cookie.

"Okay, pick me up at Pippins, I'll drop Jeep's car off and I can ride to Cottin's house in a sheriff's car and look important."

When Petey got back to Pippins he rushed up stairs and picked up

Jeep's 9mm S&W and tucked it in the back of his belt with his shirt hanging over to conceal it. He then went back downstairs to wait for Cookie. His plan was simple. He had written down the serial number of Jeep's weapon on a small slip of paper. When he looked through Cottin's house he would pick up one of Cottin's pistols. He would read off Jeep's serial number from the slip of paper in his hand to Cookie for her to write down as if this was Jeep's gun. If this situation didn't present itself he had a plan two. He would act as if he had found Jeep's gun in a drawer and give it to Cookie to document the serial number. While she was busy doing that he would steal one of Cottin's pistols and hide it in the back of his belt. He was confident one of the plans would work.

They entered Cottin's home from the rear. Petey walked into what looked like an office. It was paneled and decorated with pictures. One picture was of a farm or ranch. It was quite peaceful with the green pastures and the white fences. Finding a pistol was going to be easy, there were several lying around. Petey picked up a 9mm that looked like Jeep's and called Cookie. She was in the bedroom.

"Write this serial number down," requested Petey as he read off Jeep's serial number from the hidden paper in his hand while making believe he was reading it off the gun. Cookie pulled out her pad as she entered the room and wrote the number down. Petey then reached into his pocket, and produced the slip of paper that actually had been in his hand. Handing it to Cookie he said, "See if it matches this one. It's the number of the weapon Jeep lent Cottin. I wrote it down before we left just in case I couldn't remember what the pistol looked like. Jeep keeps the serial number and description of all his weapons in his safe."

"That's a good practice; more people should do that," said Cookie. "Most people have guns stolen that were not registered and they don't know their serial number."

"When you get back to your office double check the number just to make sure we didn't make any mistakes"

"Will do, but everything looks okay," said Cookie.

Petey stuck Cottin's newly stolen gun in his belt and said, "Jeep will be happy to get this back."

Cookie dropped Petey off at Pippins. Petey walked in the front door, thru the kitchen and out the back door. Jeep was lying low in cottage four. Petey walked in and Jeep was doing push-ups.

"I'm bored to death," said Jeep

"Here's one of Cottin's pistols and no one knows it's missing or even existed," smiled Petey.

"I'm impressed, how did you pull it off?" asked Jeep.

"Magic, use it in good health."

"You could steal second base without taking your foot off first!" laughed Jeep.

"Everything is set to go, I'm leaving tomorrow night. Bring your poor excuse for a truck up here tomorrow night after dark. I will load what I need in your bed box and slip off into the night."

Chapter 15

Cottin was staying in the woods a half of mile behind the farm. He had a class "C" RV parked in a small clearing and no one knew it was there. He would sleep most of the day and under the cover of dark he would go into the farmhouse. The farm honcho's name was Schoffman, Robert Schoffman, and Cottin called him Bugzy. Bugzy made sure the house was empty after dark so Cottin had the run of the place until dawn. Cottin made all his phone calls and plans during the night.

Cottin sat down at the desk in the den and dialed the phone. It rang six times before someone answered.

"This is Joshua. Is Abada there?"

"He will be along in a moment."

"Tell him I don't have all night."

A few minutes passed and Cottin was starting to lose it when finally a voice said, "Hello, this is Abada."

"I need another black crate," growled Cottin.

"You did not receive the last one?"

"Why would I ask for another one if I had the first one? Your pilot missed the drop by a mile. I'm surprised they found Pennsylvania, although some of your boys found it head first a few years ago."

"They were not lost, just overpowered."

"When can I have more A-dust?"

"You cannot in that quantity. I will try to mail you a thermos full tomorrow, but you must be careful handling it."

"Yea, yea, I know how to handle it," snapped Cottin.

"Don't call me, I will call you. Give me a number where I can reach you and the mailing address," said Abada.

Cottin gave him the Georgia camp's phone number and address and slammed the phone down. *Nothing was going right! I will kill Patrick and McDade if it's the last thing I do,* he thought. *They have set this plan back six months. The plan was ingenious but he was surrounded by idiots,* he murmured to himself.

Bugzy walked into the room. "I'm going to bed; do you need me for anything?"

"No, I'll wake your lazy ass up if I do."

"I've got a farm to run while you sleep all day," said Bugzy as he started out of the room.

"Get me a beer and get out of my hair," said Cottin.

Cottin was going to have to recruit a new batch of solders to deliver the contaminated water around Washington. He was sure he could get some from the camp in Georgia and maybe a few from Tennessee. He needed a new supply of bottles. He believed he had some in Georgia. He would only need a few hundred since his supply of anthrax had been greatly reduced. Cottin walked into Bugzy's bedroom and turned the light on.

"How many people do you have here at the farm?"

"Counting the cook and housekeeper we have ten. Five of them are our people and the other five are illegal aliens that do the hard labor the farm requires," said Bugzy as he sat up in bed. "I pay them under the table."

"Can they be trusted?" asked Cottin.

"They are clueless," said Bugzy as he rolled over and pulled the covers up. "Turn the light off as you leave."

Petey got down to Kendal's garage at closing time. All of his employees had gone for the day. "We need to talk," said Petey.

"I'm all ears," said Kendal.

"I need to take the truck and you have to forget that you've ever worked on it. Have you told anyone about the work you've done?"

"No, you asked me to keep it on the QT. No one knows except the kid that helped me work on it. And he has a tough time finding his way to work ever morning. Your secret is safe with me."

"Its very serious business and I'll let you know what it's all about when the time comes, but for now trust me. It's a matter of life and death."

"Here's the key, it's sitting out back with the rest of the junk. It's the only one that runs."

"Thanks, Kendal, let me buy you dinner and I'll take it out of here after dark."

"Sounds good to me, but let's not eat at that Pippin place. There must be something better than that around," smiled Kendal.

Later that night Petey drove the truck around the back of Pippins and parked it next to cabin four. As he got out of the truck he heard a voice from the next cabin say, "You make bad trade, Petey. Your other truck much better." It was Master Lee.

"This isn't mine, I just borrowed it for a friend," laughed Petey. "I'll meet you at Pippins in a few minutes and buy you a soda."

"Okay," said Lee as he walked toward Pippins, smiling. "Tell Jeep he need to get haircut and be careful. That truck not look safe."

Petey walked into cabin four and Jeep looked already to go, although it didn't look like Jeep. He had an old straw cowboy hat covering his long unkempt hair which was now blond. He wore a Lone Star Beer T-shirt and a grungy pair of Levis. And covering his eyes were mirrored sunglasses and his face hadn't seen a razor in over a week. A pair of boots that had seen better days completed the outfit. He also looked thinner.

"If I didn't know better I would think I just caught a stranger in one of our cabins."

"Hey, Pard, I'm fixin to head 'em up and move 'em out. Gonna make this place a memory as I look at it in my rear view mirror."

"You might get a job at the rodeo, letting bulls chase you and hiding in barrels," howled Petey as he held his sides laughing.

"Do you think this will fool anybody that knows me? I'm working on my Texas drawl."

"To be honest, I think it's going to work. You don't look like my friend Jeep." Petey walked over and hugged him. "Are you sure you're doing the right thing? You are going to be on your own and I don't know what I'd do if something happened to you."

"We don't have a choice, Petey," said Jeep. "Just stay available and come running if I call."

Jeep picked up the stuff he had packed along with his Remington .270 and headed out to the truck.

"Good hunting, cowboy," said Petey.

Jeep had already said his goodbyes to K.C. and B. He slipped into the truck and headed south. He had done a good job of packing and was prepared to sleep in the truck if necessary. He had a sleeping bag, clothes, food, drinks and weapons. That was all the Army had ever given him, and that had worked out just fine.

The truck was in remarkable superior mechanical shape. It looked like it wouldn't make the next fifty miles, but you can't judge a book by its cover. Once Jeep arrived in North Carolina he planned to spend a few days driving around to get a feel for the place.

Meghan was to attend a FBI meeting in Raleigh this morning. The participants would be Special Agent in Charge Tony Itzie and field agents Danny Grabowski, Al Daula and Jake Darcy. There also would be representatives from INA and the Secret Service. This was going to be an informative day. After all the introductions everyone got their coffees and took their places at the conference table.

Itzie got right to the point. "We have a hot spot north of Raleigh where we think a murder suspect is hiding. He was also involved in the killing of a Federal agent. It's a farm that has migrant workers. We need INA to go in looking for illegal aliens. This will give us the opportunity to snoop around."

"Do you want your agents to act as INA?" asked the representative from INA.

"Yes, not everyone has to identify themselves, just the agent in charge. Make a big deal about getting everyone together and give our people a chance to look around."

"This must be big, I can't remember a meeting that had FBI, ATF, INA and Secret Service in the same room," said the representative of the

Secret Service. "The CIA must be paranoid."

"They will get the minutes of the meeting excluding the last statement," laughed Itzie. "We also have reason to believe they are planning a terrorist attack on D.C. from that location."

They worked out a plan. Meghan and Danny would go in with the INA team. They were both from out of town and would be less likely to be recognized. While INA was interrogating everyone they would be free to search the farm. If the workers were illegal they would be arrested and detained. If Danny or Meghan found anything they would make note and report after the raid and a 24-7 watch would be put on the farm. Then an assault team would be assembled and after the proper paperwork was obtained the farm would be raided. The INA investigation was scheduled for Tuesday morning. Itzie felt they had a better chance of all the workers being there on Tuesday. Experience told them that drinkers don't show up on Mondays and migrant workers with money in their pocket don't work on Fridays.

Jeep spent Friday night in Emporia, Virginia. It was just twelve miles from the Carolina border. He called Petey to let him know all was well.

"Pippins," Petey said as he picked up the phone.

"Do you have topless dancers there?" Jeep said in a deep voice.

"Yea, come on over and I'll take my shirt off if the price is right."

"I mean women."

"Oh, I thought you meant men, you sound a little light in the sneakers."

"Cut the shit, Petey, I was just calling to tell you your truck is fine. I knew you were worried about it."

"How was your trip and where are you?"

"I'm in Emporia, Virginia, and everything is fine. I'm going to get the lay of the land the next few days."

"That farm is in North Carolina off route 158. B told me Danny headed down to Raleigh for a meeting. He told B that he would be working with Meghan. They think Cottin is there."

"Where is Danny staying?"

"He's at the Sleep Inn in Wake Forest, the same one where Meghan's staying."

"Thanks, Petey. Say hello to B and let me talk to K.C."

"Hang on."

"Hello, handsome, I miss you," said K.C.

"I miss you too. I'll work fast so I can get back to you. Besides, this beard is killing me."

"Beard or no beard, hurry back."

"We have to keep these calls short. I love you," Jeep said, and then disconnected.

Saturday Jeep poked around Wake Forest and the Sleep Inn. At five o'clock he stopped into Appleby's for a cold beer. He was sitting at the bar trying to get his plan worked out in his head, when Meghan, Danny, Daula and Itzie walked through the front door. He quickly put his sunglasses on and turned his head. They took a booth near the door. He had a perfect view of them from his seat at the bar. If it wasn't so noisy he could have eavesdropped on their conversation. The booth next to theirs was open. He walked over to the hostess and asked if he could sit there, he had decided to have something to eat.

As she walked him past their booth, Meghan glanced at him but showed no sign of recognition. The hostess seated him with his back to Danny and Meghan. He could now hear everything. It looked like his disguise was working.

They talked about the raid by INA on Tuesday. This gave him an idea; maybe the farm would be looking for workers on Wednesday and he could get a job. He was getting brave about his disguise and was tempted to push his luck by talking to them. He ordered and by the time dinner was over he knew as much about the plan on Tuesday as members of the raiding party. If their conversation was overheard by a stranger it wouldn't make any sense, but to Jeep it was all quite clear. He asked for the check in order to get out of there before his luck ran out. He would have his coffee elsewhere. Walking to the door he smiled and nodded to Itzie, who cordially smiled and nodded back. *This was a rush,* he thought as he walked outside. It was like being invisible. He then had a terrible thought. What if Meghan recognized Petey's Pennsylvania license plate? She certainly wouldn't recognize the truck, but the Pennsylvania plates might catch her eye. It was too late to worry now, but he must be more careful in the future. Jeep drove north to Henderson where he found an inexpensive motel for the next two nights. Jeep was actually enjoying this charade.

Cottin was on edge, he just couldn't stay here waiting and doing nothing. The A-dust would be in Georgia tomorrow. Bugzy was a jerk and wasn't much company in the evenings. Cottin decided he would go to the camp in Georgia which was more like the camp in Pennsylvania. It was more secluded and self-contained and would allow him more freedom, the problem was getting there. On the other hand, this farm was clean, there was nothing incriminating here, running an unproductive farm was not against the law.

Maybe he could get someone to drive him down in the RV. He thought it highly unlikely that it would get stopped and searched and Georgia would be a better base to work from. He would talk to Bugzy about it tonight.

The next two days dragged for Jeep. He had located what he thought was the farm, although it didn't matter. He had decided to follow the raiding party from Wake Forest. They would lead him directly to the farm. Monday was spent washing his clothes in the bathroom sink and hanging them in the shower to dry. He then decided to head to Wal-Mart and buy new underwear and shirts. "If K.C. could see me now," he laughed to himself. Jeep hated to go shopping and K.C. did most of his shopping for him.

Tuesday morning found Jeep in the lot across from the Sleep Inn; it was six thirty. He had some coffee and began his wait. Somewhere around eight o'clock three black Surburban's pulled into the lot. It was only a moment before Danny and Meghan came out of the motel and got into one of them. They started up the service road to the traffic light on US 1 and turned north. Jeep remained an inconspicuous distance behind them. He thought, "Three black war wagons will be easy to follow." He was right, in a half-hour they turned into the farm that Jeep had earlier guessed was the right one.

Speeding down the road leading to the farm house, Itzie said over the headsets "Scatter fast and don't let anyone get away. Vehicle one takes the house. Two and three cover all the outlying buildings. Let's make it quick and thorough."

Meghan and Danny were in vehicle three.

"I saw two behind the barn!" shouted Danny as he jumped from the vehicle.

"I'll go around the other way," said Meghan on a dead run. "Be careful."

They came around both sides of the barn with their weapons in hand trapping between them two very scared Mexicans with nowhere to run. Within a few minutes the INA had eleven people rounded up in the house. Using the front porch as a holding area, they started taking them into the house one at a time for questioning.

"We'll check the house last. These three buildings look like a barn, a garage for equipment maintenance and some sort of bunkhouse," said Meghan.

"Not bad for a city girl," said Danny.

"If I don't know what I'm looking for, how in the hell am I going to know when I find it?" asked Meghan with a smile.

"We'll know when we see it, anything that looks out of place. Anything that might be or lead to a hiding place."

"Do you think Cottin is here?" asked Meghan.

"Yes I do, but remember there were a lot of hiding places at the camp in Pennsylvania."

Chapter 16

It took about two hours and Danny and Meghan hadn't found a thing. The INA on the other hand had found five illegal aliens. The plan was to have the Henderson police detain all eleven, and then release the six US citizens after about four hours. That should be plenty of time for a thorough search.

The search produced very little. In the house were two handguns that were perfectly legal, they were registered to Bugzy. What seemed to be missing were the files, receipts and records that are required to run a business? The normal household bills and receipts were there.

"Look at this," said Darcy. "The phone bill shows that almost all the calls are made between nine at night and six in the morning."

"That is strange," said Itzie. "When does Schoffman sleep?"

"It looks like some of them are made to the Middle East," said Darcy.

"I smell a louse, but it's not against the law to call the Middle East," said Itzie.

"From the looks of the bedroom it looks like Schoffman lives here alone. The others commute," said Daula.

"Either he doesn't sleep or someone else is using the phone," said Meghan.

The Justice department had completed the search and was out of the house by three. Schoffman was released at three-fifteen and was back at the ranch by four.

It was four-thirty when Jeep drove down the driveway. He had observed the entire operation as boring as it was. He pulled in front of the house and walked up on the porch and rang the bell.

"What more harassment have you people thought of now?" shouted Bugzy as he answered the door.

"I don't mean to harass anybody, I'm looking for a job," answered Jeep.

"I thought you were those assholes that were here earlier. I'm not hiring anybody, get lost," said Bugzy from behind the unopened screen door.

"Okay, pal, chill out. It's not my fault you're pissed. Cut me some slack! I'm leaving," said Jeep as he walked off the porch.

"Hey, wait a minute. Come to think of it, I need a lot of help. What's your name, cowboy?"

"Cary, Duke Cary," said Jeep.

"Well Duke Cary, I hope you aren't afraid of a little hard work."

"I wouldn't be asking if I was," said Jeep.

"When can you start? I need some weeds to be cut, and a roof to be patched. I'll pay you cash, ten dollars an hour and feed you lunch."

"I can start tomorrow," said Jeep.

"We start at eight sharp. We usually quit at five, any questions?"

"When do I get paid and do you have a place I could bed down?"

"Throw your stuff in the bunkhouse. The main house is off limits and don't even come near it after dark. You might get shot," growled Bugzy.

"Okay, I'll see you in the morning at eight," said Jeep.

Jeep pulled his truck over to the bunkhouse. He had muddied up the license plate so you couldn't tell what state it was from.

The bunkhouse was not bad. It was one large room with eight beds and they were all made. There was a bathroom with three showers at one end and a well equipped kitchen at the other with two long picnic tables. It appeared to be reasonably clean and that Jeep was the only resident. Jeep would go back to his motel tonight and pick up his other stuff.

Jeep waited until after nine to head back to the motel to pick up his clothes. As his truck pulled down the road away from the farm Cottin was looking out the front window. "Who's in that truck?" asked Cottin.

"A cowboy I hired this afternoon. The Fed's took all of our laborers. All we have left of our people the cook, housekeeper and a mechanic. The two soldiers from Georgia that are part of our team headed back to Georgia right after the police released them."

"Damn, I wish you would have told me. I need a driver to take me to Georgia. What the cowboy's name?"

"His name is Duke Cary and he's staying in the bunkhouse. No one is staying there but him. I told him if he came near the farmhouse he would get shot."

"Where are you going to get more workers?" asked Cottin.

"When the word gets out to the Mexican community, they will be beating down the door for work. It might take a few days."

"What do you know about the cowboy?" asked Cottin.

"Nothing," said Bugzy. "I'll talk to him tomorrow."

"We need to talk, Bugzy. It's getting too hot for me to stay here. I think the two I sent to kill Patrick and McDade are about to make their move. I spoke to them last night .They said they couldn't wait any longer. They said the Patrick guy hasn't been around for a couple weeks. I told them to wipe out everyone at Pippins and get the hell out of there and head for Georgia. I can't get anything done working only at night. I need freedom to move around."

"What do you want to do?"

"I need someone we can trust to drive the RV to Georgia," said Cottin.

"What happens if you get stopped on the way down?"

"I have a good hiding place in that RV. There's a trap door under the bed in back. Just lift the mattress and the plywood trap and slip through, they both will close behind you and you're gone. The storage space has exits on both sides," bragged Cottin.

"Finding someone you can trust after what you've been through is going to be tough," said Bugzy.

Meghan called Petey at Pippins. "We raided the farm today, and came up empty," she told Petey.

"Where the hell is he hiding, Meg?"

"I think he's there, we just can't find him. Just like the camp in

Pennsylvania, we are missing something," said Meghan.

"What's your next move?"

"Danny and I are going to snoop around, maybe at night, I know he is there," she said in frustration.

"Do you have Itzie's approval or are you two going to freelance it?"

. "We will try it the official way, but I won't take no for an answer. One way or another I'm going to come face to face with that murdering thug."

"I sure wish I was there to take care of you."

"No, Petey, you can't babysit me while I'm on my job," she interrupted. "If we are going to have a future together you have to have faith in me. I'm a trained professional."

"That's why I want to be with you, one never knows how long the future will be, and I want to spend every minute of it with you."

"Nicely said, Petey McDade, that means a lot to me," said Meghan.

Jeep called Petey at midnight. "Meghan called earlier this evening," said Petey. "She and Danny are going to snoop around the farm."

"That's not good," said Jeep. "I got a job at the farm today and I'm living in the bunkhouse. It won't take much snooping to find me."

"Meghan is sure that Cottin is hiding somewhere at the farm."

"I think she is right, but I haven't the slightest idea where. But, Petey, we can't have her blowing my cover."

"Do you think she will recognize you?"

"She is an experienced agent, they notice things. Either she or Danny will see through my disguise. Do you know when they are coming out here?"

"I would think in the next few days. Jeep, we have other problems that I haven't shared with anyone."

"Is Pippins going broke?" Jeep asked.

"Can you describe the two characters you saw in the parking lot that Sunday?" asked Petey.

"That's easy, I don't know how tall they were, but one had red hair and the other was shaved bald."

"That's what I thought. I saw them hanging around here earlier this evening. They looked suspicious."

"Oh man, Petey, I am sure they are waiting for me to surface, but be careful, they might settle for getting just one of us. Alert Master Lee and stay on your toes."

"You're the one that's standing on your tiptoes in the manure pile, don't worry about me."

"Okay, I'll talk to you tomorrow night. Goodbye."

The last customer had left. K.C. and B were in the office in the kitchen. Petey was going to lock the front door and as he reached to turn the deadbolt the door swung open sharply, there stood Baldy and Red. "Get back inside, dickhead," said Baldy.

"Nice meeting you too," said Petey backing up.

"Sit on the bar stool," said Baldy.

As Petey started to sit on the stool the lights went out, not in Pippins but in his own little world. Baldy had hit the back of Petey's head with a blackjack. Petey hit the floor like a ton of bricks.

Red walked into the kitchen and surprised B and K.C.

"Can I help you?" said B.

"Yea, you two go out to the bar and see if you can help your friend," Red said as he pointed a gun at them.

K.C. saw Petey sprawled on the floor as she walked around the bar. He wasn't moving. "Get a wet towel, B!" she shouted as she knelt next to Petey.

"Is he okay?" said B.

"He's out cold, from the looks of it he has a concussion," said K.C.

"Can we take him up to his room?" B asked.

"Be my guest if you can manage it yourselves, but don't worry too much about him," said Baldy. We are going to kill y'all anyway as soon as you tell us where this Jeep guy is hiding."

"Help me, K.C. We can do it. His bedroom is the one on the left," she said staring at K.C. K.C. nodded and they struggled to lift Petey and half carried and half dragged him to the stairs. Red grabbed two beers and followed them. Baldy walked in front of them. They finally got him to the top of the stairs and took him into Jeep's room and put him on the bed. K.C. held the towel on his head. B said, "We need some smelling salts. I think the medicine kit is in the closet. I'll get it."

"Slow down, girly," said Baldy. "I'll get it."

"You won't be able to find it. Duh, I don't think I can escape in a closet," B said, dripping with sarcasm.

B walked in the closet and went to the back, opened the trap doors on the fire pole and slid down. She was through the kitchen and half way back up the stairs with the shotgun before Baldy could say hurry up. They both had their backs to her staring at the closet when B entered the room.

"If either of you move, you are both dead!" shouted B. "I have a twelve gauge full of Double "O" buckshot pointed at your kidneys."

K.C. opened the drawer on the night table and took out a pistol that she knew Jeep kept there.

"You are now covered twice. Drop your guns," said K.C. They both dropped their guns.

"Take it easy," said Red.

"If I'm not mistaken, in order to talk you have to move your jaw, and I consider that moving," said B. "Cover them KC."

B put the shotgun on the bed walked up behind Red and kicked him hard between the legs. He clutched his groin screaming and fell to the floor in the embryo position. She picked up his gun and said to Baldy.

"Can you get on the floor or do you want me to help you?" He dropped immediately to the floor in a spread eagle position. She kicked his gun away, walked back to the bed, picked up the shotgun and said to K.C., "Call the sheriff's office, and tell them to bring an ambulance."

The phone was on the night stand. As K.C. made the call to the sheriff's office, B picked up Baldy's gun and walked over to the back window. She opened the window and fired two shots in the air. In a matter of seconds the lights came on in both cottages. Master Lee was the first one out his front door.

B shouted down, "Grab Mike and get up here right away. The back door is open."

In less than thirty seconds Master Lee came running into Jeep's bedroom followed by Mike Austin. Master Lee surveyed the situation and smiled.

"You girls are dangerous," said Mike. "It looks like we are late to the party, Lee."

Master Lee was wearing his dobok. Baldy took one look at the black belt and started slithering toward the corner of the room.

"Who you work for?" said Lee.

"Joshua," said Baldy.

"Where he now?"

"In North Carolina."

"What were your orders?"

"Kill everyone at Pippins," said Baldy.

"How you talk to him?"

"I have his phone number in my shirt pocket."

Lee bent over and took a piece of paper from Baldy's shirt pocket and handed it to B.

The ambulance attendants were putting Petey on a stretcher when Cookie and Deputy Quigley arrived. Baldy and Red were sitting in the corner. Mike was guarding them with the shotgun. Master Lee was staring at Baldy. Red looked like he was half dead, and Baldy looked like he was scared to death.

"Here's Cottin's phone number. He sent these guys to kill everyone at Pippins according to their confession," said B.

"Who confessed?" asked Cookie.

"The bald one, he hasn't stopped talking since we took his gun away from him. It appears these are the same two guys that threatened Jeep in the parking lot that Sunday .It looks like Cottin is still trying to get even."

"Where are these guys from?" asked Cookie.

"North Carolina and they know where Cottin is hiding."

"I'll get in touch with Itzie. In the meantime these two are in my custody," said Cookie.

"I'm going to ride in the ambulance with Petey," said K.C. "Somebody call Pop, no wait, it's one o'clock in the morning. Go to his house first thing in the morning and bring him to the hospital."

"I will do it," said Master Lee.

B walked down the stairs with K.C. and whispered, "Do you know how to get in touch with Jeep?"

"We can't, he will call me this evening," said K.C. softly. "Telling him now won't help Jeep or Petey."

Chapter 17

Wednesday morning Jeep was up at six. He found a large weed whacker in the maintenance garage and was cutting weeds around the fence posts by 6:30 a.m. Bugzy showed up riding an ATV an hour later.

"So the cowboy is an early bird," he shouted over the noise. "The early bird gets the worm."

"Yea," Jeep said, shutting off the machine. "But the second mouse gets the cheese. It doesn't always pay to be first."

"You had coffee yet?" asked Bugzy. Jeep shook his head no.

"Lets go up to the house and I'll buy you a cup. Hop on the back."

Jeep put the weed whacker over his shoulder and climbed on the back of the ATV.

"Sit on the porch and I'll get the coffee. How do you like it?"

"Black," said Jeep.

Returning in a moment with two cups of steaming coffee, Bugzy said "Where you from, cowboy?"

"Next question," said Jeep as he took the coffee.

"What the matter, is the law looking for you?" smiled Bugzy.

"You writing a book?"

"Easy, cowboy, as your employer I need to know a little about you," said Bugzy.

"Single, Caucasian, high school drop-out, honorable discharge, born in Haskell County, Texas, and I'm broke, trying to work my way back to Texas."

"That's it?" asked Bugzy.

"Yep, what about you and this farm? It isn't making any money. It doesn't take a genius to see you don't have any crop or cattle. Just what is it you do here?"

"Whoa, cowboy. I'll ask the questions."

"Why don't we both keep our little secrets? You give me ten dollars an hour and I'll work real hard for you," said Jeep.

The housekeeper came to the screen door and said, "You have a phone call, Mr. Schoffman."

"We'll talk later; you might work out fine. I like people that keep their mouth shut."

Pop got to the hospital at seven-thirty in the morning and he looked very tired. "How's my boy doing?"

"He's resting. He just regained consciousness an hour ago."

"Master Lee told me what happened, Is Jeep okay?" asked Pop.

"Jeep's traveling so he wasn't there. Petey has a fractured skull."

"Is he going to be okay?"

"We don't know yet, he may have amnesia. He took a helluva blow to the head."

"This has not been a good day. Petey's mom died last night."

"Oh, Pop, I'm so sorry," said K.C.

"It's okay K.C. She had no quality of life; she couldn't feed herself and didn't remember any of us. It's really for the best. I just don't know if I should tell Petey or wait. What do you think?"

"Lets wait until we see how Petey recovers. It might be best to wait."

Dr. Hudacek came through the doors into the waiting room. "Oh Pop, I'm glad you're here," he said, sitting down on the couch. "Petey has taken a severe blow to the head resulting in some brain trauma. All we know so far is that he is awake and asking what has happened. I have asked for a specialist from Pittsburgh to take a look at him. We may have to transfer him to Mercy hospital."

"How bad is he?" asked K.C.

"We just don't know. I suspect he has some amnesia. He has swelling around the brain, which is not uncommon. When the swelling goes down we will know more. The next forty-eight hours are critical. I know that sounds like a cliché, but it's all we can do."

"Can I see him?" asked Pop.

"No," said Dr Hudacek. "I don't think he would recognize either one of you at this point. That could cause anxiety for all parties involved. It certainly wouldn't help Petey."

"Let's get coffee and then we pray," said Master Lee. "That more powerful than medicine."

"I think he's right, for now that's all any of us can do," said Dr, Hudacek.

Jeep went into the bunkhouse at noon to freshen up. He noticed a table setting on one of the tables in the kitchen. It was lunch consisting of two ham and cheese sandwiches, a bag of chips and a pitcher of lemonade. He was the only one in the bunkhouse so he washed his hands and ate lunch.

Bugzy came in just as Jeep was finishing his lunch. "I had the housekeeper make lunch for you. Was it any good?"

"It was fine. Thanks," said Jeep.

"I have someone I would like you to meet," said Bugzy.

"Any friend of yours…" Jeep mocked sarcastically. "What does he want?"

"He needs someone to drive him to Georgia."

"My truck won't make it," stated Jeep.

"Don't need your truck He wants you to drive his RV."

"He handicapped?"

"No, he just wants a driver," said Bugzy.

"What's his name?"

"I'll let him introduce himself. How's about tonight? Say nine o'clock up at the house."

"Not tonight," Jeep said stalling. "I got a date tonight that's a sure thing. How about tomorrow? Anytime tomorrow would be fine."

"I'll tell him, he'll pay good money. He's in a hurry to get to Georgia."

"Tell him to start without me," smiled Jeep. "Tell me what else you need done. I should be finished with weeding this afternoon."

Jeep couldn't wait to get away from Bugzy. He knew the friend was Cottin. He needed time to think. Should he call the authorities, or should he just walk up and shoot the SOB? He might have to if Cottin saw through his disguise. He needed to talk to Petey. He would call him earlier this evening so he would have time to decide what to do. He was finished weeding at five o'clock. He went into the bunkhouse to lie down. He was debating with himself and he drifted off. Jeep awoke with a start. It was ten minutes to seven. He would take a shower and call Petey.

"Hello, this is Pippins. How may I help you?" asked K.C.

"Hi, honey. It's Jeep, I sure do miss you."

"Oh, Jeep I'm so glad you called. We have had a little trouble. Those goons that tried to get you that Sunday tried again last night."

"I knew they would try again. Petey saw them last night in the bar," said Jeep.

"They jumped Petey as he tried to lockup last night."

"How bad did Petey hurt them?"

"They are in jail, but Petey is in the hospital. They fractured his skull."

"Is he okay?"

"He's awake, but we don't know how bad he's hurt yet. They think he has amnesia. We won't know for a few days."

"Damn, if he was unconscious, then who took down the bad guys?"

"B and me."

"What, just the two of you?"

"Yep, Master Lee questioned them. They told us Cottin had sent them. They said he was in North Carolina and they gave us his phone number. Cookie is calling Meghan and telling her where he is hiding. With the phone number, they should know where he is hiding."

"Where's B?"

"She is on her way back here from the hospital. Don't worry about us. I'm getting dinner ready and Master Lee and Mike are here now and will be until closing time. Master Lee wants Cottin to send more goons. I've never seen him upset before. It's scary."

"Okay, honey, take care. I should be home in a day or two. I love you."

"Me too you, baby. Take care of yourself," said K.C.

Things were moving too fast. If the FBI and ATF move in then he would have to back off. All Jeep wanted to do was to carry-out some county justice and get out of Dodge City as they say.

The more Jeep thought about it the more he thought he should just leave and go home. Let the Justice Department handle it. They were closing in on Cottin and Jeep would only get in trouble if he interfered. His best friend is lying in a hospital and Jeep had no idea how bad he was hurt. He should be with Petey

On the other hand this murderer had to pay for what he has done, and for what he is planning to do. This monster's brutal slaying of Mac and his wife Irma was unforgettable, what if he beat the rap in court? It wouldn't be the first time a murderer was set free. Where's the justice for Jamie and Bo. What about Petey, will he survive in one piece? What about the entire country if this nut case ever gets free again. He got into the truck and just drove. He didn't have a destination or a decision.

It was one in the morning when he got back to the bunkhouse. He knew he couldn't sleep, but he knew he had to try.

He must have dozed off, but now he was awake. What did he hear or was it his imagination? Was he awake or was he asleep? There it was again—somebody was prowling around outside. He slipped out of bed and stood against the wall. He made his way to the door. Hearing nothing he opened the door and made a rapid move to the truck. Still nothing, so he started to climb into the back to open the bed box.

"Don't move a muscle." He was staring into Meghan's face on the other side of the truck.

"Don't shoot," he said.

"Put your hands on top of your head," said a third voice from behind him. "FBI." He recognized Danny's voice.

"Let's go inside," said Meghan as she came around the back of the truck. He walked inside and one of them turns the lights on. Jeep sat on the bed and hung his head.

"What's your name?" asked Meghan.

"Duke Cary," replied Jeep.

"Are you the only one here?" asked Meghan.

"Yep, what'd I do?"

"You tell us."

"The rest of the place is clear," said Danny as he exited the bathroom.

"I work here; I just started two days ago. The day you guys raided the farm. I was looking for a job and had to wait until you people left so I could apply. I'm just a cowboy trying to work my way back to Texas." He still hadn't made eye contact with either of them.

"Is that your truck outside? It has Pennsylvania plates, not Texas."

"That's where I bought it."

"Let's see some ID," said Danny.

"I don't have any," said Jeep.

"You look familiar. I have seen you somewhere."

"I think I saw you and three guys at Appleby's the other day," smiled Jeep. "I always remember a pretty face."

"Yea, that's it. You were alone," said Meghan.

"Let's put the cuffs on him so we can search the rest of the place."

Jeep had made his decision. He was going to level with Meghan and Danny. If they hadn't recognized him, there was a good chance that Cottin wouldn't either. He might be able to help them put an end to this terrorist threat. With their support he would try to perpetrate this charade with Cottin. Of course there was always the chance they would shoot him when he embarrassed them with his true identity.

"Before you cuff me I have a question," said Jeep.

"And what would that be?" asked Danny.

"Will I still get an invitation to the Grabowski, McDade wedding?"

"What?" Meghan said in shock.

Danny grabbed Jeep by the hair and pulled his head back to get a good look into Jeep's eyes. Jeep just smiled.

"Well, I'll be damned!" exclaimed Danny. "You never cease to amaze me, first Indiana and now North Carolina."

"What's going on?" inquired Meghan.

"Take a closer look, Meghan," instructed Danny.

Meghan stared at Jeep for a second and then her jaw dropped as recognition set in.

"How in blazes did you...I should shoot you right now."

"I was afraid of that." He laughed as he stood with his arms wide open and offered to hug her.

Meghan hugged Jeep for a minute. Then she looked directly at Jeep and said, "Where's Petey? He can't be far behind you."

"Petey is back in Pennsylvania. I'll tell you everything later. Right now you two must listen. We don't have any time. Cottin is in the farmhouse as we speak. He is going to make a run for the camp in Georgia soon. Now get this, he wants me to drive him."

"He didn't recognize you either?" said Danny.

"We haven't met yet. This has all been arranged by the farm manager, Bugzy Schoffman. I'm supposed to meet with Cottin tomorrow night. I was just going to leave and not take the risk of being exposed and bring the wrath of the Justice Department down on me. But when you two didn't recognize me I thought we might have an opportunity to infiltrate the camp in Georgia. If I can pass muster when I meet with Cottin, I'll accept the offer of being his chauffeur. I think he'll ask me to join his group of misfits by the time I get him to the camp."

"Jeep, we will have to get authorization from Itzie," responded Danny.

"We don't have much time, so let's plan to beg for forgiveness rather than ask permission," smiled Jeep.

"I can't get over your appearance. You look taller, thinner, and that hair! I know women that would love to have that hair," said Meghan.

"The boots make me taller; not eating makes me thinner and the full beard hides my handsome face. And during the day sunglasses cover my eyes. I think I can fool Cottin!"

"What do you have in mind?" said Danny.

"First of all you two get out of here. Here's my cell phone number," said Jeep as he wrote it on Meghan's pad. "I will call and keep you informed as things unfold. I'll need your number and a code word we should use for a danger signal."

"I'm tired, dog tired. It should work. It has in the past," said Meghan.

"Good, now make like a tree and leave. Oh, make sure you put a tail on me and make it a good one. Now go."

Danny and Meghan walked out the door and disappeared into the night.

Jeep tried to get some rest, it would soon be morning.

Chapter 18

Petey was awake and alert, but didn't remember what had happened. Dr. Hudacek was concerned. It was early in the morning. Petey still had a serious headache, but they were trying to limit the pain relievers so they could test his awareness. He was thinking of letting Pop into see Petey.

"Now Pop, he may not recognize you. Try not to show too much anxiety if he doesn't," said the doc.

"I'll do my best, let's go."

They walked into Petey's room. The blinds were drawn, and the room was dark. Petey was awake and staring at the ceiling.

"Hey, Petey," said Pop.

Petey stared right at Pop for ten or fifteen seconds, it seemed like a lifetime. He smiled and said, "Hi, Pop, what the hell happened to me?"

You could see the relief in Pop's face. "You turned your back on the wrong guy."

"How long have I been here?"

"Two days, but the doc has been taking good care of you. How do you feel?"

"My head hurts. How did I get here?"

"K.C. brought you here."

"K.C. who?" inquired Petey with a puzzled look.

Pop snapped a look at Dr, Hudacek.

"That will be all for now. You need your rest. Come on, Pop, let's let him rest."

As soon as they were out of Petey's room, Pop said, "What was that all about?"

"I'm not too sure. He had no problem remembering you, but he didn't remember K.C. It looks like he only remembers people when he sees them. Is K.C. in the hospital?"

"Yea, she was getting us some coffee. She is either in the waiting room or cafeteria."

"Find her. I'll meet you in the waiting room," said Dr.Hudacek.

"The doctor needs to talk to you, K.C. Petey recognized me, but when your name was mentioned he didn't know it. The doc wants to take you in to see Petey. Can you handle it? He thinks he only remembers people when he sees them."

"Let's go see my friend," said K.C

As they walked into the darken room Petey was staring at the ceiling again.

"Hi, Petey, I hope we didn't wake you." K.C. smiled.

Petey just looked at K.C., "No, I've slept enough."

"Petey, look who I brought in to see you," said Dr. Hudacek.

Petey stared at K.C. and said nothing.

"Does your head still hurt?" asked K.C.

"Yes," Petey said. He was staring without blinking.

K.C. was so uncomfortable that she wanted to turn and run from the room. She thought she was going to burst into tears. The pain of knowing that her dear friend didn't acknowledge her because he didn't know her was almost unbearable.

"Is there anybody that you would like to see?" Petey asked Dr. Hudacek.

"No," said Petey. He was now staring holes right thru K.C.

She couldn't stand it a moment longer. "It was nice to see you Petey, but I have to go." Her voice was trembling as she turned and walked toward the door. She thought she was going to be sick.

"Is that you, K.C?" Petey asked as she reached the door. "Please don't leave, I'm all alone."

"I was just going to get some cold water. I would never leave you, Petey," she responded with her back still to him. Tears were running down her face and she was shaking all over.

"Only for a few more minutes," said Dr. Hudacek

K.C. wiped her nose and tears on her sleeve and turned and walked back to the bed. She sat on the chair and held Petey's hand.

"What's the matter, K.C.? Are you crying?" asked Petey.

"Allergies." She smiled and patted his hand.

Jeep was out working on broken slats in a fence. He was tired—this was going to be a long day. He was going to let Bugzy make the first move. His only concern was fooling Cottin, that and resisting the urge to blow his brains out on sight.

Bugzy walked up behind him. "How did you do last night? Did you get lucky?"

"Luck has nothing to do with it," smiled Jeep, thinking if he only knew. "Does your friend still need a driver? I might have to get going myself."

"Did you get in trouble last night?" asked Bugzy with a grin.

"Nah, how much is this guy paying for a driver?" inquired Jeep.

"He wants to meet you first. If he doesn't like you, you're back to whacking weeds," said Bugzy.

"When does he want to meet?"

"You come up and sit on the porch at nine o'clock."

"Do you want me to take a look at that roof that needs patching?"

"No, hold off on that. I don't want you starting any jobs that you won't be around to finish."

"Okay, do I get my lunch in the bunkhouse like yesterday?"

"It will be there at noon. See you tonight."

The rest of the day droned on. At five o'clock Jeep dragged himself into the bunkhouse and collapsed on his bed just to rest for a minute before he showered. He fell asleep instantly, but awoke startled, wondering how long he had slept. It was seven-thirty. He showered and drove into Henderson for a bite to eat. He arrived back at the farm at ten minutes to nine o'clock. This was just enough time to pack all his things in the bed box .(in case of a quick departure) He then removed his S&W 659 and tucked it in the back of his belt with his shirt covering it. He drove the truck over to the front porch and parked it facing the highway to expedite a hasty exit if necessary. He sat himself on the top step of the porch and waited.

Fifteen minutes later Bugzy came out the front door and sat down in a rocker looking down at Jeep. "The boss will be right out. Let me advise you—he's a no nonsense guy. Your response to his questions should be precise and respectful," instructed Bugzy.

"Whatever," responded Jeep.

"You Duke?" called out Cottin from the screen door.

"Yes sir," Jeep responded as he rose to face the door. It's now or never thought Jeep as Cottin exited the house. He looked thinner and older. He was dressed in civilian clothes. Maybe that was it.

"My name is Nicott, Mr. Nicott. Are you willing to drive me to Georgia?"

"Yes sir, Mr. Nicott," responded Jeep. Cottin looked him up and down. Jeep felt naked. He put his hands on his hips, so his right one would be closer to his pistol.

"Bugzy says you are from Texas, that right?" inquired Cottin.

"Yes sir, Haskell County, Texas," responded Jeep

"I ain't ever been to Texas, but I've seen you before," stated Cottin.

"Where are you from, Mr. Nicott? Maybe we've crossed paths." Jeep was prepared to defend himself, and kill if necessary.

"That's none of your business, son. You ever been in Pennsylvania?"

"Yes sir, I just came from there."

"Did you come from the Pittsburgh area?"

"No sir, Harrisburg."

"That's it," Cottin acknowledged. "Did you work in a gas station?"

"Yes sir," Jeep lied. "Up until a few days ago."

"That's where it was; I came through there a few weeks ago. I must have stopped at your station with that rented truck."

"I don't remember you," said Jeep, trying not to visibly sweat.

"I never forget a face. Is that beard new?"

"Yes sir, just about ten or twelve day's old," smiled Jeep.

"You see that, Bugzy, I still got it. The old lawman never forgets," bragged Cottin.

"Ah, sir, are you a cop?" Jeep asked, now trying to appear frightened.

"Relax, boy, I'm off duty as they say. You running from the law?" inquired Cottin.

"No sir, just when they chase me," drawled Jeep in his best Texas accent.

"You're going to work out fine, boy. When can you leave?"

"If Mr. Schoffman will let me leave my truck here for a few days, I can leave in ten minutes."

"How long do you want me to keep that wreck around here?" asked Bugzy.

"If I'm not back in three weeks, it belongs to you. I'll leave the registration in the glove compartment. Give me ten minutes to pack and I'm ready to run. Is it okay if I park the truck in back of the bunkhouse?"

"Yea, I'll get the RV, boss," said Bugzy.

"How much money am I going to make doing this, Mr. Nicott?"

"That depends on how many bumps we hit on the way. How does two-hundred sound?"

"Wahoo, what's keeping us? Let's go!" shouted Jeep as he ran to the truck.

Back at the bunkhouse he called K.C. for a brief moment to have her alert Meghan and Danny.

"Hi, honey, it's me."

"Hi, babe, are you okay?"

"Fine, Call Meghan and tell her I made the connection and that I am leaving for Georgia in a few minutes. How is Petey doing?"

"He's going to be fine, Jeep. We are all worried more about you," K.C. said.

"Don't worry, things are going well and I'll be home soon. Oh, and most important, I love you!"

He had to dismantle his Remington so it would fit in his duffel bag, that wouldn't take long. It would be easier if Jeep could stop laughing. He felt relieved and excited and the fact that Nicott was an anagram of Cottin was plain silly.

It seemed like Petey was improving. His headaches weren't as severe. The bone graft that Dr. Hudacek performed on Petey's fractured skull was healing. It was obvious that the amnesia would persist. What he didn't know was how long and to what degree.

"Hey, B, Jeep just called," said K.C. "Do you know how to get in touch with Danny right now?"

B just smiled and said, "I think so," and gave K.C. his cell phone number. K.C. called Danny and gave the message to Danny and all he said was great. He then reassured her that Jeep was safe, the FBI had a tail on him and he was never out of their sight. This brought K.C. a great deal of comfort.

"Hey, B, I know we have never done this, but how about you and I having a drink? I think I need one," suggested K.C.

"Works for me," smiled B. "Who's buying, Jeep or Petey?"

When Jeep walked back to the house, a twenty-eight foot RV was sitting on the driveway alongside the house.

"Wow, that's a biggin'," Jeep said.

"Can you handle it?" asked Bugzy.

"For two-hundred dollars I could drive that baby to Georgia backwards," responded Jeep. "Where can I store my duffel bag?"

"Just open anyone of those side doors, they're all storage," instructed Bugzy.

"Let's move it out," said Cottin as he came down the stairs.

"I'll call you, Bugzy. Take care of things and get some laborers working this place."

Jeep jumped into the driver's seat. Cottin preferred to sit behind him on the sofa instead of the passenger seat.

"Passenger seat too conspicuous for you?" questioned Jeep.

"You're getting the drift. If I can get to Georgia with no one seeing me, you've earned your money," responded Cottin.

"Where we headed?"

"Dahlonega, it's fifty miles north of Atlanta," said Cottin as he stretched out on the sofa.

"Do you have a map, just in case you're asleep when we get there?"

"I'd better be awake when we get there. If the boys don't see me as we drive in they will shoot you."

"If that's the case, Mr. Nicott, I'd like to tie you to the front bumper," laughed Jeep.

Chuckling, Cottin said, "That's a good one, boy."

They started down Rt 85 toward Charlotte. Jeep figured they would get there about five in the morning. He kept within the speed limit and looked for his FBI tail.

They were making good time. Just south of Gastonia Jeep had to tap a kidney.

"Can I pee in that toilet back there?" asked Jeep.

"Yep, but I think you have to get out of that seat first," roared Cottin.

"That's a good one, Mr. Nicott," laughed Jeep.

He pulled off at an exit. He went into the bathroom and sat down to pee so he could text message Meghan. "Do I have a tail?" was all it said. He rearranged the gun in his belt. It was killing his back, but he didn't dare part with it. Jeep got right back into the driver's seat and got back on Rt 85.

"Stop at the next service area. I want you to get me a cold six pack. The refrigerator is empty."

Jeep looked around as he bought the six pack of beer. As he exited the store he thought he'd better buy some gas. He stuck his head in the RV and said, "How do I pay for the gas?"

"Here, use this credit card," Cottin said.

Jeep noticed the name on the card was G. Cundiff, another stolen credit card. *Sorry, Mister Cundiff, I hope you don't get stuck for this, but I'm in sort of a spot myself,* thought Jeep.

As Jeep pulled the pump, the fellow in the next island was just finishing. As he put his pump handle away he said very softly, "I'm your tail," and walked to his car.

The RV took thirty-three gallons. Jeep looked at the receipt as he got back in the vehicle, it was seventy-three bucks. He put the card and the receipt on the table where Cottin was sitting.

"I'm glad it's your money. It took almost half of what you're paying me to fill this thing up," said Jeep.

"It's not my money," responded Cottin.

It was long past five o'clock when Cottin said, "Get off at the next exit and take Rt. 52 north." Twenty miles later Cottin directed Jeep to turn onto an unpaved road. *This must be it,* Jeep thought. Three miles into the dirt road was a gate. Jeep stopped the RV and turned to Cottin. A voice on a loudspeaker startled Jeep.

"Hello, Boss, we'll open that gate in a minute," the voice said. Suddenly the gate swung open.

"Proceed slowly from here on in, there are guns pointed at us," smiled Cottin.

This comment only heightened the anxiety Jeep was feeling. Four tenths of a mile later the headlights reflected on some buildings. *This camp is larger than the Pennsylvania camp,* thought Jeep. It appeared that it could contain a much larger population.

"You sleep here tonight, Duke," said Cottin. "Don't get out of the RV."

"Where can I get something to eat?" asked Jeep.

"Find something in the refrigerator. I'll come for you before noon."

"I'll need my duffel bag. It's in the storage area in the back."

"Okay let me get it for you," said Cottin.

Jeep stepped out of the RV behind him, watching to see if Cottin tried to open it.

There were three armed guards standing right in front of him.

"Are you carrying any weapons?" asked one of them.

"Yep," said Jeep. "It's stuck in my belt behind my back." There was no use lying to three armed men.

"Leave him alone, I just traveled eight hours with him. I know he's armed. He's not a threat. If I thought he was, he'd be dead by now." Cottin handed Jeep his duffel bag and said, "Stay inside until I come for you."

Jeep found some food in the refrigerator and pulled the privacy curtains. He checked for a signal for his cell phone. *No bars, means no signal, where is that "Can you hear me now?" guy when you need him?* A lot had happened in the last thirty hours. Thinking about the next thirty hours had heightened his anguish.

Chapter 19

Petey was doing quite well. The MRI showed that the swelling of the brain was reduced, in fact, it looked normal. The headache subsided and he was in good spirits. Dr. Hudacek was constantly testing him, hoping the signs of amnesia would disappear.

"Petey, Master Lee is here to see you. Do you feel up to it?"

"Do I know him, Doctor?"

"Yes, you do." Dr. Hudacek nodded to Nurse Boyt and she went to get Master Lee.

Master Lee entered the room and walked to Petey's bedside. He had been schooled earlier by Dr. Hudacek to say nothing. He stared at Petey and smiled.

Petey stared right back at him and then said,"What's the matter, Lee, the cat got your tongue?"

"No cats bite my tongue. See ahhh," said Lee as he opened his mouth.

Petey smiled. "That's an expression that asks why you aren't talking. I'm glad you came to see me. Are you here to take me home?"

"Not so fast," said Dr.Hudacek. "A few more days of rest and we'll see, although you are progressing nicely."

"When doctor say okay, I take you," said Lee.

Petey's recovery was going well, but the amnesia was puzzling the doctor. Physically he was ready to be released, but a few more days of rest wouldn't hurt.

It was shortly before one o'clock when Cottin opened the door and stepped into the van.

"You want to get paid?"

"Yes sir, but I have a question for you. How am I going to get back to the farm?"

"I'll give you an extra seventy-five bucks for gas and you can drive the RV back."

"What if I wanted to stay here and join this camp? It looks like an interesting group. Maybe I would fit right in."

"This is a very private community. You have to be invited to join."

"Maybe you could invite me, Mr. Nicott. I could be your chauffeur."

"Let me think about it, but be prepared to leave tomorrow," said Cottin.

"Can I get out of the RV and stretch my legs?"

"Yea, but leave the gun in the RV and don't be nosey."

After Cottin left, Jeep put his pistol by the steps inside the door and decided to take a walk. The camp was in a very steep valley. *This is rugged country,* thought Jeep. A dense forest bounded both sides of a never ending valley. It seemed to divide the mountain for miles. A refreshing looking stream snaked thru the valley. It appeared twelve feet across at its widest. It probably had a tendency to flood during the rainy season, although its banks were deep and sturdy. Jeep pondered what was best, to leave or to stay. Was Cottin going to let him leave or was his congeniality a front covering a concise murder plan? Was the FBI watching? He walked into a building that looked like the warehouse in North Carolina.

"Can I help you? You're not supposed to be in here," said a guy doing paperwork at a desk.

"Oh, I'm sorry. My name is Duke, I'm new here. I came in last night with the boss. I'm just looking for some coffee," responded Jeep. "The boss said it was okay for me to walk around."

"The next building is the cafeteria. You can get coffee there."

"Thank you, ah, I missed your name," inquired Jeep.

"Flocken, Bernie Flocken. If all you want is coffee you can take some from my pot over there. I don't think you should be walking around. You will get in trouble."

"Okay, thank you. I don't want to cause a commotion, I'm leaving tomorrow. This camp is big. How many people live here?"

"Seventy-five, more or less, there is always someone coming or going," said Bernie.

"What do you do here?" inquired Jeep.

"Fight to liberate America from the grasp of corruption that controls it from Washington."

"Wow, I have never heard it put any better. I would fight on that side. It sounds like this camp is full of patriots," replied Jeep, sounding deeply concerned. "It looks like someone needs to finish loading that van over there. Do you want my help?" Jeep walked over and began loading bottles of water in the van. It looked to him like two or three-hundred bottles, just like the ones in Pennsylvania except these were full. Jeep now knew what had to be done. He had to get out of here pronto. He said goodbye and walked to the stream and finished his coffee. As he was looking around the van pulled out of the building he had just left. It stopped near the center of the camp and three people got in while Cottin walked over and talked to the driver. Although Jeep couldn't see, he assumed the driver was Bernie—he was the only person in that building. Jeep grimaced. Had he just hastened the departure of that van by helping load it? He was sure the destination was Washington. He noted the time was two o'clock. He had to notify Meghan or Danny. Hurrying back to the RV he noticed money on the table as he entered. Sticking his gun in his back belt he surmised that Cottin was going to release him. Why else pay him? Now it was just a matter of how soon—that van had to be stopped. Acting anxious to stay while hurrying to leave was going to be an Academy Award performance.

Cottin entered the RV a half an hour later.

"I found money on the table, two-hundred and seventy-five dollars. I guess you are throwing me out. Gee, Mr. Nicott, I would really like to be accepted here."

"Go back and work the farm with Bugzy. Maybe if the reports on you are good I'll reconsider."

"When do you want me to leave?"

"Wait until eight o'clock; I want you driving at night when you're less conspicuous."

"Okay, am I allowed to eat dinner in the cafeteria?" Jeep hoped he sounded genuinely happy.

"No, stay in the RV and get some sleep. I'll have someone bring you dinner. I'll be in touch. Remember, don't leave before eight." Cottin left without another word.

In six hours that van could be in Virginia, thought Jeep. He took a folding chair he found in storage along with some literature he found on the history of gold mining in Dahlonega and climbed up on the roof. He tried to look like he was resting while he observed the movement in the camp.

He actually had slipped off to sleep for a short while. His dinner was delivered at five-thirty. He showered in the RV in what felt like a phone booth. He was fresh and ready to go shortly before seven. He took his dishes back to the cafeteria hoping to learn anything that would assist the FBI. Cottin was sitting at a long table with four people that looked like they meant business.

"I thought I told you to stay in the RV," roared Cottin.

"Yes sir, just returning my dirty dishes. I'm fixing to leave if it's alright with you."

"Yea, sure, get the hell out of here," said Cottin not aware that it was just seven."

Jeep ran for the RV and quickly started down to the front gate. As he approached the gate the loud speaker voice said, "Waiting for exit approval, it should only be a moment." Jeep poised near the gate allowing enough room for the gate to open. Jeep thought, *This gate would be easy to drive right through; it's not very formidable.* After two minutes the gate opened. As Jeep drove on he noticed the strength of the gate. It was a guard hiding in the brush with a MK 19 automatic grenade launcher.

Once on Rt 52 he headed south. He turned on his cell phone and was waiting for a signal. Suddenly a loud siren and flashing lights appeared in his side view mirror. *Just what I need, a ticket*, thought Jeep. He pulled over to the side of the road. The trooper walked up to the driver's window and suddenly Jeep thought, *Oh, no I've got a gun in my belt.* He kept his hands on the steering wheel.

"What did I do that was wrong, officer?" asked Jeep.

He smiled and nodded to the passenger window. Jeep turned and saw a grinning Danny Grabowski looking through the window at him.

"We are glad to see you are safe," said Danny.

"Did you see that green van leave at two o'clock? It was loaded with contaminated water heading to Washington D.C.," Jeep said from the rear seat of the trooper's patrol car.

"We saw it leave, but didn't put a tail on it," said Danny.

"We better find it quick!" exclaimed Jeep. "Cottin is keeping an eye on me by making me deliver the RV back to the farm."

"We will send someone back for it and take it to our office in Raleigh. Right now we are heading to a landing strip where Meghan is waiting. We have a government jet ready to take us to Washington," said Danny.

"We have to find that van, Danny. I helped load it; I won't be able to live with myself if we don't."

"Relax; we have the plate number, we will find it."

A Virginia trooper pulled the suspects over on Rt. 85 just as it departed North Carolina. The trooper announced over his PA system, "Stay in the vehicle," as he called for back-up. Suddenly the rear doors swung open and automatic fire swept the windshield of the trooper's car, killing him instantly. The van was back on the highway before the echo of the shots subsided. It pulled into the rest area one mile down the road and changed the plates. Working smoothly, the inhabitants of the van applied magnetic decals that said, "VALLY BAPTIST CHURCH." They were back on the road in six minutes.

"We just got a call that a trooper has been shot and killed on Rt. 85 in South Hills, Virginia," said Meghan as she buckled her seat belt in preparation to take off. Danny was next to her and Jeep sat facing her.

"We now have to assume they have altered the appearance of the van as well as changed the plates. Put out a call to stop all green vans going into Washington after nine o'clock tonight. As of nine tonight, D.C. is off limits to all green vans," stated Danny.

"I've told the pilot to land in Richmond. Rt 85 and 95 join back together. We are trying to limit their options for traveling north. Our local office will meet us there," explained Meghan.

Petey was allowed to wander around the hospital. He was feeling good, no headaches and the surgery wound was healing nicely. When Nurse Boyt was changing the dressing on his head Petey wanted to see what it looked like. Holding a mirror Petey noticed his head had been shaved on the top rear. "I look like Friar Tuck!" Petey exclaimed.

"Petey, do you realize that you just remembered Friar Tuck. This is wonderful," said Milly.

"If I told you I also remember Robin, Maid Marian and Little John would you let me go home?"

"We will have to ask the doctor, but my guess is yes," smiled Milly.

Dr. Hudacek was making his rounds; "Nurse Boyt tells me you are amnesia free," he smiled.

"Who?" smiled Petey.

After a few questions and the obligatory thumps on the chest and light in the eyes he said, "She's right."

.

Master Lee checked Petey out of the hospital and took him to Pippins. He was warmly welcomed back by everyone.

"Hey, Petey, how about buying a round to celebrate your homecoming?" requested Buck.

"I think I'm going back to the hospital. There must be something wrong with my hearing," said Petey. Everyone laughed and Petey told Mike to "do the house one time."

Petey asked B, "Have you heard from Danny or Jeep?"

"Just this afternoon, Danny called. Everything is fine; he and Meghan are keeping an eye on Jeep."

"Meghan who?" said Petey as he winked and laughed. It was good to be home. The phone rang and Petey picked it up "Pippins," he said.

"Is that you, Petey?" asked Jeep.

"Jeep, it's great to hear from you. Where are you? Are you safe?"

"As safe as one can be thirty five thousand feet over North Carolina, heading for Richmond"

"Sounds exciting," said Petey.

"We are closing in on Cottin, but we've had a little set back. There are some bad water bottles heading into D.C. But I'm really calling to check on you."

"I'm fine. I just got out of the hospital today. I'm going to be okay, Jeep, don't worry."

"I've got someone here who wants to say hello," said Jeep, handing the phone to Meghan.

"How are you doing, handsome?"

"Meghan! It's so good to hear your voice. Are you okay?"

"I'm just fine, but I'll be better in a few days when I see you." In the background she could hear B shouting "Is that Meghan...is that Meghan...is Danny with her? Let me talk to Danny!"

"See you soon, handsome," Meghan said and handed the phone to Danny.

"I'm getting homesick," said Jeep.

The Richmond agent was waiting as they departed the jet.

He introduced himself. "My name is Horn, Bret Horn. We've met before," he said to Danny.

"Yes, I remember, at a conference in Pittsburgh."

"We have two vehicles for you. They are equipped with police radios and on the seats you will find walkie-talkies so we can communicate offline. I'm to take Agent Williams in my car and you are to take the SUV with Mr. Patrick."

"Call me Jeep, please"

"Fine, the state police have the main arteries and interstates covered and the local police have all roads in their jurisdictions covered. We have been warned they are armed. We are to join a cadre of state troopers at exit 98 on the interstate. We are going to try and stop every green van. If the vehicle was a private van instead of an industrial panel van, this job would be impossible. At nine the Maryland and Virginia National Guard are going to close all traffic into Washington. This must be really big."

"Trust me, it is!" shouted Danny as he and Jeep got into the SUV to follow Bret.

At the entrance to Rt. 95 there were ten trooper cars lined up and at the bottom of the entrance were two pursuit cars ready for the next green van to pass. On the overpass were several spotters. Danny pulled over at the top of the entrance behind Bret.

As they listened to the trooper conversation on the Suv's scanner Danny said, "I know you are armed, Jeep but, please let Federal officers and troopers do their jobs if there is any shooting."

"Handguns are not my expertise; I will only use it in self defense. Just make sure you and Meghan protect me." He smiled.

Over the radio they heard a trooper report he was following a green van whose Pennsylvania plate was falling off. It looked like another plate of a different color was underneath it. The van was from the VALLY BAPTIST CHURCH. He gave his position as entering Hanover proceeding north on Rt 2.

Danny said over the hand held, "Bret, how far is that trooper from us? I'd like to check this one out."

"Six miles, follow me," answered Bret.

Bret made a u-turn back onto Rt. 30 and headed east at a high rate of speed. They turned left on a secondary road and Danny heard the trooper report that he was approaching Rt 30.

"Danny, Rt 2 is the next intersection," said Bret on the hand held and they should be about three miles away.

"Tell the trooper to pull them over, but be careful, they will come out of the back shooting.

Danny pulled over to the shoulder at the intersection and turned off the headlights, it was isolated. Bret went through the intersection and made a u-turn. They were now facing each other. It was getting dark quickly.

In the distance, coming up the road they could see two sets of headlights with flashing lights on the second set.

"He's pulling him over," said Jeep. The van pulled over and stopped on the shoulder of the road one-hundred yards from the intersection. The trooper immediately slammed on his brakes and backed up down the road and swung his patrol car broadside on the road and exited the passenger side. Time stood still, nothing moved, there was no other traffic. With the trooper's siren off and only the flashing lights on it was an eerie setting. The van started to move slowly as it pulled back onto the road. Bret's car turned left and started straight at the van. They were only thirty yards from each other when Bret turned on his bright lights. Gunfire erupted from the van as it started to pull around Bret's car. Bret swerved to his right and rammed the van, pushing it off the road into the ditch. Danny turned the Suv to the right and stopped directly in front of the van. His headlights lit it up. Danny exited the driver's side and ran behind Bret's car. Simultaneously Jeep dove out of the passenger door into the ditch. Lying prone and with pistol drawn no one was going to get into the woods from his side of the van. The driver tried and Jeep fired twice, hitting him both times *Bernie the rebel was now dead in a ditch,* Jeep thought. In the meantime Danny had worked his way to the left side of Bret's car. He was covering the passenger's side door as well as the rear. He looked inside of Bret's car, Bret was slumped under the steering wheel and Meghan had slid to the floor under the dash.

The trooper was hurrying toward the vehicles firing a shotgun into the rear of the open van. The passenger door was pinned shut by Bret's car. Suddenly someone came out of the window. He didn't get all the way out. Danny hit him with three of the four shots he fired.

Suddenly it was deathly quiet. The trooper was poised with the shotgun trained into the rear of the van. Danny was holding his gun on the dead passenger and Jeep was lying in the ditch looking for movement on the left side of the van.

Danny opened Bret's door. It was obvious he was hurt.

"Meghan, check on Bret. He's been hit!" shouted Danny as he scanned the van for movement. Jeep was feeling for a pulse on Bernie when he heard Danny scream

"Jeep, Hurry!"

"What?" said Jeep as he walked between the van and the SUV.

"It's Meghan. I think she's been hit."

Jeep opened the passenger side of the car. He didn't have to feel for a pulse. Meghan was dead! She had been hit in the head and chest numerous times. He groaned, turned and slid to the ground on the side of the car. Danny came around the car and stared at Jeep in horror, saying nothing. Jeep sat on the ground, his back to the car, his wrist draped on his knees, his pistol dangling dangerously loose on his right index finger and he was staring at nothing.

What had seemed like hours and was actually only minutes, the place was crowed with rescue and police. Jeep was sitting on the edge of the seat of an open door police car, his elbows on his knees and his head hanging.

Danny was giving his report to Special Investigator Itzie who had materialized out of nowhere. "The four from the van are dead. Jeep shot one, the trooper got two and I got one coming out the passenger window," Danny said. "Agent Horn is wounded in the chest and ATF Agent Williams is dead. Keep everyone away from the van. The shotgun has blasted the water bottles and the contaminated water is leaking. This whole area needs to be sealed off."

It all seems so cold and final, thought Jeep as he listened.

Chapter 20

A few hours later, Jeep and Danny were heading back to the Raleigh office, they would be there in two hours. The car was silent

"Are you going to call Petey?" asked Danny.

"Yes," sighed Jeep, "but I don't know what to say."

"I've got you a room in Raleigh. Your duffel bag is in the back. A shower and a good night's sleep will help."

"I've got to call him tonight; he would never forgive me for delaying."

"I think you need a drink first, doctor's orders," suggested Danny.

"When did you get your MD degree? The bars will probably be closed when we get to Raleigh."

"I keep plenty of medicine in my black medicine bag."

"Then why are you driving so slow? Step on it."

It was two in the morning when they got into their rooms, Jeep called Petey.

"Hello," answered a weary Petey.

"It's Jeep."

"What time is it?"

"It's after two. Petey we had a shooting down here."

"Is it Meghan?"

"Yes, she was shot."

"Is she going to be okay?"

"No, Petey I'm afraid not. Meghan was killed earlier this evening."

There was silence on the phone, and then finally, "Are you okay? What about Danny?" Petey asked.

"We're fine. There was a shootout when we stopped the van that was headed to D.C. Danny killed the guy that shot Meghan."

"Did she suffer, Jeep?"

"No, Petey, she didn't. I'm coming home to be with you. I'll be there with your truck tomorrow by three. Do you want me to call K.C.?"

"No, I'll call her if I need company. Hurry back."

It was seven in the morning and Jeep had picked up the RV at the FBI office in Raleigh and was returning it to Bugzy at the farm. He parked it alongside the house and ran down behind the bunkhouse with his duffel bag. The truck was there with the keys—he hopped in and pulled up to the front of the house, ran up the stairs and knocked on the door. Bugzy opened the door, surprised to see Jeep. "Welcome back," was his sleepy hello.

"I brought back the RV. Mr. Nicott was delivered safe and sound. I've got something to do and it might take a couple of days. Will I still have a job when I come back?"

"Yea, the boss said you did fine. Where are you going?"

"I'll be back," Jeep said as he ran off the porch.

Jeep couldn't remember what day it was as he pulled into the Pippins lot. The lot was empty, which meant it was either Sunday or Monday or Tuesday. The front door was open and Petey and K.C. were sitting in the corner booth drinking coffee. They all ran together and had a three way hug and no one said a word, but Jeep could feel Petey's body tremble with a silent sob.

"I'll get some coffee," K.C. said .She was the first one to speak. Jeep and Petey were still embracing when she returned with Jeep's cup.

They sat in the booth and Jeep said, "There's not much to tell you, it happened so fast. The agent driving the car that Meghan was in said she told him to ram the van as it started to get away. They hit it in the right front door which left her exposed. They were both shot as they sat in the front of the car. Agent Horn is in critical condition. It was a heroic act on their part."

"I want to call her parents, but I don't even know where they live. We didn't know each other very long. Why does it hurt so much, Jeep?"

"Because you're human. We are all feeling the pain of a heavy heart. I know this won't help much now, Petey, but remember, time is on our side, and it's the only healer I know for this kind of pain.

Danny will let us know about the services, what town they are in and the day and time of the funeral. We'll go together."

"Thanks, Jeep."

Jeep went up stairs. He couldn't wait to cut his hair, get rid of the beard and shower. He needed the past few days washed down the drain.

B showed up for work. They were open for dinner, it must be Tuesday.

Jeep got all cleaned and said to Petey, "Let's take your truck down to Kendal's. I owe you a paint job."

"Your car is out back, I'll meet you there."

Jeep arrived with the truck at Kendal's garage before closing time.

Kendal said, "Where the hell you been, Jeep?"

"What did Petey tell you?"

"Nothing."

"Then that's where I was," laughed Jeep

"Who cares? It's good to have you back," said Kendal.

"Can you put the truck back together again?" asked Jeep.

"Yes I can, can you give me a few days?"

"Yes I can," mimicked Jeep.

Petey pulled up in Jeep's car.

"Are we all set?" asked Petey.

"Does Kendal know what color you want?"

"Metallic blue and anything else he wants to do to it. I trust Kendal."

"Let's take a ride," said Jeep.

"Anyplace particular you would like to go?"

"Not really, Petey, as long as it's just you and me," smiled Jeep.

Jeep was just waking up and enjoying his own bed when the phone rang. He glanced at the clock, it was eight a.m.

"Good morning," said a sluggish Jeep.

"Good morning, Jeep, did I wake you?" asked Danny.

"Not really, I had to wake up to answer the phone anyway," joked Jeep.

"What? Oh, I get it," said Danny. "I'm calling to tell you about the arrangements that have been made for Meghan. The services are Friday and the funeral is Saturday morning in Altoona, Pennsylvania. That's where she was born, and that's where her parents still live."

"Petey, K.C., Cookie, Master Lee and I will be there Friday for the services and will leave right after the gravesite ceremonies, Saturday. Are you going to stop by here and pick up B?"

"Yes, I'll be at Pippins tomorrow night. Is my cottage still available?"

"Its all ready for you, just remember to tip the maid," said Jeep.

"How's Petey doing?"

"He's doing fine. It's going to take a while," said Jeep.

"Jeep, it's going to be a very impressive military type service that will tug on your heart. Meghan is being treated like the hero she was. Stay close to Petey, he's going to be emotionally moved."

"Thanks for the heads up, Danny."

"Also, Jeep, I want to thank you for that night in Virginia. I think it would have turned out differently if it hadn't been for you. I'll take you for a partner anytime."

Jeep was having coffee when Petey crawled out of bed and dragged himself into their little kitchen. Jeep poured him some coffee as he sat down. "We're going to Altoona Friday morning," said Jeep.

"Is that where Meghan was from?" asked Petey.

"How did you know?" puzzled Jeep.

"Why else would anybody go to Altoona?" smiled Petey.

"It's going to be a very emotional two days. Are you up to it?"

"I can handle it, just stay close to me, partner," said Petey.

Thursday evening and business was good. B had posted notices that the restaurant would be closed Friday for personal reasons, and would reopen for dinner Saturday night. She had posted a framed picture of Meghan and her obituary on the wall entering the dining room. She had taken the obituary from the *Altoona Mirror* web site.

Danny arrived at eight o'clock and asked Petey and Jeep to join him for dinner. Since Jeep had forgotten to eat and Petey was always hungry it made sense.

"What time do you want to leave tomorrow?" asked Danny.

"I think the evening memorial is from seven to nine," stated Petey. "It's one-hundred and thirty miles from here and that should take us three hours. If we allow time to check into our rooms and have early dinner when we arrive in Altoona, one o'clock should be plenty of time."

"As you can see Danny, Petey hasn't given this much thought," smiled Jeep.

"I'm sorry, Petey," said Danny. "Meghan was a hero; she took charge of the moment and made the ultimate sacrifice. There was nothing more that Jeep or I could do. She knew when they crashed into that van she became their primary target, and wearing a seat belt she had no place to hide, although she was unfastening it when she got hit."

"I know, Danny; I still have you and Jeep." Petey paused for a moment, smiled at them and then said, "I never was any good at making trades."

"Your friend Jeep saved me and the Virginia trooper. The driver had the protection of the van and would have been in the shadows if he had successfully exited the van."

"You don't know how lucky you were, Danny. Jeep can't hit the ground with his hat when it comes to pistol shooting," laughed Petey.

Jeep went over to the bar and brought back three shots of Black Jack Daniels. They each took one; toasting, Jeep said, "To Meghan," and they all drank.

Everyone slept in late Friday morning. The plan was for everyone to meet at Gerry's Diner around eleven. Jeep packed for an overnight stay. He noticed Petey had overpacked, "How long are you staying?" Jeep inquired.

"You just never know. It pays to be prepared," said Petey.

"Let's go see if Lee and K.C. are ready and if Cookie's here, I'm hungry," said Jeep.

"Your turn to buy, isn't it?" smiled Petey.

"I think you're right, if you take every fifth turn," laughed Jeep.

Everyone was ready and the five of them piled into Jeep's car and headed to the diner.

"Kendal called last night and said the Pennsylvania Porsche is ready. I told him we would see it Saturday afternoon," said Petey.

Danny and B were already there. They had pushed some tables together and were drinking coffee.

Everyone ordered breakfast, or as K.C. called it, brunch. The spirits were high and laughter aplenty when Petey said, "You're a great bunch of friends. I couldn't get through this ordeal without each and every one of you. You guys get it; laughter heals faster than tears, thank you."

When breakfast was over and they were all moaning that they would never eat again, Petey asked for the check. He said, "I'll get it." Everyone at the table looked at each other and in unison pretended to faint.

It was decided that Cookie would ride with Danny and B. Danny was to follow in case Jeep got stopped on the thruway, Danny could pull over behind them and use his FBI influence if necessary.

It was an uneventful trip—they arrived in Altoona minutes before three. It was decided a swim and a nap would replace the early dinner and they would eat after the services.

They all checked into their individual rooms. Jeep announced he was tired and was going to nap. K.C. yawned and everyone started laughing.

They arrived at the funeral home at exactly seven o'clock. Jeep and Petey met Meghan's Mom and Dad. Clarence and Helen Williams were greeting everyone.

"It's so nice to meet you, Petey," said Helen. "I have heard so much about you from Meghan. She was quite taken with you. In fact, she said her search was over, she had found Mr. Right."

"She certainly stole my heart, Mrs. Williams," said Petey. "She was a very special woman."

"Call me Helen, please, Petey," she said. "You know it is a closed coffin. That's the way we wanted it."

"I believe that's the way Meghan would want it also."

Petey introduced everyone to Mr. and Mrs. Williams. Then they all went in the parlor where the coffin was, surrounded by flowers. At the head of the coffin was a large beautiful picture of Meghan on a tripod. Petey took in a lung full of air to control his emotions.

The funeral the next day was an emotional roller coaster for everyone. It was almost more that Jeep could handle. At times he had K.C. and Cookie sobbing on his shoulders and was holding Petey's hand. He was glad Danny was there to comfort B. The abruptness of her death was overwhelming for everyone. The American flag was presented as a gift from the President of the United States and a star in her honor would be placed in the Justice building.

After the grave side ceremony Petey lingered at the grave. All of the mourners had departed except for their group. Jeep went over to Danny and said, "Take everyone back to the motel and wait for us, we will be along shortly."

On the ride back to the motel Jeep and Petey didn't say one word. Jeep knew Petey well enough to know that when he wanted to talk he would.

They were getting ready to have lunch before they departed for home when K.C. said to Jeep, "I have to talk to you alone. Petey told me last night he's not coming back with us. He's going to Georgia to find Cottin. He said you were welcome to join him, but you couldn't stop him."

"Oh, my God, I know I can't stop him, I don't even blame him, but it's a crazy idea."

"I think you had better talk to him while the rest of us have lunch," said K.C.

While everyone went into a restaurant next to the motel Jeep and Petey took a walk.

"What's you plan?" asked Jeep.

"I have this all thought out. I packed your clothes and weapons, as well as mine. I want you to come with me, but it's not mandatory. K.C. will take Cookie and Master Lee home in your car."

"And just what are we going to use for transportation?" said Jeep. "That is, if I agree to this madness."

"My truck, Dickey Lee and Kendal delivered it this morning," smiled Petey. "It's in back of the motel. Everything we need is in the bed box, our rifles, your fanny packs loaded with Lifesavers and even sleeping bags."

Jeep was afraid of the suddenness of the plan, but it was only a surprise to him, obliviously Petey had it well thought out.

"We can't let Danny or Cookie know. By law and job description they would have to stop us, but for K.C.'s and B safety I am going to have to tell Master Lee."

They joined the rest of the crowed for lunch. They stalled after lunch until Danny and B said they were heading back

After they left, K.C. said to Cookie, "The reason I wanted you to ride back with me was for the company. Petey wants to spend some time with Meghan's folks and Jeep is going to stay with him. I have to get back to open Pippins."

"I think that's nice, It will give both of them some comfort and a chance to talk. I think they liked Petey," said Cookie.

They all hugged and said their goodbyes. Jeep told K.C. he would call. K.C., Cookie and Master Lee climbed into Jeep's car and waved goodbye. Petey and Jeep had another cup of coffee and paid the check.

"Come on, I'm dying to see my truck," said Petey as they walked out of the restaurant and headed toward the back of the motel. There in the motel parking lot as big as life stood Master Lee with his TKD duffel bag slung over his shoulder.

"K.C. make me stay. She say I make sure we don't go to any more funerals." He smiled. "I ride in back of truck in sleeping bag. I won't get in way."

Jeep and Petey stood there staring, dumbfounded.

"I think we just doubled our forces," said Petey. "I can't think of any one more capable of covering our backs. Do you know this is going to be very dangerous, Lee?"

"I hope so," said Lee with a big smile

The three of them walked to the back of the motel where Petey's truck was parked.

The truck was breathtakingly beautiful. Its metallic blue paint sparkled under the sun and the rims supporting the new tires almost blinded you. Across the tailgate was written in gold flake "Pennsylvania Porsche."

"It's beautiful!" exclaimed Petey. "I never dreamed it could look this nice. What a great job Kendal did."

"It's too pretty to take off road," said Jeep.

"It will be the prettiest thing in the woods," laughed Petey.

"Let's go through our inventory and make sure I didn't forget anything," said Petey as he opened the bed box.

Looking through what Petey had packed it was apparent that nothing was left behind. It seemed to Jeep that all his belongings were in the box. They took a moment to organize the contents and do a quick inventory. Then they got into the truck, there was plenty of room for three in the cab.

Smiling at each other, Petey looked to Jeep and said, "The three musketeers, where to D'Artagnan?"

"To the adventure that awaits us in the south Porthos," replied Jeep.

"D'Artagnan was not musketeer," smiled Master Lee. "He was wannabe, the three musketeers were Aramis, Athos, and Porthos. What..." he said looking at Jeep and Petey, "you think Dumas story not translate to Korean?"

Jeep and Petey could not stop laughing. This man was truly amazing, and this was going to be a fascinating escapade.

Chapter 21

Cookie and K.C. arrived with no time to spare. K.C. was late in starting dinner. Hopefully her assistants had gotten everything started. K.C. was always training interns that her alma mater kept rotating through Pippins. The two she was presently working with were exceedingly competent and she really had no reason to worry.

Danny was going to stay overnight. When he heard Petey and Jeep had not come back, he decided he would fill in for them. He quickly found out no one was quite sure what either of them did.

Jeep called at seven, he knew that it was the peak hours for K.C. in the kitchen so he kept the call very short.

"That Master Lee stunt was clever," Jeep said.

K.C. chuckled. "I talked with him about staying with you earlier when Petey told me he was staying. He didn't have to be asked twice. He bolted from the car telling Cookie that he wanted to see more of Altoona and he would take the bus home."

"If you get a chance, talk to Danny and see what the FBI's next move is concerning Georgia. I'll call again tomorrow, I love you."

"Me too, you," she said and hung up.

Later, after everything was locked up, B, Danny, K.C., and Mike Austin were sitting having a closer (Last beverage of choice for the evening). They were talking about the events of the last two days.

"What's everybody doing tomorrow?" asked Danny.

"I've got to pick up a load in New Stanton," said Mike, "and deliver it to the Speedway in Toledo, Ohio. I'll be back in time to help behind the bar Tuesday for dinner."

"Great planning, Mike, you won't miss a minute of work here," said B.

"Where are you off to this coming week, Danny?" asked K.C.

"I'll be in my office most of the week concluding the paperwork on Virginia, and then, if I guess right, Itzie will have us back to Georgia to close in on Cottin," said Danny.

"I'll be glad when that's over. I still don't feel safe, and I won't until that destroyer of lives is locked up," stated B.

"My plan is no plan," laughed K.C. "I might work on some recipes tomorrow if I'm feeling creative, if not I might take a nap."

They all exited from the rear door and retreated to their cabins. *B was going to save some mileage on her car tonight*, thought K.C. as she set the alarm and locked the door. This week had been an emotional drain on everyone. The positive is the weather is getting warmer.

The three were in an unusually good emotional state considering the past week and the sinister chore that lay ahead of them. Although they knew where they were going, they didn't have a precise plan about capturing their prey. Jeep was the only one familiar with the camp and its surrounding terrain, as well as its armed population.

"Let me know if you get tired driving and I'll relieve you," said Jeep.

"I don't think I'll ever get tired of driving this baby," replied Petey.

"Can we stop soon? I think Oriental bladder smaller than Caucasian bladder," announced Lee.

"We're entering Winchester, Virginia, I'll look for a rest area," said Jeep.

After making their pit stops, Master Lee went to a remote spot of the rest area and went through twenty minutes of stretching and warm ups. It looked like he was shadow boxing against ten guys. As they got back into the truck, Lee said, "Sorry for delay, but I need to stay loose."

"Keep the weapons loaded and Lee loose," said Petey. "It sounds like a plan to me."

Just north of Richmond, Petey asked Jeep for the exit number that the shooting took place. He wanted to see where Meghan died. Jeep gave him directions and soon they were at the precise location. There wasn't any visible indication that anything extraordinary had happened there.

"Are you sure this is the spot?" asked Petey.

Jeep was standing by the ditch; he looked down and saw something. He picked up a spent 9mm cartridge. He held it between his fingers and showed it to Petey.

"You are standing at the precise spot where Bret Horn's car was," confirmed Jeep.

They decided to get a motel south of Petersburg. It was getting late and suddenly they were all very tired. They grabbed some burgers and had a meeting in Petey's room. "Boys, we need to do some careful planning. The first things we need to do is establish is our objective. Cottin is the primary objective. Do we capture him and turn him over to the authorities or does one of us have other plans?" asked Jeep while looking at Petey.

"No," said Petey. "I will do this by the book. I wouldn't get you or Lee involved in a murder."

"Number two; there are a lot of citizens in that camp. Do we have a stealth plan to slip in and take Cottin or are we prepared for collateral damage? Number three; what do we do with him after we confiscate him? Ponder these questions while you try to sleep tonight. We will talk about them tomorrow. Now we had all better get some sleep, goodnight."

They took advantage of the free continental breakfast the motel offered and got back on the road.

"Did everyone sleep last night?" inquired Jeep.

"Yes, I sleep on floor," said Lee.

"When I finally got to sleep, I slept pretty well," said Petey.

"I was thinking of stopping at the farm, I have an idea that maybe I will be welcomed back into the camp. I know Cottin will recognize us once he sees us, but if we play our cards right it will be too late."

"Only plan is good plan," smiled Master Lee.

It was shortly after nine in the morning when Petey pulled his truck into the farm. Jeep walked up on the porch and knocked on the door. Bugzy answered the door and said, "What do you want?"

"Hi! Mr. Schoffman," said Jeep.

"Do I know you?" asked Bugzy.

"Come on, Mr. Schoffman, it's Duke, Duke Cary."

"Well, well, boy, you sure do clean up good. I guess there is hope for your generation yet. Do you want your job back?"

"Well, that's part of it. I have two friends with me who are also willing to work," responded Jeep as he waved for Petey and Lee to join him on the porch.

"What are their names?" asked Bugzy.

"Bo and Jamie," said Jeep, thinking fast.

"The biggun looks strong, but what can the little Jap do?"

"He's Korean and stronger than he looks."

"I was rice farmer, good worker," said Master Lee amusing himself.

"You know I need the help, same deal, bunkhouse, lunch and ten dollars an hour."

"Mr. Schoffman, I would like to talk to you later if you have the time," said Jeep.

"Come on up to the house after six. We can talk then," said Bugzy as he closed the door.

"I didn't even know I was looking for a job," said Petey. "Oh, and by the way, who am I, Bo or Jamie?"

"I am Bo, it's easier to spell," said Lee.

They got settled in the bunkhouse, it looked like three other laborers were living there. Jeep asked the mechanic what needed to be done. He found them all something to do and they went to work for the rest of the day mending fences, cutting grass and weeding.

At five, after they washed, Jeep told Petey and Lee to go pick up some dinner and bring it back and he would talk to Bugzy.

Shortly after six Jeep knocked on the screen door of the farm, the front door was open.

"Come on in, Duke," said Bugzy from somewhere inside. Jeep walked into the living room and from behind him he heard Bugzy say sit down. Jeep turned around and Bugzy was pointing a pistol at him.

"What's going on, Mr. Schoffman?"

"Sit down I said," Bugzy repeated with authority. "Who are you and what do you want?"

"I'm Duke and I want to go work for Mr. Nicott in Georgia," said Jeep.

"That's bullshit, you had better level with me or I'll shoot you right here. That's what I was told to do."

"Who would tell you to shoot me?"

"The boss, I told him you were back and looked different. He asked what had changed. I told him what you looked like now and that you had two friends with you. When I gave him their description, he went nuts."

"I don't understand," said Jeep trying to figure out his next move.

"The boss said your name is Jeep Patrick and you are trying to kill him. And that your friends are Petey and Lee. And I should be careful that Lee is some martial arts expert. I told the boys in the bunkhouse to bring them up to the house when they get back. Fortunately, one of the laborers said he is a black belt in Karate."

It was twenty minutes later when Jeep heard the truck coming down the gravel driveway.

"I'm so hungry I could eat a horse," said Petey

"If you like horse you would love dog," smiled Master Lee.

"I never know when you're joking. Do you eat dog?"

The headlights showed four guys waiting outside the bunkhouse, the farm mechanic and the three Mexican laborers.

"We have a welcoming party," said Petey. "Staying alert means staying alive, Lee."

"Mr. Schoffman wants to see you two," said the mechanic.

"Tell him we will come up right after we eat. I'm very hungry," said Petey.

"He said right away."

"I said after I eat!" growled Petey.

Master Lee had worked his way around to the front of the truck standing off to the left of the mechanic. The mechanic pulled a pistol and pointed it at Petey.

"Oh, that is such a big mistake," groaned Petey.

Almost instantaneously Lee lunged into the air kicking the gun hand, sending the pistol flying. Spinning around, Lee's foot caught the mechanic on the side of his head. He fell immediately and lay motionless. Lee turned to face the three laborers. One took a fighting stance that looked aggressive.

"You are student of martial arts? Very nice, but hold your hands up higher and widen your stance," instructed Lee as if he was addressing a student.

He mimicked the laborer only holding his hands higher.

"Like this," Lee smiled.

He then took down the other two laborers with a loud shout and a few selected lighting fast punches and roundhouse kicks.

"See, now you try on me," Lee instructed the petrified not so aggressive looking third laborer.

The poor man looked terrified, then turned and ran off into the field, disappearing into the night.

"Jeep might be in trouble. I'll go around to the back of the house, you go to the front," said Petey.

"They will be up here any minute," said Bugzy. "I just heard the truck return."

Jeep was sitting in a straight back chair in the parlor and Bugzy was standing in the foyer holding the gun on Jeep and the front door was to his left. Petey worked his way around back to an open window at the end of the hall. The hall led back to the front door. The screen door opened and slammed shut. Bugzy turned toward the door. "I'm over here," Petey said through the window. Bugzy swung around one-hundred and eighty degrees to face the back window and Master Lee slipped through the front door and kicked Bugzy in the back of the head. The blow snapped his head. He staggered forward and tried to turn around but his body wouldn't cooperate. He was out on his feet. Master Lee walked up and took the gun away from him. Lee struck him in the abdomen, letting out a loud yell and Bugzy fell flat on his face and curled into a ball.

"You didn't kill him, did you?" asked Jeep.

"No, he only wishes he was dead," said Lee.

"Are you okay?" said Petey as he came through the front door. "What went wrong?"

"Bugzy called Cottin and described the two guys with me. He also told him I looked different. Cottin put it all together and told him to kill us. Bugzy said our names were Jeep, Petey, and Lee so I guess the jig is up now that he knows we are coming after him."

"Maybe we should try the Deputy Porter trick and have Bugzy call Cottin and tell him the deed is done," said Petey.

"We can try, but it didn't work last time," sighed Jeep.

"Keep an eye on this guy, Jeep, Lee and I will get the other three resting by the bunkhouse. We'll bring the burgers up and eat here. I'm famished."

They had everyone tied up and in the bathroom when they sat down in the kitchen to eat their dinner.

"Hey look, I found some beer in the fridge, and some other good things, how about some ice cream for dessert?" laughed Petey.

"The housekeeper and cook will be here first thing in the morning. What do we do with the prisoners?" asked Jeep.

"Release the two laborers, they were just in the wrong place at the wrong time," said Petey.

"What about Bugzy and his helper?"

"Let's just leave them for the cook and housekeeper to find. We can leave them in the bunkhouse, it might take someone longer to find them there," suggested Petey.

"Can we call Danny and ask her what we should do with them? Maybe we should have the police hold them on assault charges." said Jeep.

"We were trespassing on their property," suggested Petey.

"You have a point, but let's tell Danny and make it his problem."

They left Bugzy and the mechanic tied securely in the bunkhouse bathroom and headed for Georgia. They figured they would have a twelve to fourteen hour head start before they were found, even if Danny decided to do nothing. It was before eight p.m. when they headed south for the camp.

"Well, Cottin knows we are coming, and that doesn't bother me one bit. Let him worry about the apocalypse," said Jeep.

"What does that word mean?" said Lee.

"His expectation of imminent destruction," smiled Jeep.

They rolled through the night taking turns driving and sleeping. They pulled of the road just outside Dahlonega and waited for daylight. What they were looking for was a secluded site in the Chattahoochee National

Forest that was within a few miles of the camp. A place they could establish a clandestine camp and hide the truck.

At dawn Petey drove the truck deep into the woods following Jeep's direction. "How much further? The trees and scrubs are scratching my beautiful truck," announced Petey.

"I don't think we can go much further. See if you can find a clearing that offers some sort of protection," said Jeep.

They came across a thirty foot group of large boulders and rocks.

"This should work fine. I saw a stream behind these rocks," said Petey.

"We are in the foothills of the Blue Ridge Mountains; there are a lot of streams and waterfalls. Beware of holes in the ground. They mined for gold here twenty years before the California gold rush in 1848. Also, there are a lot of tunnels," informed Jeep.

"Is there any gold left?" asked Lee.

"Yes, but it would be too expensive for any mining company to dig it out, so keep your eyes open. One-hundred and fifty-five years ago the gold lay on the ground and they just washed it off with big pressure hoses. I'm telling you this because the ground around here can be dangerous. It can be filled with holes, tunnels and offers loose footing. You guys set up a base camp while I try to find where Cottin's encampment is located."

Jeep started walking up a ridge that he thought was bordering the camp. If he was correct the encampment lay in the next valley. Upon hitting the highest point of the ridge he started proceeding up to toward the mountains. Jeep paused and popped a Lifesaver in his mouth and wondered if he should have brought his rifle with him. As he was catching his breath, he heard faint noises—he believed they could be coming from the camp. Noticing the ridge was falling off steeper on his left, he continued with caution. He was confident he was on the right track as he proceeded slowly in a crouched position. Seeing the road first and then the gate he halted, knowing somewhere below was the sentry on the loudspeaker that controlled the gate, as well as the guy with the grenade launcher. He retreated ten yards and marked the spot with a pile of broken branches and started back down. He timed himself on the return trip; it took twenty-five minutes to reach the base camp that Petey and Lee were establishing.

"I found Cottin, at least where he lives. I certainly hope he is still there!" exclaimed Jeep.

They had established a very effective base camp. The front of the truck was partially hidden in the rocks. The bed of truck was covered, and a lean-to was stretched from the truck to a couple of saplings, enough to keep them dry in a storm.

"What food we have is in the bed box. We are good for a few days," said Petey.

They planned and prepared most of the day. The thought was to slither into the camp after dark, seek out Cottin and snatch him. The one shortcoming of the plan was they did not know his whereabouts. Jeep had his Remington and Cottin's 9mm that Petey had acquired with his magic act. Petey had his Weatherby and Colt. Master Lee had his self-assurance.

The plan was to traverse the ridge above the guard gate and negotiate the hazardous slope into the camp. They agreed to stay thirty yards apart, thus reducing the risk of more than one being spotted at a time. Master Lee would lead the way, he was the silent one. Petey would try to stay thirty yards to his right, he was the reserve power. Jeep would stay back thirty yards, he was the shooter. They still had to decide should they go during the daylight hours and determine Cottin's whereabouts or wait for dark and take pot luck?

Suddenly Jeep decided. "I'll go four hours before dark and scout the camp. I've been trained to lay motionless and observe. Petey, do you still have those glow sticks that you use hunting?"

"Yea, I've got a dozen of the multicolored small ones."

"I will leave a trail of glow sticks for you to find me. They last six hours. They will only be visible the last two, for you to find me. That will give me four hours of daylight to determine his location and then Lee will lead us to him. I will leave shortly after four and expect you two to find me by eight thirty."

They all agreed this was the best approach. Jeep spent the time leading up to four o'clock making a makeshift Ghillie suit (a camouflage suit that helps snipers blend into the terrain) and applying mud to his face.

"Hey, let me do that," said Petey. "One of life's pleasures is rubbing mud in your face." He laughed.

Jeep slipped out of camp moments before four, wearing his Ghillie suit, he disappeared after twenty yards.

"That camouflage suit work. He gone," said a surprised Lee.

Jeep made his way back to the broken branches landmark he had left. He proceeded cautiously along the ridge, breaking and placing glow sticks every thirty yards. He made sure they were under leaves or behind trees so the could only be seen from the uphill side looking down.

There wasn't a lot of activity in the camp. Moving very slowly and looking for traps or alarms, Jeep proceeded to within fifty yards of the cafeteria and burrowed comfortably into the earth. He popped a Lifesaver into his mouth, the game was on. He was hopeful that during the next three hours Cottin would have dinner in the cafeteria. He took pleasure in knowing that he was invisible to anyone further than fifteen feet from him.

Petey and Lee worked out their plan, finding out what the other would do in certain situations.

"If one or two discover me, don't help me. If three or more jump me at once and they are armed, well, then you may help," said Lee.

"Well, if they discover me, come running," said Petey. "I'll take all the help I can get."

They spent the rest of the waiting time covering the truck with brush and hiding the camp from view. It would be unfortunate if someone stumbled across the camp and was waiting for them when they returned with their prisoner.

Following the glow sticks was an easy task, so much so that they had to constantly remind themselves to slacken their pace and remain quiet

It took a great deal of discipline for Jeep to resist the urge to slip closer to the camp. Finally he saw Cottin walk into the cafeteria. He checked his watch, it was almost seven. *What will I do at the moment of truth?* Jeep thought. When he and Cottin come face to face, will he do the right thing and resist the urge for vigilante justice.

It appeared that a lot of men were eating late or Cottin was having a meeting. The building had numerous people in it, too many to attempt to abduct Cottin. As Jeep waited, he started thinking that maybe the morning would present a better opportunity to find where Cottin was sleeping and snatch him at dawn. This idea became more appealing as the obvious meeting dragged on. He heard Petey and Lee sliding down the ravine wall. They were ten yards behind him when he heard Petey whisper, "He wouldn't go any closer than this."

"I'm here." Jeep motioned and kicked his feet.

"We would have tripped on you before we saw you," said Petey as they slid alongside of him.

"Cottin's been in that building three hours," murmured Jeep.

"What's next move?" asked Lee.

"Lets find out where he sleeps and take him at dawn."

"Sleep here?" questioned Petey. "I should have brought a pillow!"

"Spread out for the best view of the camp and watch to see where Cottin sleeps."

Lee went slightly back up hill to the left and Petey moved off to the right. They settled in for a long night.

In another hour Cottin exited the cafeteria and walked directly to a foot bridge. He crossed the stream and entered a cabin on the far side of the ravine. In fifteen minutes another person, a female followed his footsteps to the cabin and knocked once on the door. She was admitted immediately. Jeep smiled and thought, *Enjoy, you bastard, it's the last time you will have female companionship for a long time.* Sometime after midnight the cabin door opened and the female visitor left, Cottin was now alone.

Chapter 22

Itzie had the FBI assault team meet at three thirty in the morning a mile from the entrance of the camp. Danny Grabowski, Jake Darcy, Al Daula and Sobalsky were all part of the team. The plan was straightforward, enter the camp at dawn with force, contain or eradicate all resistance and arrest Cottin.

"Remind the armored personnel carrier of the grenade launcher at the gate," stated Itzie.

"Do we consider gender?" asked Darcy.

"All citizens are to be considered armed and dangerous. Our recon missions have indicated no children are in the camp. If residents take up arms against you, let God guide your hand. Our intelligent report states, no friendlies in camp."

"We go at dawn," said Daula as he put on his Kevlar helmet and vest.

This assault team was better armed and protected than our Marines at Iwo Jima.

It was almost dawn; Jeep, Petey and Lee were in their proper positions. Master Lee was starting to move toward Cottin's cabin. Suddenly gunfire erupted in the distant along with a few explosions. The camp was alive with activity instantly. It was obvious the people were schooled in case of an attack.

Lee moved quickly for cover. Jeep saw Cottin exit his cabin with a rifle and head for the ridge behind his cabin. He vanished into the woods as if he was on a mission.

"Slip back up the hill and observe whose shooting. If it's the FBI attacking the camp, you may assist with cover fire only, but by all means, Petey, don't let them know we are here. I'm going after Cottin, he has already slipped away," ordered Jeep.

Petey and Lee started up the hill scurrying for cover, knowing they had to remain clandestine.

"It looks like the FBI is going to ruin all our fun. Let's head back to the truck," said Petey. As the two of them climbed up the ridge they stopped to observe the firefight below.

Jeep headed up the ravine away from the gate and all the fighting. Covering three-hundred yards he knew he was out of sight of anyone in the camp. He then found an easy place to cross the stream. He headed up the ridge toward the mountain trying to climb higher and faster than Cottin. Jeep knew high ground was to be his advantage even though he didn't know Cottin's position.

The resistance was far more than the FBI expected. Not only were the citizens abundant in numbers, but in ordnance and ability. The FBI's force was more skillful and would be successful, but the cost of lives on both sides would be greater that estimated. Danny had ducked behind a building and didn't notice the person coming up behind him. The man was only four feet behind Danny when he leveled the shotgun at Danny's neck. He suddenly groaned and fell to the ground. Danny turned around when he heard the noise. It was obvious this man had been stopped a second before he blew Danny's head off. Danny looked around to thank his teammate, but he was all alone. He broke into a sweat, he was a second from eternity, but he was still alive and didn't have a clue as to how or why.

Petey smiled at Master Lee, "I don't think Jeep could have done much better."

"Danny don't know he have guardian angel," said Lee.

"Let's wait another moment to see if he needs more help," suggested Petey.

Jeep had reached the top of the ridge; the gunfire down below had died away. Cottin was starting down the other side when Jeep saw him. He smiled to himself; this was going to be very enjoyable. He fired a casual shot at him. Cottin dropped to the ground immediately in fear of his life. Jeep started down the slope in Cottin's direction. "Stop shooting, I'm the law protecting the perimeter, come out where I can see you. Who are you?" called out Cottin.

"I'm the pale rider bringing you judgment day."

Fear set in as Cottin scrambled to his feet and started to run, Jeep fired again this time close enough for Cottin to sense it. Dropping to the ground, he cried out, "Come out in the open, give me a fair chance."

"Like you gave Mac and Irma?"

"Who?" screamed Cottin.?

"Or Bo, he didn't have much of a chance lying in the hospital."

"Who are you?"

"The equalizer, when a good soul is murdered on its way to Heaven, I make sure the offending soul goes to Hell," expounded Jeep.

"I'm hurt, your last shot hit me," lied Cottin.

Jeep could see Cottin searching, swinging his rifle back and forth looking for a target.

"No, you are not hurt yet," said Jeep, moving after he spoke. He was now less than forty yards from Cottin as Cottin fired, missing Jeep by twenty yards to his left. He had no idea where to look for his target.

"Lay the gun down, Joshua, or I will kill you slowly."

"You know my name!" he screamed and started running down the hill. He stumbled and fell twenty feet into an old mine shaft. He let out a piercing shriek when he landed.

Jeep lost sight of him immediately, but he was sure he knew what had just happened. Cautiously he approached the crevice on his belly. Peering into the gap he saw Cottin lying on his back in a great deal of pain.

He was whimpering, "Help me."

Jeep searched around and soon found the entrance that was covered with overgrowth. Taking a flashlight out of his fanny pack he searched the tunnel. He could see Cottin laying about fifteen feet up the tunnel. He turned off the light and broke open a glow stick and held it under his chin. Laughing to himself he knew it would give him a ghoulish look. He entered the tunnel and said in his most scary voice, "Joshua, Joshua

Cottin, your time has come." Jeep could hardly contain himself from laughing. Cottin was crying.

The FBI was rounding up the stragglers, they had two wounded. The camp had suffered six fatalities and nine wounded. The state had brought in two prisoner transportation buses. After the buses had left, they began to search the camp. This camp was a bonanza of weapons and subversive equipment. The dissidents in this camp could supply many armies of radical militants. After an hour of searching the camp Itzie said, "Congratulations, men, I am sure this will turn out to be the biggest cache of illicit ordnance, drugs and chemicals ever found in the continental United States."

Petey and Lee had seen enough and didn't want to risk being seen, so they headed back to the truck. They broke camp and prepared to leave. Petey was sure the authorities would search the surrounding area and they couldn't risk being observed. They would stay in the Dahlonega area until Jeep returned. They just had to stay on the move and out of sight of familiar faces.

With the Ghillie outfit and the glow stick lighting up parts of his face, Jeep was a ghoulish sight to behold. As he walked up to Cottin he could see that he was unable to move, he probably had a broken back.

"No! Someone help me, please," he cried. "I can't move."

Jeep leaned over and looked onto his eyes. It looked like they were going to pop out of his head. He shrieked and fainted. Jeep wondered if his heart had stopped. It looked like Cottin was doomed, he couldn't be moved and his legs were twisted in a strange manor. Jeep took a bottle of water out of his fanny pack and dampened Cottin's face with it. He was regaining consciousness, his eyes looked at Jeep, but they didn't focus. *Maybe he has a concussion?* thought Jeep.

"Cottin, can you hear me?" asked Jeep.

"Yes, who are you? Get me out of here," replied Cottin.

"It's Jeep, Jeep Patrick, You're in bad shape. You can't be moved. If I try, you would die very painfully."

"Jeep, you have to help somehow," pleaded Cottin.

Jeep gave him a drink of water. "Can you move your arms?" asked Jeep.

"Yes, but I can't feel anything from my waist down," coughed Cottin, blood appearing in his mouth.

Jeep pondered for a moment and fiddled with Cottin's pistol he had. He knew the only way for Cottin to get relief was to do the honorable thing and take his own life.

"Your only hope is to eat your gun, if you have the grit," said Jeep.

"You mean kill myself?" blubbered Cottin.

"I'm afraid it's your only choice," said Jeep, handing Cottin his pistol.

"You bastard, you ruined everything," said Cottin as he pointed the gun at Jeep. "Everything was on course until you and your friend Petey interfered. We could have brought this country to it knees. We could have gotten rid of all the incorrigible, the minorities, the unwanted, the self-righteous religious freaks, the pious fags and the cowards. We could have built a new America," lectured Cottin heinously.

"America doesn't have to be rebuilt, we just have to keep improving on what we have," said Jeep.

"Well, now, sucker, I have the upper hand. I only wish I could kill that friend of yours Petey. Do you have any last words?"

"Only that you remind me of Andy Griffin's deputy, Barney Fife. He didn't have any bullets in his gun either," smiled Jeep.

Cottin pulled the trigger and listened to the weak click it made. He moaned and dropped his arm to his side.

"Now listen, asshole, you don't deserve a second chance, but I'm going to give it to you. I'm going to give you a bullet when I leave. I will be gone before you can load it in the pistol. It's your only hope," stated Jeep.

"I'll load this gun before you get ten feet away," snarled Cottin.

"Just remember to reassemble it first," laughed Jeep as he removed the slide action and barrel.

The light from the glow stick cast an eerie radiance in the cave.

"You are heartless," moaned Cottin.

"Maybe so, but I did know some people that would have helped you. The McLaughlin's, Jamie, Bo, and Meghan," he said as he walked from the cave.

Jeep started down the ridge avoiding the camp. He stopped to remove the Ghillie suit when he heard a gunshot. *The sniveling coward probably missed,* he thought as he continued back to the truck camp.

Lee and Petey had stopped at a roadside produce stand and were buying some fruit when the FBI black SUV's went speeding past. The windows were tinted so they couldn't tell if Danny and the others were among those departing.

"I think it's a safe bet they are gone," said Petey.

"Let's just drive back and forth on the road," said Lee.

"I will. Let me drop you back at the campsite in case he returns there."

Lee was waiting at the old site when he saw Jeep coming off the ridge. Jeep walked up to Lee and hugged him.

"It's over Lee, let's go home. Where's Petey?"

"Him on road. We meet him," said Lee.

It was less than a ten minutes wait on the shoulder of the road when Jeep saw the Pennsylvania Porsche cruising down the road toward them.

Jeep loaded his weapons and gear into the bed box, climbed into the cab with Lee and Petey and said, "Home, James, and make it quick, I need a shower." It was nine thirty in the morning. Jeep looked at his watch "I'd like to be home by nine this evening."

Taking turns driving they revisited all that had happened as they pressed for the sanctity of home. It was starting to get a little ripe in the cab, but it didn't deter them from their objective. The truck pulled around back of Pippins and Jeep looked at his watch.

"Nicely done, James."

They unpacked everything into Lee's cabin. They all showered and freshen up at Lee's. The story was all worked out with K.C. Jeep entered the back door into the kitchen. He and K.C. had a heartfelt embrace and a quick kiss. Jeep walked into the bar.

"Where have you been hiding Jeep?" asked Buck.

"I've been in the kitchen helping K.C," he said and winked at Mike.

"Oh, there you are," said Petey as he walked through the front door. "I've been looking all over for you. We've got to talk. They both sat in the corner booth smiling like the cat that ate the canary."

Petey whispered to Jeep, "I've got to get some sleep."

Epilogue

One year later...

Danny and B's wedding day was a beautiful sunny day. The wedding was at noon at St.Bernard's and the reception was being held at Pippins. It was being catered by students of the cooking school. K.C. was maid of honor and Jeep was best man. The bridesmaids were Cookie, B's sister and her best friend from high school. Petey, Darcy and Daula were ushers.

B wanted the wedding held in Pennsylvania because it was her home. Her mom and dad had moved to Sun City in South Carolina. plus having it here was less of a financial burden on her friends.

It was a great choice to have it at Pippins. The food at the reception was exceptional and plentiful. An epicurean delight and the deal on the booze couldn't be beat.

Pippins was closed to the public and the entire restaurant was an extraordinary party.

Jeep and Petey were in their corner booth reflecting on the past year. Petey had taken the news about his mother's death well. Because of the amnesia, he had a tough time recalling her. Petey said, "The last few years Pop told me that mom didn't recognize any of us, and now that she is gone I can't remember her. It doesn't seem right."

"She loved you, Petey. That's what's important," comforted Jeep

Buck had quit drinking. He still showed up every day to help sweep, only now he was paid off in diet soda. He was talking about getting a real job.

Mike Austin might be having the most fun at the reception. Jeep had rented a piano and Mike was providing the music. Everyone was enjoying his repertoire of songs, but Mike was enjoying it the most.

Gov had expanded Gerry's diner and the service hadn't suffered. It was still the best breakfast joint in the county. Dickey Lee was winning turkey shoots all over Pennsylvania. He was the second best rifle shot in the county.

Cookie looked beautiful in her bridesmaid gown.

"That is the prettiest sheriff I have ever seen," shouted Petey as she walked up to the bar for a refill. She was now officially the county sheriff and the boys couldn't have been more proud of her.

Jeep looked over and saw the FBI agents Darcy, Daula, Itzie, Sobolsky and Bret Horn having a wonderful time. Bret had an office job working in D.C. He had lost a lung and had limited neck movement as a result of the shooting, but he was still with the Bureau and that was all that mattered to him.

Jeep paused and reflected; the two agents from the Justice Department that had been killed were both from ATF. That was the department of the government he and Flip had first contacted.

If Jeep was to believe the newspapers, his good friend and lawyer was becoming a Judge. He remembered when he was a shortstop with good range and hit for a good average named Flip, now he was the Honorable Judge Robert Flockvich, but he still had a problem going to his left.

Dr. Hudacek and Nurse Milly Boyt were having a grand time dancing. What friends in need those two had been a year ago. They deserved to have a pleasurable time. Milly was obviously having more fun than she had at her junior prom.

Kendal's business was going strong. With all the attention on TV about restoring and customizing cars he had grown to ten full-time employees. They all joked with him about when he was going to have his own TV program. His work was very high quality.

B's mom and dad, Joan and John, looked tanned and rested. South

Carolina was being good to them. Pop was really enjoying having family around. He was boring anyone who would listen with Petey and Jeep stories and what great kids they had been.

Overhearing one of the stories, Petey said, "I think he is suffering from my amnesia or we have two brothers that we don't know about."

Danny sat down with the boys and said, "Do you realize it's been a year already since the trouble here and in Georgia? A few things still puzzle me."

"Like what?" asked Jeep.

"That anonymous phone call about the dead body in a cave that turned out to be Cottin. Did you know he attempted suicide and botched it up? Although we didn't find him right away, forensic said he didn't die from the gunshot wound, he died from internal injuries. My question is why he had only one bullet?"

Jeep and Petey looked at each other and shrugged their shoulders and smiled.

"Maybe he was broke," replied Petey, laughing.

"Another thing that bothers me," said Danny.

"Shoot, Sherlock," said Jeep.

"Remember I told you about the guy that was going to blow my brains out from behind and someone mysteriously shot him."

"Yea, you said that happened in Georgia, right?" asked Petey.

"Yes, well CSI unit told me he was shot with a .300 magnum shell and no one in the raiding party was carrying that caliber. But I was thinking, you have a Weatherby that shoots a .300 magnum, don't you, Petey?"

"Yep, and it's a powerful weapon, but it won't shoot from Pennsylvania to Georgia," grinned Petey as he got up to dance with Wanda.

"Well, I don't know how many other times you boys saved my life, but I just want to say thanks."

"You're welcome," Petey and Jeep said in unison.

"But they not save you from reckless act you commit today," laughed Master Lee from a nearby barstool.

Lee's TKD School was growing in leaps and bounds, and so was his love life. He was now dating a Korean girl he had met at tournament in

Uniontown. If you looked up the definition of friend in the dictionary, Master Lee's picture was next to it.

Jeep would always say about Master Lee, "You didn't always see him, but he was always there when you needed him. If trouble comes your way, just look over your right shoulder and there would be Master Lee ready to help."

Later, as the party was winding down, Jeep was sitting in the booth with his arm around K.C. "Well, honey, I suppose you would like to do this someday."

"Do what?" She smiled.

"Cater a big party." Jeep laughed and ducked as she swung at his head with a loving swat.

They were all having a closer at the bar and Jeep was acknowledging everyone with a toast. "B, K.C., Gov, Cookie, Flip, Kendal, hey, wait a minute, Kendal why don't you have a nickname?"

"Kendal is my nickname," he said.

For all of you that have enjoyed the adventures with Jeep and Petey, but never got the opportunity to dine at Pippins, K.C. has included a couple of her recipes from the menu.

K.C.'s Mini Meatloaf

1lb. ground beef
½ lb. ground pork
½ lb. ground veal
1 package of onion soup mix
¾ cup dry breadcrumbs
2 eggs
¾ cup water
2 tbsp. basil
2 tbsp. flat parsley

Preheat oven to 350
In a large bowl combine all ingredients
In muffin tin make six meatloaf balls
Bake uncovered 20-25 minutes until done. Let stand five minutes before serving.

Filet Minon

Preheat oven to 450
Heat cast iron skillet on burner set on high
In dry pan sear steaks for two minutes on each side (depending on thickness)
Place skillet in oven for four-five min.(rare or medium)
Remove steaks and let sit for ten min. (handle is hot)
Whiskey Sauce
Using same skillet (handle is hot) let cool to medium. With pan off burner add four oz. of whiskey of choice and deglaze pan
2 tbsp. of Dijon mustard
Reduce sauce over medium heat and pour over steaks and serve

K. C.'s LASAGNA

12 oven ready lasagna noodles
½ lb. ground beef
½ lb. ground pork
2 eggs
15 oz. Ricotta cheese
4 cups of shredded mozzarella cheese
½ cup grated parmesan cheese
4 ½ cups of Italian sauce
1 medium onion
1 clove garlic

tbs butter preheat oven to 375

Spray 9 X 13 pan with cooking spray

In medium skillet melt butter, sautee onions and garlic add beef and pork in skillet brown and drain.

In medium bowl beat two eggs, ricotta, two cups mozzarella and parmesan

Pour one cup sauce in bottom of baking pan

Place four lasagna sheets on bottom slightly overlapping them

Half the Ricotta mixture

Half meat mixture

1 cup mozzarella

1 ½ cups Italian sauce

4 lasagna sheets

Other half of Ricotta mixture

1 ½ cups Italian sauce

4 lasagna sheets

Remaining meat mixture ½ sauce top with 1 cup of mozzarella

Cover tightly with foil. Bake 50-60 minutes until bubbly. Uncover and top with remaining Parmesan cheese and cook five more minutes or until cheese is melted.

Let rest for 15 minutes before cutting.